the

DEVIL'S

playground

ELIZA
FREED

Brunswick House
New York

Brunswick House Publishing
244 Madison Avenue
New York, NY 10016
First Brunswick House ebook and print on demand edition: November 2015
The Brunswick House name and logo are trademarks of Brunswick House
Publishing, LLC.
The publisher is not responsible for websites (or their content) that are not
owned by the publisher.

Manufactured in the United States of America
ISBN *978–1-943622–00–9* (ebook edition)
ISBN *978–1-943622–01–6* (print on demand edition)

also by Eliza Freed

For Vivian.
You are pure light . . . and awesome.
I love you.

There were times when I felt completely alone.
Even when he was standing right next to me.
He would tell me that's ridiculous.
He would convince me I never felt it.

one

I SCANNED THE BALLROOM OF the Downtown Club in Philadelphia. Brad was standing near the bar, laughing with his high school friends, the ones he rarely saw anymore. He towered over most of them. His six-foot-three body an anomaly among his childhood friends. His height matched his power. He could stare you down with his jet-black eyes, or melt you with them, and he always knew which way to proceed. Most people were at his mercy. I was at his side.

I barely smiled, but Brad caught it and winked at me. He kept watching me as he half listened to his friends talking. There was little Brad didn't notice.

"Meredith, I want to introduce you to my father," the bride said, pulling me away from Brad's stare. I stood even straighter. The introduction was the reason I'd been excited about the wedding. It was why I'd spent weeks finding a dress. And it was why I'd barely drank a sip of alcohol the entire day. The bride's father was Judge Warren of the U.S. Court of Appeals. He was an Army veteran and Harvard Law grad who'd made his way to Philadelphia and an appointment to the Third Circuit. One didn't fall into that position.

I followed the bride across the dance floor. My Norwegian cream skin, the same as my mother's, was perfectly highlighted in the light-green dress I'd saved three months to buy. I'd been told before that I was angelic. Looking, at least. My skin and light eyes—not quite green, not quite blue—had garnered comments from passersby even as a child.

"She's beautiful. Why she looks like an angel."

My mother would take me aside each time and tell me *they* say that to everyone. "You're no prettier than anyone else, which is fine, because beauty will get you nowhere."

Beautiful or not, I'd capitalized on others' views of my appearance since they'd first noticed me. I knew what colors looked best, what cuts of clothing to wear to accentuate my lean figure. I wasn't voluptuous or petite. I was statuesque. At least that was the word my mother's boyfriend chose when he'd inappropriately blocked the doorway to my bedroom to discuss my future plans.

I'd been high at the time, like the rest of my senior year. I'd skipped school as much as I could and had driven the three and a half hours east to the shore. I wasn't challenged by my coursework, not inspired by my teachers, and easily ranked in the top of my class. If it wouldn't have killed my father, I'd have dropped out and surfed every day.

I was sitting on the floor of my room, leaning against my bed, and he was standing at the foot of it. I hadn't noticed the thirty extra pounds he carried around his waist or the bald front of his head until that day. He was a drycleaner. My mother had brought him home for dinner after having a pair of pants tailored at his store.

He picked up my bra from the hamper and held it to his nose. He closed his eyes and tilted his head toward the ceiling as he inhaled deeply. He ran his fat fingertips over the lace at the edge of the cups and pressed the silk against his cheek. My stomach churned with disgust. No one—man or woman—had ever made me feel that afraid.

His grotesque leer had made me want to change something. Something bigger than anything I'd ever imagined while swimming in the ocean, or lying on the sand. I stopped getting high and started making a plan. It started with locking my bedroom door every night until I moved in with my father.

"Dad, this is my friend, Meredith." Judge Warren turned and paused at the sight of me. The candles' soft light highlighted the chiffon crossed at my chest and tied behind my neck. "She's an attorney with the Justice Department."

His eyes widened, and he took one step to my side, blatantly appraising me in front of his daughter. She smiled to put me at ease, but I wasn't uncomfortable, I was prepared.

Game on.

The judge and I spoke of his path to the bench. We went all the way back to his military service, and I memorized every word he said. Judge Warren was the human equivalent of a tufted leather chair in a warm, ornate library. He was broad and upright, commanding attention, but reserved. He was a powerful man, whose generous smile relaxed you immediately. And to me, he was fascinating.

I was intelligent and interested and, above all, innocent in my intentions. I would not sleep with this judge to get ahead. But I would learn from him in whatever limited time I was allotted.

When he asked for my business card, I presented him with the one I brought with me. It'd been placed in the side pocket of my purse, all by itself, waiting for the judge to request it. I promised to have lunch with him the following week. He wanted to discuss my future, the one he knew would be bright. The judge had found me "remarkable." My work here was done.

I walked back to our friends, still high from my introduction. Two pregnant wives anchored the table; waters with lemon rested between their swollen fingers. One was due that month, the other the next. Both were uncomfortable, tired, and annoyed by the shots their husbands poured down their throats and chased with beers, and I couldn't bring myself to sit with them and listen to their complaining. My life was too short.

"Do you want to dance?"

My body relaxed at the sound of his voice. It would forever be recognizable. I turned to find Brad standing just inches behind me. His smile was collusive. He was saving me from this table of lost joy, and it reminded me of the first night we met. He had rescued me from a guy hitting on me in a bar. He'd walked up and asked me if I was ready to leave. And without even knowing his name, I'd left with him.

"Yes," I said, and he took my hand in his and led me to the dance floor. The orchestra slipped into a slow cadence, and Brad held me the way he had a thousand times before. I'd been dancing with him for four years. Through weddings and promotions and thirtieth birthday parties and drunken holidays together. We'd been to the mountains, the islands, and to Europe, and we hadn't found a reason to stop dancing. But this would be the last dance for a while. The babies were beginning to come; the parties were beginning to end.

Brad leaned in as he whispered in my ear, "Frank and Tom were just telling me how lucky I am you haven't begged me for a baby yet."

"Is that how it works? We women beg you for your DNA to make the perfect baby?"

"According to them." He laughed and pulled me closer. "You smell amazing." He wanted me again. He'd had me when we woke up that morning, and again in the shower before the ceremony.

Brad's needs were simple. He wanted me, and power, and money. Not always in that order. Brad didn't care about changing the world. He cared about running it. But somehow we worked. Our goals were completely different, but the road we traveled to reach them was perfectly balanced between us. I forgot what we were talking about and let Brad lead me.

"I saw you wrap His Honor around your finger. I almost felt bad for the man." The smile on my face hid my disappointment. Lately, I'd sensed tiny moments of jealousy from Brad. Not jealousy of other men, but of me. As if he feared I might eclipse him. It reminded me of my mother. "Do you want to have a baby?"

I leaned back to see if Brad was kidding. "You want to talk about babies now?"

"Yes. You're twenty-nine. I'm thirty-one." Brad kissed me again. His eyes lit up with the same excitement of the days we'd set our wedding date and settled on the condo in the city. Brad liked when things were decided.

"I have so much left to do."

"None of our friends died when they had their babies," Brad said, pointing out the obvious, of which I was still not convinced.

"I don't want to have a baby just because everyone else is having one."

"You won't. You've never given a fuck what everyone else is doing. It's part of your charm." Brad admired me with the strangest expression. He was right next to me, and yet felt so far away. As if suddenly he didn't know me at all. "You're beautiful," he said, but *they* say that to everyone.

The song ended and took the discussion of babies with it. Brad and I walked over to the windows overlooking Independence Mall. The Liberty Bell was lit up, proclaiming our independence on this hot summer night. Brad handed me a glass of champagne. He put his arm around me and stared out the window as well. I leaned into him, feeling him solid beside me and forgot the last few minutes. No, it was not time for babies. We were on the verge of something brilliant.

two

NINE YEARS LATER

"MOMMY, CAN BRIAN HAVE A snack?"

I'd started locking the bathroom door, but I was too nervous to lock it while I showered. What if one of them fell and hit their head and bled to death while I was shaving my legs? What if I couldn't hear their screams, or their banging on the door? No matter how old they got, I never felt sure they'd be okay.

"Brian who?" I told Liv never to open the door for anyone. No one was allowed in the house. *Do. Not. Open. The. Door. Do you understand me?* I said it every time I got into the shower.

"This Brian." Through the fogged shower glass I could see Liv and the four-year-old boy from across the street staring at me in the shower. Brian was not fazed by my nudity.

I opened the shower door and stuck my head out. "Brian, can you wait in the hall for a minute?"

He shrugged and walked out of the bathroom, probably wondering what was taking so long with the snack.

"I thought I told you not to open the door?" My teeth were clenched. She would be the death of me.

"I didn't. I unlocked it, and then *he* opened it."

"It's not funny, Liv!"

"He's hungry. And that's not funny, either. You fed that dog the other day. The one that was lost."

"Brian's not a lost dog. He has a kitchen across the street."

"Does that mean no snack?" She had the sweetest face, that of an angel. And even though I knew that she knew exactly what she was doing, it was impossible to be mad at her.

"I'll be down in a minute."

As I walked into the kitchen, James told Brian hot dogs were the gross part of pigs. "Like all the stuff you'd never want to eat on a pig." Brian insisted he didn't want to eat any part of a pig, and Liv told him he had to eat a pig to have bacon, and everybody loved bacon. It seemed every conversation was some equally mind-numbing variation on the gross parts of a pig. I tried not to listen. *How much can one woman take?*

"You know a hamburger is made from a cow," James said.

"Milk, too," Liv added.

"Nobody likes milk."

"Lots of people like milk. Mommy, don't lots of people like milk?"

I nodded my head and grabbed three bowls from the cabinet. I poured goldfish into the bowls and took a handful for myself. My hair still had soap in it. I was in my robe. I wanted to be standing under a hot shower, not feeding these tiny people fish.

"Without milk, there'd be no ice cream."

"That's not true."

"Yes, it is."

Brad walked through the door. His eyes were glassy. He had that goofy I'm-kind-of-drunk smile on his stupid face. "Hey, Brian! What are you doing over here?"

"He's scavenging for food," I said.

Brad's smile disappeared. He looked like he wanted to disappear. My nasty tone was ruining the afterglow of his golf outing. I couldn't even pretend as if I cared. At least not until I rinsed the soap from my hair.

I carried a glass of water to my plant dying in the foyer and watered it. It continued to die. It couldn't stand hearing about the gross parts of the pig either. "Why can't you live?" I asked the plant, and heard Liv walking around, searching for me.

"Mommy, can you make ice cream without milk?"

My eyes bulged at Brad as I walked back into the kitchen, and then I closed them tightly, attempting to shut all of them out of my mind.

"Man, you're an angry woman," he said without an ounce of sympathy.

"It's because I can't be clean. Even inmates are allowed a shower. Not me, though."

"Go shower now. I got this." He opened a beer and sat down at the island. "Do you want me to shower with you?" He winked.

God, I hate you.

❧

I DID SHOWER. I SHOWERED for forty minutes. I was in no rush to be anywhere else. We were always late whenever we left the house, but that was because I never wanted to be where we were going. I had 77,000 miles on my car. Three hundred and ninety-eight were to places I wanted to be. But who was counting?

After the shower, I put the kids to bed. I sat on the couch and listened to Brad's day. Who he golfed with. What business was conducted. How it affected him. He didn't ask a word about my day. He'd stopped a long time ago. He'd stopped after the thousandth time he'd returned home to find me unhappy.

His arrival was usually timed perfectly after I'd cooked dinner, listened to the kids' riveting conversation while we ate, cleaned everything up, and completed elementary school homework. I packed their lunches and signed their assignment books. Tomorrow's outfits were picked out, and notes were written. Permission slips were signed and money was paid. And then Brad would walk through the door and wonder why I was miserable. *Don't you want to hear about my day? I cleaned two fish tanks and plunged the toilet.*

I wanted to *need* to take a short shower. I missed having someplace to be. Having something to talk about that was about my life and not Liv's and James'. I let my mind drift to when the next interesting thing in my life might occur. Five years . . . ten years . . .

Maybe I'll cut my hair.

three

I PEELED MY NAME TAG off the paper and slapped it on my chest as I entered Mrs. Hughes' first grade classroom. Tagged. I was it. Mrs. Hughes was talking to the class over the whispers of the unicorn mother. She wasn't actually a unicorn; that would be noteworthy. She was the creator of the famous unicorn cupcakes for her daughter's birthday the year before. Her shaving of pretzel rods into horn shapes to be iced and dipped in colored sugar had been repinned thousands of times, making her a mythological creature in our town.

I stayed on the outskirts. Not because I didn't like her, or the other moms who continued to talk while ignoring the teacher. I was pretty clear on the fact the unicorn was never going to like me. I've never thought of snacks as art. For Liv's last birthday, I'd sent in brownies she'd helped me bake. The box kind.

Liv caught sight of me and beamed with pride. I waved to her, thankful for the reminder of why I subjected myself to elementary school field trips. The year before, the girl who was terrified of bridges had sat next to me as we'd crossed the Ben Franklin Bridge into Philadelphia. I thought I'd talked her through it, but by the time we hit land, she'd thrown up all over us.

I scanned the class for the little gephyrophobiac and stopped on the only man in the room. How I hadn't seen him immediately was a bit terrifying. Had the Pinterest Princesses completely dulled my recognition of testosterone? He had my full attention now. He was tall, standing behind Allison Pratt. *Broad shoulders, too.* His hair was dark, slightly long, and pushed back from his face. Everything was dark about him. His hair, his eyebrows, and the just barely there beard and mustache. Everything but his eyes. They were a light green, and impossible to look away from. He had that wildcard factor. As if he could be an oral surgeon or a park ranger, and you wouldn't have guessed or been shocked by either.

I recalled Liv telling me Allison's dad was a police colonel. I knew she had part of that wrong, but he did possess that unmistakable *I can make this the worst day of your life* expression cops often had.

Colonel Pratt waited for the shock to pass from my face and put me at ease with a slight tip of his head while I imagined all the tickets a friendship with a police officer in my small town could get me out of.

The unicorn must have seen his gesture, because she rushed over to engage me in conversation. Or was it an interrogation? I was the stranger from out of town no one knew anything about, but God knew these people kept trying. "Hello, Meredith," she said, placing her body in my line of sight. Forcing me to address her.

"Hi," I said, trying to engage. It was always an enormous effort. "Excited to visit Philadelphia?" I went on the offensive.

"I'm exhausted. I was up all night hot-gluing our name tags." She reached to the short-legged table next to us and picked up a lanyard with a piece of cardstock hanging from it. It had rocks and stones glued to it and "Mrs. Walsh" written in the center. I was pretty sure the unicorn hadn't discovered masturbation.

"I . . . uh, actually got one from the office when I signed in." I smiled and nodded my head as if this was the end of the conversation.

The unicorn reached up to my breast and ripped off my name tag. "Don't be ridiculous! Here," she said, and put the rock chain over my neck. She walked away, and Colonel Pratt silently laughed by the windows.

I held up my collar for the day and mouthed, *where's yours?* To which he responded with more silent laughter. The teacher ended her speech about today's rules, and Liv ran over and wrapped her arms around my waist. She squeezed me tight, and I instantly felt bad for the kids whose parents weren't here. Liv was lucky I didn't work.

My lunch was collected, and I was lined up and herded onto a school bus. Liv and her friends scored the back seats, and I took a small two-seater three rows up. It was close enough to deliver the evil eye if necessary, but far enough away to let her sniff freedom. The colonel sat catty-corner from me, and the unicorn took the seat next to him. She was still talking . . . always talking, that one. Until Mrs. Hughes asked if we would mind spreading out. The unicorn moved to the middle of the bus; the colonel didn't move a muscle.

I placed my bag in the seat next to me. It was a two-seater for two little people and I made it my own. I searched through my bag for my earbuds as Mrs. Hughes yelled over the children that every seat needed to be filled, and the consolidation began. I pulled my bag onto my lap, dreading who would join me and praying they wouldn't throw up on me before we arrived.

The colonel stood. He was the biggest person on the bus and yet he had a gentleness about him as he moved back and sat down next to me. I slid against the window, giving his shoulders the extra room they required. The sides of our thighs touched. In my mind it was more of a caress, and I couldn't stop the sexual thoughts from racing through by head. *I wonder if he likes to be on top. How big is he? Does he talk during sex?*

I noted the wedding ring on his finger, and the unicorn taking her new seat with two little boys. She glared at me with the same disdain she reserved for the mothers who bought pre-packaged party invitations.

"You're going to get us in trouble," I whispered, and ignored the view from the front of the bus.

"Impossible." He leaned toward me and let his legs flow into the aisle. He was clearly unconcerned with all of the judgment on the bus; his attitude was a dip in the ocean on a hot day. He smelled of some thick mix of mahogany and a fresh soap scent that only heightened his masculinity. I told myself it was the scent I was attracted to, not him. The way my heart raced with him next to me made me feel half-animal. "Besides, Tommy What's-His-Name has already asked me three times if I've ever killed anyone. I figure the conversation will be better back here."

I tried to hide how excited I was that he was there. I tried to hide it from myself and him. "Thanks. Liv told me you're a colonel in the police army."

He laughed at her boggled description. "Not quite." He was a steel beam dipped in maple syrup. An innocent smile and sweet eyes atop an alarming physique.

"Have you ever killed anyone?"

He stopped moving and stared directly into my eyes. His were the color of water in a green glass, cool, and light.

He disarmed me.

"I'm Vince." He held out his hand to me.

"Meredith." I slipped my hand in his, and his warmth reminded me of the first time Tim Reynolds touched my breast in high school. He'd shaken my father's hand when he'd picked me up and then had parked in the woods and slipped his hands up my shirt. I was safe with Tim. He was as honorable as he was aroused. I think he joined the marines after graduation. I hadn't thought of him in at least ten years. I wondered what happened to him.

I wondered if I was blushing.

The Franklin Institute was a science museum full of inter-active exhibits about how things worked inside your body and out in the world. I survived it with my four little friends. My nametag was intact as I climbed the stairs of the school bus home. The boys in Liv's class began the "same seats" chant, and I took my seat against the window.

Acting on an archaic habit, I checked my email on my phone. There were none. I dropped my phone in my lap, more disappointed in myself than the empty inbox. I always strug-gled to keep up with my messages. But now that I no longer worked, if I got three a week, not about my children, that was busy.

The colonel sat two seats in front of me, and his seat in-trigued me. His seat selection and the width of his chest. The boys continued the "same seat" chant, and he moved back.

"Don't let them bully you," I said, liking the feel of his thigh against mine. His body made me want to run away with him and do naughty things. I pressed my shoulders against the cold bus wall and tried to stop the heat from spreading through me. I tried to make sense of what was happening. Because this wasn't my first field trip, but it was my first one like *this*.

"I was only trying to give you some room. I like this seat."

I lowered my voice and tilted my head down so no one could read my lips. "You're going to upset the room mothers' squad."

"You don't like them, do you?"

What's not to like? I watched the other exhausted moms file into their seats. *Why do they piss me off so much?*

"They're okay." It was difficult to like what I was working so hard not to become. "I love my nametag." I held it up with a disingenuous smile.

Vince watched me with a look of sympathy and curiosity. "Do you work outside the home?" It was the gentlest way to ask the question, and I still hated it.

I sighed. "No. I don't work."

"Well, today was work. I felt bad you had Curtis Wright in your group. He's notorious."

"I know. Why does Mrs. Hughes hate me? He kept hiding from me." I laughed a little, trying not to let anyone hear me. "Why does he do that?"

The colonel leaned in and whispered, "That's how he gets attention."

"Oh. I thought he was just unlikable." I nodded. "Attention makes more sense," I said in the colonel's ear, sure he should have moved his seat.

"He's unlikable, too." The colonel leaned back, and I turned my body toward him and rested the back of my head on the window. I was aware of the angle of my chin and the arch of my back as I pushed my hair behind my ear. My voice was higher and lighter than usual. I recognized it as foreign, but couldn't stop myself. My head tilted when I laughed. I swear I even flipped my hair once. I was an idiot. For this juvenile behavior, I should have hated myself, but I was too busy worshipping him. I couldn't stop. Even though I'd known him only for a few hours, I cared about his opinion. I craved his attention, and a silent part of me recognized those weren't the only things I wanted from him.

Jeannie Holland tapped the colonel on the shoulder from her seat across the aisle and asked him, "What do you think is worse, having a seagull poop on you at the shore, or having a dog pee on you at the park?" While the colonel weighed in, I closed my eyes and memorized the sound of his voice.

The ride back to school wasn't long enough.

four

THE SCHOOLS WERE GOOD. SCHOOLS plural was over-stating things. There was only one district in the entire town. Most of the people there were the third or fourth generation to graduate from the same high school, the same building.

I'd promised myself when I merged onto the highway twenty years ago, leaving behind my mother and her dry cleaner, that I'd never live in the country again, but now there was more to think about than just me. What was best for James and Liv came first. Always. And our city lifestyle wasn't the picturesque childhood Brad and I had imagined when we'd picked out their names.

I'd suggested the suburbs. Brad had insisted on the country. But if Brad was moving me to Dinkville, I wanted to do it right. Buy a house in the middle of nowhere and not see a neighbor ever. Maybe an old farmhouse, something with a story of its own. Brad had wanted a house in the newest development. Something with no story to tell because it even bored itself. He'd finally worn me down, and since he had no time to fix anything, new was the least frustrating path. There were mature trees surrounding each mini-mansion, and I pretended we were secluded.

We had a three-car garage for our two cars, and five bathrooms for the four of us. It was sterile, void of all personality, and it was my sanctuary. The kids and I had been deposited the same way passports were put into a safety deposit box. One like all the others on the wall.

At first, we'd had lots of parties. Everyone in the neighborhood had been very welcoming. But at our last one, the man from next door had pulled me into Liv's play kitchen, jabbed his hard dick against my hip and tried to kiss me. I lost interest in getting to know the neighbors. Them, and their hard dicks.

I ran my hands over the hangers in my closet. It was almost as big as my bedroom in the house I grew up in. I found the navy linen shirt dress I hadn't worn since the spring before. It was short, and I paired it with beige wedge sandals. The First Grade Patriotic Program was a big day out for me. *Why am I the only one living in this house who has no life?*

Nothing had been more terrifying than quitting my job. I'd promised myself three things:
1 I would stay in shape.
2 I would read and not lose my connection to the world.
3 I would not start fucking the UPS man.

It took about nine weeks to realize these goals were harder to maintain than I'd thought. Especially after the first few *packages* had been delivered. I never read; barely watched the news. I had some strange connection to our mailbox, as if it might hold some surprise key to my existence, delivered every day around two. I was a passenger—no, I was the driver in my children's lives.

But even with only the mail for excitement, unemployment had been a relief. James had thrown up in the middle of the night the eve of my first day off. I'd spent the morning washing sheets and sipping tea, pleased my sick child could relax in his own bed with his mommy there to take care of him. It was right. It was how I thought motherhood should be. But the moments of gratefulness had been replaced with bitter boredom as Brad dressed for work each day, and I put on my uniform of yoga pants, a tank, and my favorite hoodie in time for carpool.

I backed out of my garage bay as my phone dinged with a text.

B: Not going to be able to make it. Caught in a meeting.

"Tell her yourself," I said, and threw my phone on the passenger seat. I shouldn't have been surprised. When I'd heard Brad promise Liv that morning that he wouldn't miss the patriotic program, I'd forgotten to tell her not to get her hopes up, that we always came second. I forgot I was all she had. I pulled onto the country road and let my mind drift back to my neighborhood.

Despite the events of our last party, I was still close with a few of the women. On the nights Brad came home before ten, we'd walk the neighborhood together. One time I'd actually borrowed milk from the woman next door. I bought her a gallon to replace it, and after I'd gotten home from morning carpool and yoga, I took it over. I walked into her house the same way I had a dozen times before. She was spread eagle on her kitchen island with a young guy standing between her legs. He was shoving a banana into her and chanting, "You will eat this when I'm through." My feet were frozen in place. I couldn't turn my head. I'd only ever put a banana in my mouth. It was perverse. It was interesting. The guy turned to me, and I recognized him as the director of the morning childcare program at the school.

I ran home and called Brad. My heart raced at the attraction across the street. Brad didn't answer. He'd probably been in an important meeting. It was the first time I'd masturbated while the kids were at school.

THE FIRST GRADE PATRIOTIC PROGRAM was famous in the town. It was the equivalent of a celebrity tree lighting, or a presidential debate. I parked behind the last of the cars, at least two blocks from the school. Half the town was already there. I leaned my head on my car window and closed my eyes in the warm sun until the banging on my car window startled me, and I jumped in my seat.

"What the hell are you doing? You can sleep at your house." Jenna banged on my window again. She was the only person I'd met in the town who I was thankful for. I knew I was going to love her when she'd shown me the marijuana in her pool bag last summer.

"I was thinking. Something I can only do when my kids are in school," I said as I got out of the car. I shoved the car door shut and clicked the lock button on my key fob. "This music program is cutting into my coherent time."

"Did you at least find something patriotic to dress her in?"

"Does her Christmas tulle skirt, a tank top tied at her waist, and the blue streaks in her hair count?" I asked. The wind picked up as we walked the two blocks to the school, and I detected the smell of cigarettes on Jenna. I liked that she had secrets. It made me think she could probably keep mine. Not that I told her anything. Not that I had any.

We were twenty minutes early, and the auditorium was already full. We waited in the hallway for more chairs to be brought in. Jenna was taken from me by the unicorn, who had important PTO business to discuss with her. Some discourse among the fundraising committee had to be dealt with immediately.

"Psst," I heard, and glanced over my shoulder at the art room. The colonel was standing by the doorway and motioning me toward him. I looked behind me, assuming he was talking to someone else, but there was only me in his line of sight. When I turned back, he was smiling at me, waiting for me. My breath caught, and I reminded myself to breathe. *Get a hold of yourself, Meredith. He's Allison's father. That's it.*

I walked over, and he pointed through the window into the art room. A little boy with paint covering his hands was trying to wipe it on his shirt and only succeeding in getting it all over everywhere.

"He's my smart one," the colonel said, and laughed in my ear.

"Book smart?" I asked, and watched as the little boy wiped his red hands across his jeans and stared in wonderment at his predicament. "He's ready for the patriotic program."

"His mother is going to kill him." Reality spoke, and I listened carefully. I leaned away from the colonel.

"I should find a seat," I said without looking up. I felt his breath near my cheek for a split-second, and then I walked into the gym. Jenna had a seat saved for me on the aisle.

"Everything okay?" she asked as I sat down. *Do I not seem okay?*

"Yeah." I tried to sound nonchalant, and Jenna either bought it or was letting me off the hook. Or maybe she was high.

"I saw you talking to Chief Pratt." Her voice was even and completely void of any accusation.

"He was on the field trip with me last week." Jenna was still uninterested, so I pushed. "What's he like?"

"He's a decent guy. If you're into the cop thing. He graduated with John." With all the seats filled, people were starting to line the walls of the auditorium. Vince got up and gave his seat to an elderly woman. "Supposedly his wife is the salt of the earth, but everybody says that about me, too."

The colonel's wife caught my eye across the aisle; she was now sitting next to an elderly woman she didn't seem to know well. Mrs. Pratt wasn't thin or fat, her face was completely void of makeup or color at all, her hair was back in a perfunctory ponytail, her shoes were ugly, and I wondered if she was fucking the UPS man, because based on appearances, she was everything I never wanted to be. Salt of the earth . . .

five

"YOU SAID YOU WERE GOING to commit to Cub Scouts. It's all dads there." I regretted the statement immediately. He couldn't help having a dinner with the CFO. Brad didn't decide when his boss came down from Manhattan.

"I work. That's what I've committed to."

Unlike me . . . Deep breaths. He didn't mean to be a dick. It just came naturally to him. Brad finished tying his shoes and headed downstairs to the workout room while I texted babysitters so I could accompany the Cub Scouts on their tour of the police station next Thursday without Liv complaining the entire time.

What will I have for dinner? My boss never takes me out.

Brad's hours were late that week, and I was left with soccer, lacrosse, and math facts to fill my time. I was writing out a check for the Cub Scout membership fees when James jumped over the bottom three steps, dressed in his uniform. Liv was telling me a long story, not stopping for me to even nod, and I realized I wrote the check out to her teacher by mistake.

"Can you give me a second? I have to write out this check," I asked her as nicely as possible while I wrote "VOID" across the front of the check. She continued to talk, standing over me, drilling her words into my head until James interrupted her.

"It's a good thing there's no negative-twelve-dollar bill," James said, and I just wanted to put my head down on the counter. I actually shook my head trying to process it, but then he explained. "If you tried to buy something for twenty bucks, you'd have to give them your negative-twelve-dollar bill, plus thirty-two dollars more." I closed my eyes. "That would be terrible."

It was a miracle, but I finished the check and made Liv promise to behave for the sitter. I followed James to the third bay of the garage and hiked up my sleeveless maxi to climb into my Escalade that I didn't even like. Brad had insisted. I'd wanted something small. Something not sucking the life out of the environment . . . and me. But he'd said, "You're a mom. You need the extra seats to drive the kids' friends around."

I looked back at my nine-year-old in the third row of the enormous vehicle as the image of Brad in his mystic black metallic pearl two-door flashed in my head. *You're a mom . . .*

The fear of God was placed in the scouts by their leader. Manners, hand-raising, quiet while the officer was speaking. James banged his sneaker on the wall until his leader paused and glared at him. I was pretty sure we weren't making it out of there alive. My interest in appropriateness faded daily.

We followed our leader through the barracks door. Wide-eyed, the scouts took in the lobby, while I took in Colonel Pratt. He was in uniform, and he should wear it twenty-four hours a day. Suddenly my bitterness for being forced there faded as my eyes lingered over the stripes on his shoulders and then fell to each button of his shirt and finally landed on his holster. The children and the other adults in the room seemed to slip away as my breath echoed the slow pace of my inspection.

James stomped on my foot as he rushed by me to be first

through the door and ripped me from my admiration. We were escorted to a holding cell and then to an interview room, where the colonel asked, "Has anyone ever met a police officer before?"

Hands flew up toward the ceiling and before I could react, the colonel asked James when he'd met an officer. He hadn't, that I remembered.

"I've met three when they pulled my mom over for speeding."

I closed my eyes as our leader, and the rest of the men with me, laughed out loud.

"Three separate times?" the colonel asked, turning his attention to me with disbelief.

"Yep. Once in New Jersey, and twice on the same day in Maryland."

The colonel shook his head a little, and I lowered mine. "Did your mom get a ticket?"

"No," James innocently admitted.

"Never? Not one of those times?"

"The policemen were all really nice to her," James said.

"Figures! Of course she didn't get a ticket," Richie's father said, and I retreated to the back of the crowd.

The colonel turned the kids' attention to the table in the middle of the room and tugged at the handcuffs attached to the table by chains. "I think we should interview your mom about these tickets. Who wants to see Mrs. Walsh in handcuffs?"

Richie's dad's hand shot in the air, followed by the kids erupting in cheers. The colonel held up the cuffs, staring at me, waiting for me to come. James gently pushed me forward, finding the whole thing hilarious, and I could already hear him retelling the story to Liv and anyone else who'd listen.

I left the safety of the back wall and sat down at the table. With his back to the scouts, the colonel smiled at me, and I raised my wrists to the table. He handcuffed them, and his fingers brushing against my wrists hardened my nipples. I leaned forward, letting my dress fall away.

"You're blushing," he whispered, and I said nothing.

"So, Mrs. Walsh," the colonel began as he sat in the chair on the end of the interview table. "It seems you have a propensity to speed. That you're a repeat offender. Is that an accurate statement?"

All eyes were on me. I was back in the courtroom. Adrenalin coursed through me, followed by an intense longing.

"I'm invoking my right to remain silent and requesting counsel."

The colonel paused. His face held no reaction. He was a gifted interrogator. The scouts and all their dads just stared at us as my eyes fell to the handcuffs, and the colonel turned to the scouts. "Does anyone know what your right to remain silent means?"

The scouts all raised their hands at the same time, and their answers were all wrong. The colonel took his time explaining my rights and answered all their questions. When I finally looked up, Richie's dad was staring at my cuffed wrists. His mouth was open and his chest rose with deep, inappropriate breaths. Another officer ushered the boys outside to see a police car as the colonel released my wrists.

"Either you've committed a lot of crimes, or you've worked in law enforcement."

"Yes."

He sat on the table next to me with a pleased expression on his face. "Are you on Facebook?"

"This is an odd interrogation," I said and rubbed my wrists.

"You're not a fan of questions?"

"I love questions. Not fond of answering." Not wanting to annoy him, I asked, "Is there a way to escape Facebook? I mean, how will I know when everyone goes to Disney?"

"Exactly, we're trying to figure out as a department how we

can leverage social media, but I don't know a lot about it."

"Perhaps joining yourself is a solid first step." I followed the colonel outside and used the last few minutes of our visit to memorize every inch of him in his uniform.

When all the kids were in bed, and Brad was still not home, I changed my Facebook profile picture to the most flattering one I had. There was no question he was coming. I wanted to look my best.

six

THERE WAS AN APPEAL TO Colonel Vincent Pratt. It wasn't only his physical appearance. It was that he continued to surprise me. He didn't friend me on Facebook. I watched as he friended the rest of the town, knowing he knew I was there, and he didn't friend me. When it would have seemed almost rude, he liked one of my photos. It was more dangerous than friending me. It was a secret message telling me he wouldn't expose my intrigue to the public, but rest assured he still knew I was out there. There was nothing ordinary about him, and there was already plenty of ordinary in the world. Plenty in my own home. In my own bedroom.

It was Saturday. So before swim practice, Brad would mount me. He was leaving that morning for a weekend in Boston with his high school friends. I would be on my own. A few seconds after his eyes opened, Brad lifted the covers, slid over next to me, and rubbed his hard dick against my back. I was dreaming of a police officer I had no business thinking about. Brad pulled my shoulder, laying me on my back, and spread my knees before climbing between them and entering me.

"How's that for a good morning?" he asked.

"It's something," I said, and stared at the ceiling above us.

He pushed my legs up, my knees even with my back, and rammed into me as I imagined waking up next to law enforcement. Eventually, Brad came, and my legs were released. He rolled off me and caressed me between my legs. His finger found my clit and played with me, and I tried to pay attention.

"It's your turn, baby." He only called me baby in bed. I tried to remember what he called me out of bed, but it seemed we rarely spoke. I think he called me Meredith. I silently pledged to begin paying attention. I should know what he called me. He should call me something.

"Come for me," he said, and broke through my concentration on all the wrong things.

"I'm sorry. I just have a lot on my mind."

"Like what?" he asked, and removed his hand.

"Like the end of the school year, and swim team, and teachers' gifts, and summer plans. I know it sounds silly, but it's all swirling around up here." I tapped my finger to my temple.

Brad got out of bed and walked into the bathroom.

I heard the shower turn on and touched myself, letting my fingertips play in a new way. I wouldn't fall into the same old routine with the colonel. I roughly ran my hand across my nipple, and then squeezed it as I watched, and the warmth building inside of me clenched down. I remembered the way the colonel's uniform stretched across his chest. It wasn't too small; his chest was just not an average size, even for a policeman. I pressed one finger into me, and I saw his eyes watching me. They were telling me to come. That he wanted to see it. The heat increased with the movement of my hands, and I arched my back and came in Brad's bed and in my mind.

☙

ON MY SECOND TRIP BACK to town for swim practice, I marveled at my luck in having kids in both practice times. I was going to have to communicate with some other moms and get in on the carpool. The colonel's police car was parked on

28

the side of North Main Street when I pulled into town. I didn't wave. It seemed uniformed police officers never waved while in their cars.

On my way out of town, I passed him again, and my Facebook notification lit up with a message.

V: Are you running some type of illegal taxi service?

Even that seemed like more fun than two separate swim practices, I thought. I responded back.

M: Is that what you're staking out North Main for?

V: I looked into your background.
I know you were a U.S. Attorney.

M: Sounds like a judicious use of our tax dollars.

V: Also explains why you're so evasive.

M: My kids are on the swim team. I drive to the pool a lot in the summer.

V: Do you always go on the weekends?

M: I try not to, but this weekend my husband's away.

V: Do you not like the pool?

M: It's very nice. Your kids would enjoy it.

V: That's not what I asked. How do you feel about it?

M: I feel trapped there.

I ran my thumb across my phone's screen and let the words sink in. I never complained about the pool outside of my head, but I hated it there. On sunny days, I sat and listened to the hens of Riversbend, New Jersey discuss every other woman around them. I counted the years until my kids would lose interest in it, and I imagined hiring a nanny to bring them so I could go to the shore every day alone.

After lunch, we piled into the car and returned to the pool. The Escalade knew the way without me steering. My kids' excitement was barely stunted by the lifeguard's yells to "Walk" as soon as they set foot on the sidewalk. We were the first to arrive. I drug a lounge chair onto the lawn and dropped my bag down next to it. I hoped to remain an island. I took off the appropriate cover-up I'd invested in to ensure my virtue was intact by August and walked to the diving board. I was actually thankful for the boring-ass monokini I was wearing. It would stay on as I went off the board.

I walked to the edge, bouncing hard, enjoying the uncertainty beneath my feet. At the end, I stared down into the deep water. There was a horseshoe at the bottom, left from the night before. It was pointing up, and when I looked up, I saw Vincent Pratt walking in with his kids in tow, and Richie and his dad. The colonel was under the shade, at least fifty yards away, and I could tell by the way he carried himself that it was him. I turned my back to the water, bounced twice, and did a back flip.

I stayed underwater as long as possible. It would be the last peace of the day. When I emerged, two women and the unicorn were pulling chairs next to mine on the lawn. I dove down again, not willing to face my reality.

My friends, or dysfunctional team as I sometimes thought of them, were taken with bitching about the swim coach, so I was spared the critique of every other woman's bathing suit. I lied and said I was exhausted, and they sympathized with me for having to do *everything* with my kids since Brad worked so much. Yes, *everything* was too much for me.

For a break from the intellect-enhancing conversation, I went to the bathroom and bought a watermelon water ice. My steps were small and slow as I made my way back to my chair. When I passed Richie's father and Vince, I waved and wondered if they, too, were discussing our swim team's need for personalized flip turn instruction.

"Why don't you have a seat?" Richie's dad asked. It was like he read my mind and wanted to save me from the present.

I'm going to, I thought. I'm going to sit right down with these two men, in front of the whole pool, and talk to them about something. I don't care what. But it wasn't these two men I wanted to sit with. It was Vince.

"Sure. I just need to get my cover-up." The word was ridiculous. Why would someone cover up at a pool?

"No, you don't," Richie's dad said and made it seem as ridiculous as it was in my head. Or maybe it was because the idea was actually ridiculous. I sat down next to him, across from Vince, and felt the stress leave my chest as I exhaled. "Brad working?"

"Actually, he's away with his high school friends this weekend."

"What? Lisa won't let me go anywhere."

"Are you not trustworthy?" I asked, already knowing Lisa was the most jealous person in town.

"I'm completely trustworthy. Unless you're offering something."

I looked across at Vince, and we both ignored the comment. Before a response was needed, Lisa's best friends came and sat with us, and even though I was sure they were there to keep an eye on things, we all fell into an easy conversation, which eventually landed on identity theft. It was the perfect topic for my female counterparts to hang on every word from Vince's mouth. It was a great mouth.

"I get so much fake email as it is, I'm not sure I'd recognize a hacker," one woman said.

"Just never click on a link," Richie's dad chimed in, begging for attention. "That's how all the viruses invade."

"I just set up a trash email account," I said, and everyone turned to me, shocked I was participating. "It's an address I give to stores, newsletters, and anywhere else that's not of a personal nature. Then I check in there once in a while, but I never open anything . . . it keeps it all out of my way."

The woman to Vince's left deemed this idea brilliant and took out her phone to share it on Facebook.

"Interesting," Vince said, and I let my eyes linger on him. *I want to see you come.* I stood and returned to my hen house. I threw out my water ice cup and sank into my lounge without a word to my team. I took out my phone, and there was a Facebook message from Vince.

> V: *When you got up, Rita made a comment about you walking around without a cover-up.*

> M: *Did you defend my honor?*

I sent back and peeked in his direction. He was smiling as he read from his phone.

> V: *I would have, but Richie's dad was all over it, or he'd like to be.*

> M: *Now that you've experienced it firsthand, can you*

understand my thoughts on the pool?

V: It's a bit of a cage. I actually hate thinking of you here. I wish you never had to come back.

M: I'd miss the water ice.

No reply. I turned and acted like I was listening to the ladies discuss the school's dress code as I watched Vince through my sunglasses. Next week, I needed to take some time and figure out what I was doing, because there was not a thing right about it, and Vince had to be told that. I watched as four moms stopped by to talk to him. Richie's dad basked in the attention. He'd found the perfect pool wingman if there even was such a thing. The women laughed too loud; one awkwardly climbed onto the picnic table next to Vince, while another adjusted her cover-up and watched her competition shamelessly reapply lip gloss. It was totally pissing me off. He said something to them with his gentlemanly smile and got up from the table as if he was taking a call, and I got a new message.

V: What is your "fake" email address?

M: Why? Do you have some spam to send me?

V: Still waiting patiently.

I put on my black cover-up that hung loosely to my knees. It was your basic prison-issued standard uniform. I called for my brood and packed our enormous pool bag. I needed my phone, sunscreen, and a towel. This bag was forty pounds. I handed it to James, and he dragged it most of the way. As I passed the picnic tables, Richie's dad asked if I was returning tomorrow.

"I'm not sure," I answered, and could tell Vince knew I was lying.

"I love your cover-up, Meredith," the woman sitting next to Vince said, and I looked down at it. Branded with boredom.

"Thanks," I said, and escaped. When everyone was buckled in the back of the car, I sent Vince a message.

M: I.will.never.read.this.8@gmail.com

As Exhibit A of my boredom, I checked my spam email three times that night. Around 9 P.M., there was a new email from You.will.read.this.8@gmail.com.

V: I hate your cover-up.

I laughed out loud and permanently deleted our Facebook messages. We would now be emailing.

seven

THE COLONEL'S EMAILS WERE SPORADIC at first. Always under the guise of seeking information that would help the town. Did I think the new traffic light by the cemetery was helpful? What were my thoughts on armed security at the school? I wouldn't let myself appreciate them. I didn't allow myself to check for them during the day. I wouldn't be that mother. That time belonged to Liv and James. But I thought about him constantly.

I walked through each room of our home, examining the tall ceilings and bone-colored walls, trying to determine what the most absurd part of it was. The coldest corner of the house. There were so many to choose from, but I was captivated by the front staircase. It was open and wide and led straight up to a landing before turning for the last three steps. There was a half-moon balcony that served no purpose outside of baffling me as to its value. Since Rapunzel didn't live there, and no opera performances were scheduled, it seemed a bit over the top.

I moved a dining room chair to the front door, sat in it, and stared at the odd staircase. My aura of thought, the annoying sound of peacefulness, must have pervaded the house, because within minutes I heard tiny footsteps.

"What are you doing?" Liv asked, not sure what to make of me sitting there.

"I'm looking at this staircase."

She walked over, climbed into my lap, and stared at it, too. "What about it?" she asked, having no patience.

"I think it's odd."

Liv stared up, noticing the staircase for probably the first time. "I'm hungry," she finally said. She leaned up with her arms around my neck. "Can I have pasta for dinner?"

"You always want pasta."

"I love it. Isn't there anything you love so much you want it every day?" she asked, and her sweet little eyes melted me in my seat.

"I feel that way about you and James. I love you so much I just want to be with you forever."

Liv caved into my chest in a state of pure bliss. She tightened her arms around my neck until it hurt. *How could this surprise her?*

I squeezed her tight. "I love you, Liv."

"I love you, too, Mommy." She kissed me with her tiny pink lips, and I smiled the same way she did moments ago.

The staircase caught my eye again. "What do you think about painting the stairs?"

"Can I paint them?"

"No. We need a professional stair painter. You can watch them and learn how they do it."

"Can I dye all my hair pink?"

"No, but I'll make you pasta for dinner." I put her on the floor in front of me.

"Why can't I have pink hair?" she asked as I slid the chair back into the dining room.

"Because you already have blue streaks in it, and you're seven. You've got to be satisfied with what you have," I said and watched as the staircase caught Liv's eye again. She turned to me to say something and paused. I braced myself for the return lesson on being satisfied.

"Pasta," I said, not wanting to face her judgment.

MY DAY'S AGENDA CONSISTED OF a party on a farm. We arrived a few minutes early, which was rare. I kept the kids in the parked car with me and told them to look at the horses, that maybe they would get to ride one. I took out my phone and texted Brad, asking if he thought he'd be back from his team-building golf tournament in time for dinner. As I hit send, Liv and James started their latest debate on whether a bomb's explosion could be felt in Connecticut if detonated near us.

"You guys need to stop playing video games."

"Why?" James asked.

"Because what child sits around thinking about bomb explosions?"

"It was in a book I read," he said, and they both continued their argument. I needed to go out to dinner. I couldn't eat another meal alone with them. I checked my phone for a return text. There was none.

Cars filled the parking lot. Lots of kids were invited to this one, and their siblings. Liv's classmate was the birthday boy, but James was happy to be included. I signed into my junk email on my phone, and there was one from the colonel.

V: How's the horse party?

My head shot up looking for him.

M: Are you following me?

V: Yes. I just pulled in. Allison was invited, too.

"Okay, kids. Let's go," I said into the back seat, immediately halting their pointless conversation. I hopped out of the Escalade and straightened my dress. The colonel, his wife, and their three kids piled out of his truck. Of course, the whole family was there. I scanned the other party goers on the cloudless, humid, Saturday afternoon, and lots of couples were with their children. The whole family was invited.

I wanted to go home.

But Liv took my hand and dragged me toward the barn. She and James were my whole family.

I pushed that realization down.

Way down.

And I plastered a smile across my face as Liv led me into the barn with James close behind us. There were wooden tables with food lining one wall, and hay bales and benches to sit on lining another. Adults congregated in small groups as the children were herded to the side to be given vests and sheriff badges. They were told of every detail the party would entail. I eyed the punch bowl and assumed it was non-alcoholic. *Where is Jenna?*

As if on cue, she entered the barn through the wrong door with a child in her arms, one hiding behind her leg, and another whose eyes were glued to her phone in his hand. Until he dropped it, and she had to reshuffle everyone to pick it up. She sent the kids to the herd and bee-lined to me in the corner. "Thank God you're here," she said. She pushed her hair out of her face, but it fell right back in front of her eyes again. She ripped a hair tie off her wrist and secured her hair back in an unkempt ponytail. She opened her tote bag and rested it on her hip as she searched through it. Her movements were almost violent.

"I was just thinking the same thing."

"Aaron shit his pants right before we left." My face twisted in disgust. "He's eight. Who the fuck has an eight-year-old who still shits his pants?"

"It's never happened before," I said, knowing this was a "special" occasion.

"Just makes it weirder," Jenna said, and produced a little airplane bottle of vodka from her purse. "Can you get me a glass of punch?"

I laughed until she joined in. It was a rough ride to get there, but we were together. "Of course," I said, and left her in the corner of the barn.

I nodded at the unicorn. She was listening to all the kids' instructions. She was involved. I blankly smiled as I swept the rest of the crowd. The colonel's wife handed a child to him, and he lifted the little boy easily into his arms. There was always something hot about a guy with a child in his arms. His wife took out her phone and snapped a picture of them. It was much less hot when the guy's wife was around. The picture was all over Facebook before the day was over.

I poured two cups of punch and found Jenna before we were all moved outside. The kids were taken off the fence five at a time to climb onto horses and be led in a circle by an adult. I leaned against the fence and sipped the punch concoction Jenna mixed. My lips pursed at the excessive vodka barely mixed with the punch. "Whew! That was some morning you had."

"You have no idea. He shit his pants." She downed the rest of the punch in her cup. "I need another. You ready for a refill?"

"I'm good. You're going to need a ride home."

"I can't go back there. Get a sitter and come out with me tonight."

"I don't know if—"

"Tell Brad my kid shit his pants. He'll understand." Jenna walked away, and the fence around me filled with other parents watching their kids go by on horses.

"Mommy, take my picture. I named this horse George," Liv yelled, beaming from atop her horse.

"Didn't it have a name?" I called over the fence.

"He likes mine better." Liv leaned toward the fence, and I snapped her picture. "I love you," she said and continued on her ride past me.

"Look, Mom! No hands," James said as he neared the fence.

"Please be careful."

James rolled his eyes. I took a picture of him, too.

I checked my phone's email, because apparently I was bored. Okay, that was a lie. I wanted him. I wasn't bored, I was needy. The two emotions were becoming interchangeable, and I was becoming incapable of fixing myself. There was only one email, from the colonel.

V: Will you be riding today?

M: Not dressed for it.

V: I'm glad you're not.

"Stop texting Brad with that stupid grin on your face," Jenna said, and I looked up to see the colonel watching me. "People are going to think you're having an affair if you walk around that happy." I hid my eyes. I was sure he heard it. "Did you tell him we're going out tonight? Because we are."

"No. I didn't tell him. Where do you want to go?"

"Anywhere I can sit outside and have a drink. How about Savannah?"

"Georgia? Will I be back in time to pay the sitter?"

"Definitely not."

eight

I PICKED UP JENNA. AFTER your kid shit his pants, sobriety was a high bar. I was happy to drive. We headed to the golf course, but the parking lot was filled with familiar cars.

"Oh God, please not here," she moaned, and I turned west toward the river. I nodded as Jenna rambled on about her horrendous hoard of sons. I was a safe place. I knew she loved them, and if there was anything left of her sanity by the time they left, she'd be very proud of the work she'd done with them. "Where are we going?"

"McFadden's?" I asked as we headed over the bridge toward Philadelphia.

"At the Phillies Stadium?" She was in shock, as if I'd kidnapped her.

"Is that okay?"

"Yeah. It's just, like, actually somewhere. I'm not used to crossing the county line without an act of God occurring first." Jenna turned up the music, and we rode up the highway with our windows down and the radio blaring. "Can I smoke in here?" she yelled, taking cigarettes out of her bag.

"No." I shook my head.

Jenna turned the music down. "Figures. You're such a prude. You know I only hang out with you because you laugh at my jokes."

This made me laugh, proving her point. "I know."

"We should get crazy tonight. Let our hair down. When the visiting team's bus pulls out, let's flash our tits at them."

"No."

"Again . . . I don't know why I'm here." Jenna started laughing before she finished the statement.

⌇

THE LOTS AT THE BASEBALL park were full, too, but full of anonymity. I paid the twenty-five dollars to park and walked past the endless cars. The game started at 7:05; the only tailgaters left were the ones without tickets. The bouncer checked our IDs at McFadden's, and Jenna beamed, even though we were clearly over twenty-one. We filed through the crowd to the outdoor area and ordered beers, and I inhaled deeply the air of freedom as Jenna lit a cigarette.

Jenna perused the crowd as if she'd never been to a place as interesting. She was on the run after the day she'd had. She took long drags of her cigarette, and I pointed my face to the rising moon. When she stomped the butt out on the ground, she tapped the shoulder of the guy next to her.

"Would you mind taking our picture?" she asked, and I almost fell over.

I smiled, still confused. Jenna had never taken a picture of us before. I watched in shock as she posted it online and tagged me. "I thought you hated people knowing where you are," I said.

"That's when I have no place to go. We're actually somewhere tonight." Jenna hit send and smiled at me. "Suck it, Facebook."

We watched the game from the televisions at McFadden's. I'd never watched the game on my television at home, but it was almost like being in the stadium. I mean, we paid for parking. And it was a lot easier to get a beer in McFadden's than in stadium seats. Jenna easily made friends with the guys next to us and had them take two more pictures as we all drank three more rounds. It was then I realized she was drunk. She functioned so well, making me question how often she was sober.

I left Jenna with her new friends and headed to the bar for another round. I leaned on the counter, waiting for the bartender. When he returned, he recognized me and began opening beers and placing them in front of me.

"Am I drinking too much?" This was the second round I'd bought Jenna and our new friends.

"I'm just a great bartender," he said with an air of pride in other areas. "Six again?"

"Yes. Thank you." He opened the sixth beer and took my money to the register for change. Past the register, I saw Vince. He was standing with three other men, two of whom were familiar. They were all talking, engrossed in their conversation, but his eyes were on me.

The bartender returned with my money, and I left a tip, collected the bottles in my fingers, and headed back to Jenna without a word to Vince. I delivered the beers and checked my phone for emails. There was only one.

V: I swear I'm not stalking you.

He'd read my mind. I wrote back:

M: That's what all the stalkers claim.

V: Go to the bathroom. Meet me at the inside bar.

I gave Jenna the bathroom signal. She barely responded, but she understood. The air conditioned air chilled me as I walked inside. Vince was waiting for me at the bar, dressed in cargo shorts, flip flops, and a Phillies tee that was just this side of fitting. I could almost feel his chest beneath my fingers. I rubbed them together as I closed the distance between us, suddenly aware of my favorite jeans and tank top, which seemed fine for the golf course, but not enough for Vince. I'd become accustomed to wanting to impress him.

"This is a surprise," he said.

"It is, right?" I asked, and Vince chuckled, and even that was hot.

"It is. I promise." His smile lured me in. I couldn't take my eyes off him. Every other person in the bar who I was in danger of knowing somehow completely faded away. My heart raced with the excitement of him, of *this*. It was a foreign mix of need and abandonment that should have terrified me but instead, filled me with life.

"Don't you think you're taking this whole 'I'm hot' thing a little far?" I waved my hand vertically in front of his body, and he laughed again. "I mean, the ridiculously hot body, barely contained by your Phillies tee, the slightly long black curls popping out from under your hat . . . What's next? Motorcycle? Firearm strapped to your leg . . . twelve-inch cock?"

Vince raised his eyebrows and stared at me, amused. "Do you always say what you're thinking?"

"No."

"I'm happy you're impressed, but I swear I thought I was only going to see the guys I came with."

"It's just too much." I sighed and took a sip of my beer. "How long have you been here?"

"We were watching the game, but the Phils look terrible, and I saw on Facebook you were here."

"So you *are* stalking me?"

"It's not stalking if you put it on Facebook." The mention of the post reminded me of Jenna and that she probably shouldn't be left alone too long. "I need to get back."

"Back to the group of guys you're hanging out with?"

"Back to Jenna. I think she's had a long day of drinking.

Pony parties, you know."

"It feels like a week ago I saw you there. Are you going to the pool tomorrow?"

"I hope not." I turned to walk away, and Vince grabbed my elbow. His gentle grip sent a jolt through me.

"Don't go yet."

I looked at the television above us and the crowds on the sidewalks heading to their cars.

"It's the bottom of the ninth."

The sight of his hand still touching me caused a physical pain. The need to touch him was greater than my recollection of my role on this Earth. My God, I just wanted to feel his chest. And because I had no self-control, I wrapped my arms around his neck and hugged him. A goodbye hug like I'd give to any guy friend, or a friend's husband, except I barely knew Vince, and this hug's sole purpose was to etch in my mind forever the feel of his body against my own.

Jenna was close to belligerent. I should have taken her home an hour before. Apparently, while I'd been in the bathroom, rounds of shots had been consumed. I said goodbye to our companions and led her out of the bar. When she realized we were leaving, she argued she wasn't ready to go and tripped, finally slumping on the sidewalk at my feet.

I crouched down, trying not to draw attention to us or her inebriation. The last thing I needed was a call to Brad asking him to bail me out of jail. I had her halfway to vertical when she fell down again, this time almost taking me with her. Vince flew out of McFadden's side door and helped her to her feet.

With us all standing, he turned to me for direction on what to do next, but I was still shocked by the sight of him.

"Which way to your car?"

Yes, of course, the car. I started walking toward our parking lot. Vince wrapped an arm around Jenna's waist and support-ed her as she propelled them both forward on wobbly legs. I followed, carrying our purses. When we crossed the street, the police officer directing traffic did a double take, and Vince nod-ded at him, sending some silent cop signal that I was thankful for.

I unlocked the Escalade and opened the front passenger door for Jenna. Vince ignored me and lifted her into the back seat. He buckled her seatbelt as if she was one of his children and then stepped up into the passenger seat.

"What are you doing?" I asked, leaning on the open car door.

"Yeah! What are you *do*-ing?" Jenna loudly formed words in the backseat.

Vince was as comfortable in this mess as he'd been on the bus to the Franklin Institute. "I'm helping you get home. I'm a public servant."

Jenna laughed hysterically in the back seat and then fell over until her head hit the seat next to her. There was a strong chance I'd need his help. Resigned, I closed his door.

We pulled out of our parking spot and stopped in the line of cars trying to exit the lot. Vince helped me merge with the behemoth vehicle I never wanted. When we were finally on the Walt Whitman Bridge, I exhaled, feeling the worst of the night was behind me.

"You know who you look like?" Jenna said as she rested her head on the side of Vince's seat between us. "This cop in our town." She hit my arm too hard. "Doesn't he look like the chief?"

I took the opportunity to survey Vince's shoulders and chest. Vince smiled, and his light eyes danced in the oncoming headlights. His legs were spread, his thighs too wide to hold to-gether, his hands resting in his lap, connected by muscular arms to the chest of a god. I dragged my gaze back to the road in front of me and swallowed hard. My body was ultra-aware of the air around me. Everything seemed to be touching me with him this close.

"A little," I said.

"The cop is cuter," Jenna declared, which made Vince and I both laugh. "No offense," she added.

"Oh, none taken." He was a good sport.

"The chief is cute. Huh, Mer?" I eyeballed her in the rearview mirror, thankful I hadn't confided to her how I felt about this man . . . and his chest. "Like, mount-him-and-make-him-scream-my-name cute," Jenna said, and hiccupped loudly. "Fuck. I hate the hiccups."

I closed my eyes for a second and shook my head. *Please, let her pass out.*

Jenna slapped Vince on the shoulder. She leaned up again and hiccupped into the front seat. "Meredith wouldn't fuck him. She's a prude. She won't fuck you either, you know?" She leaned up further and stared at the colonel like she'd never seen him before. "Who are you? You look familiar."

I took my hand from the steering wheel and rubbed my temples. She was going to be sick tomorrow.

Ten miles of hiccups, and Jenna finally passed out in the back seat.

"Sorry about her. You know, mom of three boys," I said, as if that was the universal excuse for public drunkenness.

"She's fine." The kindness in Vince's voice put me at ease. We crossed the river and left the highway, and the back roads filled the car with darkness.

"Do you think he's cute?" Vince asked, and I stopped breathing for a minute.

"The cop?" I turned toward his silhouette. "Or you?"

"I'm starting to enjoy your inability to answer questions. It's fun," he said, and the sarcasm dripped from his words.

"Here to please."

WE RODE IN SILENCE THE rest of the way. I pulled into Jenna's driveway and looked at her in the back seat. I shook her leg, but she was passed out.

"Do you mind getting in the third row? I don't want her husband to see you. Or anyone to see you." Vince started to say something but stopped and got out of the car and climbed through the back door into the third row. "Try not to leave any DNA behind."

I leaned into the backseat and tried to rouse Jenna again. I sat her up and opened her eyelids, but her eyes only rolled further back in her head. Without a better idea, I took her phone out of her purse and called her husband's number.

"Where the fuck are you?" he answered.

"Hey, John." I tried to keep my voice light. This was not a big deal. "It's Meredith."

"Is Jen alright?" He was panicked, and that was a good sign.

"She's fine," I rushed to say. "She's actually in my car in your driveway. I just need a little help getting her inside."

"Fuck," he grumbled close to under his breath and hung up.

"He's coming out," I said to the backseat, which appeared to hold no one.

John turned on the front light and pulled a sweatshirt over his head as he stomped out the front door. He softened slightly when he got closer to the car. We stared into the backseat together. "What the fuck?"

"I know." I scrunched up my face, not sure what to say or how to defend us.

"Why do you look so good, and she's . . . this?" He pointed into the back seat, and then leaned over and unbuckled Jenna's belt. He lifted her up and over his shoulder.

"I was the driver."

John carried Jenna inside, and I followed with her purse. I left it on the table Jenna always left it on, right inside the door, and closed the door behind me.

By the time I reached the Escalade, Vince was back in the front passenger seat. It felt so normal having him there . . . with me . . . in the car Brad had picked out and paid for. I climbed in, put the Escalade in reverse, and turned around before driving down Jenna's long lane.

"Why aren't you as drunk as Jenna?"

"Because she's beating her brains out for her kids to have the perfect childhood," I said.

I am selfish.

"And what are you doing?"

"Fucking things up." I turned to Vince, whose face was barely visible in the dim light. He reached over and paused, resting his hand on my forearm. I wanted him to rest it on my breast. The heat from his touch spread through me. It warmed my arms and my legs and traveled up my neck until it was almost unbearable.

"You're not fucking this up."

I stopped the car at the end of the lane and looked at his hand, which now caressed my skin. "Are you my children?"

"No, but I've seen your daughter smile. She is pure light, and air, and confidence, and that doesn't happen by accident."

"It doesn't happen when people get divorced, either." For once, Vince lost his carefree demeanor. The truth hurt. "Where to?" His eyes bore into me. "I mean, where do you live?"

I couldn't do this alone . . . I could have pulled out the *your wife* card, but I kind of hated her. For no reason I hated her, except she got to live with Vince, which apparently wasn't that great, since he was a dick and touching my arm in my car. Jackass.

"You're a jackass, you know?" I said.

"I thought I was cute."

"You're a terrible husband."

"That's unfair."

"Really? Let's call your wife and ask her."

He sat motionless, staring at me in the wake of my ugly words. "How about just drop me off at the police station. I'll check on things there."

nine

SCHOOL ENDED. ANOTHER YEAR DONE. First and third grade would forever be a memory. The very next day, I set the alarm to get the kids up for swim practice. No one loved to swim more than me, and I still didn't want them on the team. Swimming should take place in the ocean or a lake. With nature. Not in a lane, after setting an alarm, during the summer. Brad felt it was a great activity for them. I thought we could try sleeping in and having our Saturdays free, but in the end we would spend our summer learning how to dive off a block . . . at 8 A.M.

❧

FOR THE FOURTH OF JULY, Liv scored us an invite to her friend's house on the parade route. She in her red-and-white striped dress and blue hair, and I in my white eyelet maxi dress, arrived with our stadium chairs and bowl of fresh-cut watermelon and blueberries. I put it on the table next to the fruit bowl carved out of a watermelon, complete with a rind star handle and star-shaped fruit inside. *Why, people? Why?*

"Oh, Meredith. I brought fruit, too," Alexis's mom said and waved at her art project.

"You sure did. How clever."

"Pinterest."

"Of course." I turned and walked away.

Brad walked the parade with the Cub Scouts. I told myself it was because he was a good dad, but watching him shake hands on his way down the street made me think he was considering a run for office. Which was silly, since he had no time. *He works.*

I made James stop and take a picture with Liv, and for fun I took a picture of Brad. He rolled his eyes because he was no fun. Officer Pratt walked—in full uniform—behind the World War II veterans, and I took his picture, too. And then to cover the evidence, I took sixty-seven more pictures with the excuse that I wanted James to see the parade since he missed it as a participant. The colonel looked right at me without an ounce of recognition. We hadn't spoken in nine days. Not since the Phillies game, and it was a constant dull tone in the back of my mind. An almost ache of what might have been.

I checked my junk email every day, but he never wrote, and that was the way it should be. But it was making me miserable. Or I was miserable and it was making me realize the depth of it. I wanted to talk to him. I wanted him.

I survived the quaint parade by hugging the curb. The rest of the ladies hovered in the shade of the weeping willow tree, discussing God-knows-what. Probably me.

Brad and James met us, and we all walked over to another Cub Scout's house for a picnic lasting until the fireworks at 9:30 P.M. Brad was hot and miserable and finally took my suggestion to go home and take a shower. I grabbed a beer and set up my chair near the keg with a perfect line of sight to the pool, which was then blocked by three women with fake smiles and endless comments about everyone else's children.

Jenna finally arrived and saved me. She moved her chair close and drank from her oversized travel cup that was a staple with her presence. I drank my warm beer conservatively until the colonel's wife walked through the back gate, then I downed my cup. I needed to talk to Brad about moving.

Mrs. Pratt had her youngest's hand firmly in hers as they crossed the lawn. He was lubed with sunscreen, buckled tight in a life jacket, and tossed into the pool with the other kids. Her daughter slipped into a tube and jumped right in, while her older son searched for someone his age. I kept an eye on the gate, waiting for the colonel to arrive, but there was no sign of him, so I filled my beer.

Jenna knew Mrs. Pratt. Everyone knew everyone from around there. She introduced me to the colonel's wife, and I leaned on Jenna's social graces, which I recognized as a point of weakness for me. *Since when did I need to lean on someone?* Mrs. Pratt, or Lynn, as she told me to call her, was frazzled and overwhelmed and almost incoherent.

"Where is—" she began, and then forgot the rest of the sentence as her daughter jumping into the pool stole her attention. When she turned back, she smiled absently and never finished her question, having completely forgotten she ever began it. It appeared she had too many kids, but as the conversation turned to the parade and dance troupes and tee-ball, I realized she was a product of her own activity list.

My team's conversation quickly moved to the bad kids we should avoid, and I had as much time for that as I did for the swimsuit police at the pool.

"I don't know what's going on with my Nolan," Nolan's mom said about her perfect son, whom I always found annoying. "He was talking back and arguing the other day." She shook her head, unable to put the pieces together. "Yesterday, he punched a boy at the pool. I'm sure the boy did something to make Nolan hit him, but still, it's not like him. I can't figure it out."

"Have you considered the fact that Nolan's an asshole?" I asked, and every woman within five feet of us gasped as their eyes fell on me.

Nolan's mom tilted her head, lifting her ear toward me, trying to hear better what I said, since she *clearly* heard that piece of wisdom wrong. I shrugged, and she stood and walked away, followed by every other woman except Jenna.

"What the hell was that?" Jenna asked. Her mouth hung open as her head shook. She watched Nolan's mom storm away before she turned her attention to me.

"That kid is an asshole."

"So what? Half the kids here are assholes, just like their parents. Since when do we go around telling them?" Jenna and I watched the other women console Nolan's mom on the other side of the pool. "You have to go apologize to her before her head explodes."

"I'm not apologizing."

"What has gotten into you? The last few days you've been . . . angry."

"Everything okay?" Vince's voice cut through me, and Jenna and I turned to see him standing behind us, concern covering his incredibly hot face.

"Everything's fine," Jenna said. I couldn't take my eyes off him. He was some lost memento, a stuffed beagle from the state fair I had clung to as a little girl on the moonless nights. The nights when I was alone. "I was just telling Meredith why we can't actually tell the parents of asshole children that their children are assholes." The colonel's mouth fell open, and then a smile spread across his face. "It's not funny! Meredith, you've got to go over there right now and apologize before this thing spreads."

I took a deep breath, not really caring about Nolan's mom or her asshole son. But when Brad walked through the gate, I knew I had to clean it up before he got involved.

I walked to the lethal injection of my stay-at-home-mom life. She was angrily whispering to several of her minions, and

I gambled the best course of action was to take them all on at the same time.

"Hi." I shook my head sympathetically. "Please forgive me. I don't know what is wrong with me. Of course, Nolan's not an asshole. *I'm* an asshole. It's either the heat, or every holiday since my parents died—" I threw the dead parents in out of desperation, "—or exhaustion, but I'm not myself either. Seriously, it's not Nolan you should be worried about, it's me."

She softened immediately. Partially because she was a nice person, but mainly because I had given her a tidbit of information about myself. Something she could share with others. "Meredith, I'm so sorry. We had no idea your parents are deceased." *Who's we?* "That must be so hard."

"It been a few years now. Some days I just get into this funk, but I shouldn't be spreading it around. Do you forgive me?"

"Of course." She sounded like she genuinely forgave me. I turned and saw Brad introducing himself to the colonel, and I searched the table behind Nolan's mom and her mob for more liquor.

"Are those Jell-O shots?" I asked, pointing behind her.

"Yes! Let's all do one."

The crowd gathered and vodka-laced Jell-O healed the wound I'd created with my honesty. Nolan was in the pool, splashing a little girl in the face until she cried, and then he called her a baby and splashed her again. I picked up a handful of Jell-O shots and smiled before walking away.

The picnic continued without me insulting anyone else. I watched as Brad and Nolan's mom laughed about something. I was just happy to see she was really over it. At least for now.

I kept my distance from the colonel. It made it easier to watch him. My anger dissipated with every turn of his head, every word from his mouth. He was incredible.

Asshole Nolan splashed a little girl playing with Allison and Liv, and Liv yelled at him and punched him in the face. I was out of my chair, practically spilling my beer, trying to reach her before Brad saw. Nolan was crying at the side of the pool, obviously not letting it go. The colonel pulled him out of the water and told him to take a deep breath. My eyes were on Liv, who was completely unrepentant. I could hear her already. "He deserved it." I would have to muster the motherly words on how we didn't hit people, even when they deserved it.

"Real men never make a girl, or anyone else, feel bad to make themselves feel strong. You understand?" I heard the colonel saying to the little asshole. "You're better than that. Know it." He touched Nolan's chest with two fingers as the boy nodded. I was paralyzed. "Now go apologize and be kind. Wait until you see how many kids want to play with you when you're kind."

Nolan dove into the pool and apologized to Liv and her friend, which did nothing for the lesson Liv needed to learn, but I let it go because I couldn't let go of the colonel. I watched as he stood next to the pool and kept an eye on Nolan until the children were returned to harmony.

Without warning, James walked over to me and hugged me causing my white eyelet dress to become see-through, which was not going to fly. It was lined, but the dark circles surrounding my nipples were just visible enough to give everyone the mental image of the rest of me.

"Sorry, Mom," he said, and since the damage was already done I hugged him again. Even without caring about my areola, James could sense the additional work he'd caused me. Brad looked up from his conversation, and I pointed at each of my breasts. His eyes widened. He nodded as I gave him the signal I was driving home to change. I grabbed my keys and slipped through the gate to safety. I hit my stride in the side yard and felt as light as a feather when my hand touched the car door.

"Leaving already? Surely there are more assholes who need to be informed."

My head dropped. *What? Is he everywhere?* I turned to face him and watched as the colonel's gaze caressed every corner of my exposed body in my soaked dress. "My loving son hugged me when he got out of the pool." I could have crossed my arms. I could have turned away. But his eyes on me made my nipples hard, and I wanted him to touch them.

"I watched you work your magic on the mavens. Impressive," he said, finally moving his attention from my breasts to my eyes.

"I'm used to a jury."

"I want to see you again. I feel like I owe you an apology."

"You owe me nothing. That's how I know there's nothing to apologize for."

"I want there to be something," he said.

He said it, and I stopped breathing.

When I finally exhaled, I couldn't keep a smile from spreading across my stunned face, and I felt myself leaning closer to him as my cheeks flushed. I was a fucking moron. And I recognized all of it was nonsense. I was married. I was bored. This was nothing but a dangerous distraction. It was the devil's playground.

"I've got to go." I climbed into the Escalade and drove away, watching Vince in my rearview mirror until I reached the stop sign.

Don't do this, Meredith.

ten

LIV WAS SO TIRED, SHE slurred her words as she said she loved me. Her arms, usually tight around my neck from not wanting me to leave her bed, could barely hold on.

"I love you, too," I said for the forty thousandth time and turned off her lights.

Brad and I met in the hall between Liv's and James' rooms.

"Are you coming down?" he asked, but I couldn't tell if he had a preference in my location.

"Yeah. I'll have another beer with you." I wanted to talk to him. I wanted him to hear me. I wasn't sure what the problem was exactly, or what the solution was, but I needed him to admit there was a problem. An issue . . . with me.

Brad disappeared down the stairs, and I threw my shoes in my closet. Two walls of shelved shoes lined the walk-in. Brad would say I was crazy for complaining. He was almost bitter at how perfect my life was. But he couldn't spend ten hours with the kids without them annoying him. On the rare occasion he was there for homework, it ended with his jaw clenched and the kids in tears. How he could berate me for not basking in this life never made sense to me.

I walked down the stairs, determined to find some common ground. Brad handed me a beer, and I followed him onto our back patio. We hadn't used it yet this summer, hadn't even lit the fire pit.

"Maybe we should have a party," he said and sunk into the outdoor sectional as if it was his bed. Brad had consumed just enough beers to be pleasant.

"Who would we invite?"

He laughed, but it was actually a serious question. His peers from work? The neighbors? "That was a great crowd tonight. Let's invite them. Maybe get some crabs, or have a shrimp boil. Or both." He stretched his legs out to the coffee table in front of him. I'd forgotten how tall he was.

"Maybe," I said, hoping he'd forget the whole thing by tomorrow. A party sounded like more work for me. Work I had no interest in doing.

"Seriously, Meredith. It doesn't have to be a big deal. We'll send out an email, get a keg, and a few bushels of crabs."

"What if it rains?"

"What if there's a tsunami? God, you are such a downer. It's like you hate having fun anymore."

I pursed my lips and refused to respond. I was there for a reason. I needed his help. Even if he was a dick, he was the only dick I had. "Speaking of what I am . . . I've been feeling lost lately."

Brad's relaxation drained from his face and he stopped drinking his beer. "What do you mean, lost?"

"I don't know. Since I stopped working, I don't really have a purpose. Nothing that is challenging me. I have no passion."

Brad laughed. It wasn't light and amusing. It was demonic, and I braced myself. "You think I have passion? You think I like working sixty hours a week?"

"Why, when I bring up the fact that I'm feeling lost, do you immediately tell me about you?"

"Because you act like you're owed something. That you should not work, and do yoga, and look great, and yet still be challenged." He said this dramatically, filled with disdain. "Your *passion* should be explored." He was making me sick. Making me hate him. "That's not real life, Meredith. Some of us have to work."

I got up and walked into the house. I wanted to pack my things and drive away. The anger seared through me. I would never fuck him again. *His dick can shrivel up and fall off before it touches the inside of my mouth.* No good, motherfucker, boring-ass lay was going to tell *me* about passion?

I lay awake, trying to find a way out of my marriage. But every thought led to me seeing Liv and James only every other weekend, and I couldn't live that way. I wouldn't make them live that way. Liv packing her stuffed bunny every other Friday to take with her to wherever her father was living. I wouldn't even let myself consider who he'd be living with. I forced my mother's dry cleaner from my mind. No one else was ever going to tuck my children in.

Period.

I'd find something that fed my soul to fill my time when they were at school. I would thrive. I would grow if it killed me. I would stay with their pompous father, who didn't deserve me, or them.

I was still awake when Brad skulked into the bedroom and plopped onto the bed. He pulled the covers over his shoulder and rolled toward the wall before I heard his breathing steady. I took a cleansing breath and let the teachings of yoga fill me. I was grateful. I was healthy and in control. I would make this work and exchange with the universe positivity.

I DREAMED THAT NIGHT THAT Brad died in a car accident and when I woke up, I was fine with it. But when I spooned Greek yogurt into a bowl and topped it with blueberries and granola, Brad watched me sympathetically.

"Do you want to go to the shore today?" he asked.

I almost spit the yogurt right out of my mouth. Surely he had several things more important to do than go to the shore with me.

"What do you think, guys? Want to go to the shore today?" he asked the kids, clapping his hands and riling them up.

Liv and James immediately jumped out of their breakfast chairs and began dancing around the kitchen. I couldn't remember the last time we'd gone somewhere as a family. *Well played, Brad.*

It wasn't until we were in the Escalade heading east that Brad told me we'd been invited by the unicorn at the picnic yesterday.

"Really?" I was still trying to process the invitation, let alone Brad's interest in going.

"Yes. Really. Believe it or not, people want to be our friends. She seemed nice."

"Lacey's mom, right?" She'd never *seemed* anything but annoying to me. Oh wait, she was also a huge gossip.

"Yeah. You know what she told me?"

"I can't imagine."

Brad checked the backseat in the rearview mirror and, satisfied the kids were unable to hear him through their headphones, he leaned toward me. "That Vanessa is fucking one of the guys who runs the before-school daycare program at the school."

I rolled my eyes. I would have told him that months ago if he'd picked up his office phone when I'd called.

"What? You don't believe it?"

"I think she talks too much. What business is it of hers if Vanessa is fucking the daycare guy?"

"Vanessa's a whore." Brad's tone was nasty and dismissive. He'd gone from light gossip to judgment faster than I could keep up.

"Who cares?"

"I know I watch her husband leave every morning so he can get to work while her ass is still in bed. He needs to make enough money for her to stay home and fuck some guy fifteen years younger than her while her kids are in school every day. Sounds like a whore to me."

I was pretty sure Vanessa got up early every morning. I turned toward the window and smiled, thinking she'd need time to primp before the young man showed up with his banana. Something about the affair made me like Vanessa even more. It was as if she was throwing up her middle finger at her husband and the rest of the world. I wasn't able to reconcile her actions with my own thoughts on cheating, but she was fearless. She'd lost ten pounds, had gotten a tattoo, and had a huge smile on her face every minute of the day.

"I hope when her husband finds out, he makes her life a living hell." Brad's voice was rough, his tone as nasty as the scowl on his face.

"Sarah should mind her own business." Brad watched me with disappointment in his eyes. My thinking the unicorn was a judgmental bitch was somehow judging him. Brad didn't like to be judged. He was perfect. *He works, for God's sake.*

❧

WE ARRIVED AT THE SHORE house, Sarah's rental for the week, and there were no spots on the street. Brad dropped the kids and me off in front of the house and left to search for a parking spot.

I faced the house and took a deep breath. Before I'd settled my nerves, the unicorn and her three children came out of the house. Her kids were excited to see mine, and she was shocked to see me.

"Meredith, you came!" *I did.* "Where's Brad?"

"He's parking. This was so kind of you to invite us down for the day."

"Nonsense. Everyone is welcome. Half the town is coming down." She corralled the kids into the backyard and took me inside to show me a small corner in the living room where I could leave our bag of dry clothes. I placed the box of donuts we'd picked up on the counter and put the store-bought veggie tray in the refrigerator. I felt like giving the unicorn more to talk about was part of the gift. *Gasp, she doesn't even slice her own cucumbers.*

We stayed on the beach long past the guards leaving. Liv and James frolicked the entire day. In the water. Out of the water. They built in the sand, rode the waves, and played paddle ball and Frisbee. And when they needed something, they asked me. I reapplied sunscreen and doled out juice boxes. I stayed by the water while they swam, and all the while Brad was talking to some of the other dads. They were laughing and sharing stories about their jobs. Their careers they'd worked so hard to achieve. Two of the men were attorneys. Certainly I had more in common with them than Brad, but he never once mentioned my career. The one I'd left behind.

Faced with the choice of taking my spot with the women or playing with Liv and James, I frolicked right alongside my children. By the end of the day, Liv and James were exhausted. They covered up in towels and lay on our blanket, whispering stories of idiocy to each other. *What's the craziest thing you've ever seen? What would you rather be, a shark ninja or a ninja shark? Would you rather never eat again, or never sleep?* Their conversations were tolerable with the ocean strumming behind them.

With everyone settled, I walked to the edge of the water. I'd waited all day, taking care of my children, and listening as the ocean called me to it. It was calm today, the breakers a small barrier between me and the horizon. I walked out, raising my knees high to climb over the waves, and then I dove in. I emerged on the calm side of the set and floated on my back. The water washed away the sand and cooled my hot skin. I was alone in the ocean, and it was better than any adult with me, including my husband. Hadn't these women ever worked? Had they forgotten what it felt like? How could they be so happy being this? Their husbands' wives. Their children's moms.

What the fuck is wrong with me?

The waves picked me up and floated me over them. The ocean loved me. And in the silence of it, I heard exactly what was wrong with me.

I wanted Vince to touch me.

There, I'd said it. He'd been on my mind all day. I'd tried to bury it in the sand, but I *wanted* him.

eleven

BRAD MADE US ALL WALK the eight blocks to the Escalade. He grumbled about what a nightmare it had been to park it, and I somehow kept from pointing out that he'd wanted the ridiculous car in the first place. The kids dragged their boogie boards on the sidewalk. The scraping sound grated on me, but I pushed it out of my mind and thought of the ocean. I'd endured the entire day for a twenty-minute swim alone.

We loaded everything including ourselves in the car, and as we pulled away from the curb, Brad closed all the windows and turned on the air conditioning. *Why can't we feel wind?* I pointed the vents pummeling me with cold air in every direction away from me and read the news on my phone. I mentioned a few stories to Brad, but he was tired and silent and a giant dick like usual, so while I sat right next to him, I wrote the colonel an email:

> M: *I went to Sarah's shore house today, and she didn't make me wear a name tag with shells and small sea creatures glued to it.*

I laughed. And then, aware of my surroundings, searched for a lie about what I found funny, but Brad kept his eyes on the road and never asked.

After a few more news stories, I went back to my email and

was relieved to find the colonel's reply:

V: I know.

M: How do you know?

V: Because now I'm on Facebook. Beautiful day, according to the photos. And Richie's dad.

I hit the home button on my phone and found the Facebook app. It had a little red circle with the number twenty-six in it. I'd never had twenty-six notifications before. I braced myself and I opened Facebook. Sarah King Lawson had tagged me in an album. *An album?* I clicked on it, and photos of today came up in full color. Most were pictures of the kids. My kids, Sarah's kids, and all the others at the shore that day. One picture had me on all fours, working on a sandcastle with Liv and James. I was partially covered with sand, and the camera angle stared right down between my breasts. I was looking to the side at Liv, who was laughing hysterically, and I remembered the exact moment. She had told me a joke she'd made up about a hermit crab. It wasn't very funny. I'd told her it needed a little work. She'd placed her hand on my shoulder and reminded me how awesome she was, and then she'd almost fallen over laughing.

There was one photo I knew Sarah had taken. It was all the adults, except her, sitting in a row of beach chairs. It was innocent enough. The last picture was of the ocean with me standing in front of it, staring out to the horizon. My suit was high on my butt, the bottoms of my cheeks peeking out, and my back was bare. My hair blew in the ocean breeze. I couldn't stop staring at it, and for the life of me, I couldn't figure out why she'd ever post it. She must not have realized I was in it. There were already twenty-two "likes" and eleven comments. I opened them. Most were about the ocean, some asked how long Sarah was going to be down there, and Richie's dad had commented, "Beautiful!" which I found suspect. I hit the home button and closed Facebook.

I emailed Vince again.

> M: It didn't really happen unless it's posted on Facebook.

He immediately responded:

> V: I'm beginning to understand that. Some people are on there a lot. And from the comments on one of the photos, the entire world now knows how long Sarah will be out of town.

> M: Are you planning on staking out her house?

> V: Why? Do you want to join me?

"Mommy, can I play on your phone?" Liv asked, and I hit the home button with a little too much urgency.

"No."

"Why?"

"Because I'm playing on it," I said, but lowered it to my lap and watched the houses as we passed them on our way back home. *I wonder where the colonel lives.*

ॐ

AFTER I UNPACKED THE CAR, the cooler, and our beach bag, I made sure the kids had showered and finally took one myself. The absence of the sand and salt water saddened me. Even with the unicorn, a day at the shore was better than any other day. I watered the plant that insisted on dying. I perused my book shelf, wanting something to read, searching for someplace else to be in my mind.

Tomorrow Brad would be back to work, and I'd be back to swim practice. And no book was going to take me away from that. I climbed into bed, my wet hair hanging down my back, and I signed into my email. There was one from Vince, and I clung to it before I even opened it.

V: Your daughter looks just like you.

M: Covered in sand?

V: Yes, and comfortable.

M: According to her, she's awesome.

V: According to me, so are you.

I closed the emails and went to sleep. I didn't wait for Brad to come to bed and turn the television on some show I couldn't care less about. I didn't leave a light on for him. I lay in the dark and closed my eyes, letting sleep have me. I dreamed I was laughing at a joke the colonel told me, and then Liv starting laughing with us. When we finally calmed down, Liv told me I was pretty when I laughed. She said I was awesome like her.

twelve

WHEN I AWOKE, THE FACEBOOK notifications were still coming in. Most were likes of the pictures I was tagged in, but one comment was from an attorney I used to work with, Christine Donahue. She asked me to meet her for lunch, and my heart fluttered. I couldn't comment back fast enough that I would meet her anytime, anywhere. We switched to email and set up a date for the following week to have lunch in Philadelphia. It was the equivalent of a drunken weekend in Spain at this point.

"HOW'S THE MOM THING GOING?" Christine asked. She'd never married, never had children, and there were times when I thought she might be the smart one.

"I'm getting used to it," I answered as honestly as possible. "But I don't want to talk about that. Tell me everything about the office. Every case, every attorney, every investigator. I hope you have time for an extra-long lunch, because it's been too long since I've talked to anyone."

Christine almost satisfied my bottomless need for information. She was detailed and accurate, exactly like her case files. Lunch was a tiny glimpse into my old life, and I reveled in it through two glasses of wine. Just putting something other than a maxi dress on was exhilarating. I was going someplace with actual napkins. There was no picnic table in this restaurant, and as I scanned the dining room, not one child.

I didn't care if I seemed desperate. I couldn't. That was the definition of desperate, wasn't it?

"Have you made lots of friends now that you're off?"

"A few. Stay-at-home moms are different."

She tilted her head to me sympathetically. "I'll bet you're more alike than you think. It's like the thieves and the hookers. Their needs aren't so different from ours. Their actions are just a bit misguided. You have to find some common ground."

"Do I really have to?"

Christine laughed at me as she shook her head. "Are you sure you're okay? It's not like you not to connect. You had the entire judicial system eating out of your hand when you were with us."

"You guys loved what I was serving," I said, and reminisced about the people I worked with. The attorneys, bailiffs, judges, even the defense attorneys, they were all such wonderful characters in the artful play I called my career. Now the talent pool seemed shallow.

Or maybe I was just a bitch.

We finished our lunch with Christine telling me about the new man she was seeing. He was divorced with two small children, and he and Christine hated his ex-wife. Yes. She was the problem. I nodded, and dramatically winced as Christine told me the ex's demands of the children's time. I was properly appalled at how much money the ex needed to live. But in my heart, I feared someday I would be her. Christine asked—told—me to get my kids raised and come back to work as soon as possible. Brad had just taken over the London offices. It was going to be a while.

thirteen

INSTEAD OF MY WEEKEND MOUNT with Brad, I rolled over and grabbed my phone. I signed into my email, desperate to hear from Vince. Before I hit enter, I took a minute to evaluate my situation.

He was fire, and I was playing with it.

I was not a cheater. These were the actions of a vacant housewife starved for attention. I needed to build my own life and not search outside of my marriage for fulfillment. I was too smart for this. And my family deserved better.

Deep breath . . .

I hit enter, and relief flowed through me at the sight of his email address. Without hesitation, I opened it.

> *V: Are you going to the pool today?*

> *M: Why?*

> *V: I just asked because I like to waste my time knowing you'll never answer.*

> *M: My brother and his wife are taking my kids to Dutch*

Wonderland for the day, and my husband won't be back from London until this afternoon, so I'm running away.

V: Tell me where so I can run away with you.

I stared at the screen. It was a pivotal moment. Words needed to be said. The tone had moved from parental peers to *A few glasses of wine, and I'll tell you what I think about when I touch myself.* I wrote:

M: You shouldn't follow me. You'll find yourself lost and drowning in regret.

V: Where?

M: I'm going to The Point, where they don't care if I cover up.

There was no response. And there shouldn't be. *This* needed to be done.

❧

THE ROAD TO THE SHORE was a mix of small highways and small towns. I played classic rock music from my phone and sang along with the windows down and my hair blowing in my face. I watched the clouds pass above me, and I convinced myself I was happily married and Colonel Vincent Pratt was a bad idea. One I couldn't seem to get out of my head. He wasn't your garden-variety letch. He didn't ogle me. Something about him gave us merit. He was so good, so this couldn't be wrong.

Brad deserved better than this. Liv and James deserved better. I deserved better . . . and I was not even going to start with the Pratt family. I wondered how many affairs he'd had. It was never the first. Men who cheated, cheated. And according to Brad, women who cheated were whores.

I was over-qualified to be a whore.

With only ten miles to the back bay, I pulled a six-month-old roach from my beach bag and lit it. I inhaled, sucking in as much of the sweet smoke as possible, and then forced in another two small puffs. I dropped my lighter in the console next to me. The purple crystals covering it caught the sunlight and spread white dots throughout the interior of the Escalade. *My very own disco dance floor.* I inhaled the last drag off the roach, tossed the miniscule paper out the window, and drank a huge gulp of water. My high sunk in as I drove over the bridge to Ocean City. I took the first right I could and headed out of town and to The Point, where the inlet connected the ocean to the bay. Where a person could hide from the world.

While high, I climbed the dune and Vince didn't seem like an issue. He'd said three nice things to me. He was entertaining. Really, what had occurred that was so significant? *Nothing.* I was making more out of it than there was. I needed to relax. Jenna was right. I was a prude. The wind caught under my sheet, blowing it over my eyes until I lowered it to the sand and watched it flutter into waves. I secured two sides with my shoes and one with my bag. I folded a towel as a pillow and lay on my back, watching the clouds float by, and I was happy. I was satisfied. And I was alone.

I retied the string on my bikini bottom. The suit was white and small and fit perfectly. Five-days-a-week workouts, only to be covered up. What sense . . . the bikini would have caused mayhem at the pool. I think Fox News might have received a report of it.

The sky was bright, and my eyelids became heavy after a while. I shut them and let sleep take me back to the shore in my twenties. When I would lie on the sand with at least ten other people and talk about the antics of the night before. Law school had drained me, and the summer at the shore while I studied for the Bar had restored me back to myself. In my dream, Brad was on the beach with me, but I didn't know him that summer. He was annoyed I was smiling so much and asked me to stop. I woke up and opened my eyes, suffocated by frustration.

Was the Meredith Brad married really me? Did he ever truly know the girl I was at the shore for the summer? I rolled over on the blanket and racked my brain for all the moments of genuine laughter with Brad. We'd celebrated our achievements. There'd been tremendous success in our marriage. At first for both of us, but now just for him. We'd huddled together as we'd buried our parents one by one. We'd worked like dogs. Long nights at the office and at-home breastfeeding. We were two of the most driven people I'd ever met. Perfectly matched intellectually, and yet worlds apart motivationally.

Did we ever laugh?

Ugh. Who cares? I sat up, pissed at myself. This was more stay-at-home mom angst, and I wouldn't be dragged into it any more than I would compete to be the head room mom. I stood, shaky from the sun and the weed, and ran into the ocean. The waves crashed against my thighs, and I let them push me toward the shore. When the set passed, I ran in deeper and dove into the cresting wave. I floated on my back and cleared my mind. Yoga had taught me to separate my body from my thoughts. I was at one with the moon as it directed the waves, and I floated over the currents beneath me, listening to the breakers falling on the sand.

The first thought to pop into my mind was sunscreen. Specifically, the fact that I had none on. My face felt burnt. Which was impossible, I hoped, but I still needed to get out of the water. I swam until I could stand, and walked out.

Vince was sitting on a small towel next to my sheet. I was

supposed to say something, I think. But instead, I studied the muscles that rested between his shoulder and his neck. His knees were raised, his forearms rested on them with his fingers threaded in front of him.

He didn't smile as I walked toward him. I braced myself for a cheesy comment of how I looked in my bathing suit, but it never came. Instead he shifted his weight and leaned back with his hands resting behind him, and I stopped breathing. His stomach, which I had imagined a hundred times before, was on full display. He'd worn a t-shirt to the pool, and now I knew why. He'd have to fight the women of our town off of him if they saw this.

"I saw you do a backflip at the pool," he said, tentatively staring at me as if a debate was raging in his mind. I smiled at the idea of the flip. "You're different in the water. You're peaceful."

I stayed still above him. "My father used to say I was half fish, only satisfied when I was wet." Vince studied me as I spoke. "He chose the name Meredith because it means 'guardian of the sea.'" I dried the water dripping down my back from my hair and thought of my father. *What would he think of me now?* The painful longing for him returned. "He used to take me in the ocean as a little girl, and my mother would yell at him not to take me so deep, but I could swim as soon as I could walk and I always had to be the farthest person out."

No one could come between me and the ocean. And now Vince was sitting on the sand and knew it, and I'd never told Brad any of it. The memory belonged to me and my father. I'd buried it in my heart when I buried him.

Vince's wedding ring caught my eye. It was a plain silver band. "Have you ever cheated on your wife?" came flying out of my mouth, shocking us both. Scared of his answer, I turned away and sat on the sheet. I took to the task of slathering myself with sunscreen.

"No," he said, and I wanted more than anything to believe

him. He was too good to cheat. He was perfect in my mind, and I'd leave him there to have him stay that way. "Should I bother asking you?"

"I haven't. And I never want to." That was as clear as it was going to get. There should have been no ambiguity, regardless of what my eyes told him to the contrary.

"Because it's morally wrong? Because of your children? Or are you afraid of a scandal?" he asked, and I wanted to know if this was the order of his conscience.

"You didn't ask if it's because I'm in love with my husband."

"Because I know that's not the reason."

"I don't cheat because it's typical." I leaned over to him. "It's too easy, and I'm better than that." I was. I was better than that. Than whatever *it* was. I sat back, resting on my hands behind me, and stared out at the horizon.

"Do you mind?" Vince asked, motioning toward my sheet.

"Quite the opposite." I moved over, sharing my space. I recognized the mixed signals. I wasn't going to have an affair with him, but I wasn't going to lie to him either. He could figure it out. He lay beside me. He rolled my towel into a ball and rested his head on it.

After a few seconds, he raised his head and stared at me. "Your towel smells like marijuana."

In that moment, he reeked of Brad. Brad had never gotten high a day in his life. He found it appalling. Had he known me when I'd spent the summers riding waves and getting high, he never would have wanted me. Now, I was lucky to smoke pot once a year.

"Is that probable cause to search my bag?"

"It's my job." His words were thick with regret. I was no longer perfect in his mind. Lucky him.

"You'd put me in a cage, too?" I asked and returned my stare to the water. "You can search my bag if you want. You have my consent." The word "consent" floated between us, now a part of our situation. The colonel lay still. "When you were little, did you dress up as a police officer for Halloween?" I asked, imagining him as a little boy.

"Every year. What were you?"

"A mermaid." I looked back out at the sea.

"Mermaid, attorney, they're close."

I laughed, and Vince joined me. "Yes. Practically identical."

"Why did you stop? Working? You're obviously still a mermaid."

"I showed up at court with spit-up running down my back. My babysitter quit in the middle of a trial. The stomach flu." His arms stole my attention, and I let my eyes follow them to his shoulder. "Ear tubes. Tonsils. Swim lessons. Sick parents," I recited, my eyes still focused on his neck. "Not seeing Liv for one waking moment of her first birthday." Vince rolled onto his side, hanging on my every word. "And my husband's constant calls asking if Sunday through Thursday next week worked for him to be in London. One of us had to quit."

"Did you ever talk about it being him?"

"He makes more money and he has no patience."

"Sounds unfair."

"Once a woman has children, nothing's fair anymore." He took it in, milling it around in his head and probably the head of his children's mother. "That goes for all women. Whether they work or stay home, have one child or ten. Once you become a mother, your life is no longer your own. That's the way it should be, right?"

Vince stayed silent. How could he answer that question? I couldn't, and I was a mother. I lay back down with my face to the sky. The endless summer sky I was under with the gorgeous colonel, complaining about my life.

"But most women would kill to be in my shoes, and I try not to take it for granted."

Vince stood and held out his hand for me. "Come in the

ocean with me, Meredith."

"It's rough," I warned.

"We'll swim out past the breakers. Out to where it's calm."

I scanned the beach to my right and my left. The only people left were a family packing up their carful of gear. They'd be gone soon, too. I placed my hand in his, determined there was still a way to turn back.

We walked into the deserted ocean, him following me. A wave crashed onto us, pushing me back against his chest. It fulfilled my growing need to touch him, but still my body wanted more. It wanted his hands on me. Everywhere. Vince put me back on my feet in front of him, and the waves pushing against us replaced the idea of touching him.

"We're going to have to make a run for it," I said.

"I'll follow you," he said, and I turned toward the waves. I let one pass and ran before the next set formed. I dove through it and came up past the breakers, watching Vince dive in. He was a good swimmer. That mattered.

We stayed out too far and floated with our toes in the air. The lifeguards carried their stand to the top of the beach and waved before leaving for the night. It was time to go back. Back to my life. To Brad's life. Vince was standing in the water watching me.

"Come here," he said, and I couldn't move. The look in his eyes had lost its curiosity. He'd answered all his questions.

I swam over, and he pulled me to him. My chest tightened. I was internally torn between the overwhelming need to feel his body against mine, and the instinct to run before I ruined my life. He wrapped my legs around his waist and I rested my hands on his arms, and we floated together over the waves. They lifted him first, pressing his body into mine in a slow, sensual rhythm. I let go of every rational thought in my head and leaned back, letting the back of my head float on the water and the moon direct our movements. Vince's finger ran from my neck, down the center of my chest to the top of my bathing suit bottoms, and I closed my eyes and exhaled.

Everything was silent, but the ocean around us. As if the sea wanted us to be together. Vince raised me up, and I looked down at my legs, my body touching his. My gaze rested on his stomach and I let myself forget the currents around us. I was so far from my life. So far away.

"Just for a minute," he said, bringing my eyes back to his, "I don't want you to think I have a plan . . . or some idea of what I'm doing now, or next." I swallowed and parted my lips to breathe. "I've never done anything like this before. You have to believe that."

I should have nodded, or spoken, but instead I stayed perfectly still. We weren't going to have an affair. I was never going to see him naked. This would be the last conversation about this, and I wanted to savor it.

"But I haven't been able to stop thinking about you since Philadelphia, and the things I want to do to you are far from typical."

My eyes lowered to his lips until he placed them on mine. He wasn't sweet or gentle. He was the colonel and he took exactly what he wanted. I wrapped my arms around his neck, needing him closer, feeding the cravings for him since he'd sat with me on the school bus. I was barely cognizant of his tongue in my mouth, energy flowing through me stealing my morality. His arms encircled me like heavy timber, forcing me toward him, and yet we floated over the waves as if nothing could sink us.

I was pulling him closer to me, letting my body dictate my actions. It wanted him, and it would have me risk everything to have him. Vince kissed me until his hard-on jabbed into me. It was a warning of the inevitable, and I jerked away from him. He took my arms and held me to him, not letting me free. My body was on fire. The water flowing against it left me chilled.

"You follow me to the shore," I said, fighting to catch my breath. "And kiss me in the ocean. What else will you do?" He waited, and the water lapped against us. "Will you push my top to the side and take my breast in your mouth?" Vince's eyes never left mine. I leaned back, my vulgarity gaining strength. "Will you take off my suit bottom and fuck me right here?"

"I'll do all of that." The words hammered from his mouth. His chest heaved, and I looked out at the horizon, defeat floating between us.

"You'll turn me into your whore. Into the town whore."

"It could never be like that."

"It is *always* exactly like that," I said and pulled away. Vince released me, his eyes searched mine for some understanding as he rose and fell over the waves. His jaw was locked in frustration. "I need to go home."

I swam forward and caught a wave to shore.

Vince stayed in the water. He faced me as I dried off, and I wanted to go back in. I wanted him to fuck me right there. Which was exactly why I needed to leave. I found my skirt and put it on before taking off my bathing suit bottoms. I threw them on my towel as Vince walked up next to me. I squeezed the water out of my hair and lowered a bandeau over my head. Vince stayed silent. What else needed to be said? I turned toward the ocean and untied my top, removing it out from under the bandeau. The touch of him between my legs while we floated in the ocean lingered in my mind. I watched the waves come to shore, and wanted him more. I sighed as I dragged my tank top over my head. I rolled the bikini top and bottoms up in a towel. The deep silence sank between us.

We were too good to have an affair.

We both knew I was right.

fourteen

WE WALKED OVER THE DUNE, Vince following me. His truck was parked in front of the Escalade. I opened the driver's door and threw my bag across the seat. I climbed in and shut the door without saying goodbye. Vince opened his truck door and stood between it and his truck. He dropped his bathing suit to his ankles and stepped out of it. His tan line stopped just above the curve of his perfect ass, and I reached my hand to my mouth and exhaled. I was in awe. He brushed the towel across his skin while the muscles in his back and upper arms flexed to his body's whim. A hot sheen covered my skin as Vince twisted just enough for me to catch a glimpse of the dark hair trailing from his belly button to his penis.

"Man, he's good," I whispered to no one.

I found my phone in my bag and took a picture of the back of him. He turned, half laughing at the sight of my photography, and I forgot everything about the ocean. That is, everything but how he'd felt between my legs.

Vince put his suit in a plastic bag and zipped it into his backpack. He stepped into shorts, and I exhaled the air I hadn't realize I'd trapped in my lungs. He walked back to my door and leaned in the window, very cop-like. I lowered all the windows, figuring it smelled like pot.

"Miss, can I see your camera?"

"No, officer. You may not."

"Did you just take a picture of my bare ass?"

"Yes. Yes, I did. It's lovely," I said, remembering every inch of it. "But you already know that. Thus the baring of said ass."

"I'll follow you home." His police demeanor was replaced with his easy smile I couldn't get enough of.

"No. I'll follow you. That way I can get high." He froze, the blood rushing to his face, and I recognized the phrase "seeing red" in action. "I'm kidding! I do have some trouble with the speed limit, though. Following you will force me to take my time."

He nodded, tapped my door with his open palm, and walked back to his truck.

I followed him as we pulled onto the street and drove away from the shore. From the first place he'd kissed me. *First.* I drove without an ounce of concentration on the road. I played my wedding song. It was a stupid song. It had no meaning even back then. Its only purpose was filling the void of our song on the wedding checklist.

I remembered every touch of Vince's hands on my body. Both nipples hardened from my memories. I thought back to the Franklin Institute, and the spring concert, and his first emails, and his talk with Nolan about how a man treats a woman, and every breath I watched him take in my presence. I shifted in my seat, my body restless and wanting him.

I recalled every inch of his naked body I'd just seen by his car. I left the windows down and turned the air conditioning on to cool me. I started to combine the images. The colonel on the school bus naked. The colonel in the parade naked. The colonel, the colonel, the colonel . . . An hour passed, and I was ready to run my car into the back of his truck and fuck him on the side of the road.

When we merged off Route 55 onto Route 40, a car got between us, and I felt some relief. Brad's face, and how nervous he was when he'd proposed, flashed through my mind. I held up my fingers, my engagement ring eyed me back. *I loved this ring, and I loved him putting it on me.* I let the sun dance over the stone inside my Escalade. Brad had known me so well. He'd known I'd never want a diamond. The extravagant stones, especially back then, were surrounded by violence. They were blood diamonds and a huge waste of money. When he opened the ring box, and it was a blue topaz, I knew I'd found my soulmate. Funny how that feeling faded, but the topaz never did.

I passed the credit union on the edge of Riversbend. The sign out front said 6:41 P.M., eighty-one degrees. The sun was low in the sky, making it hard to see out the windshield. The traffic light turned green before we fully stopped, and Vince accelerated through it.

I could see the car coming from the side road. It was going too fast, speeding toward the intersection. I banged my hand on my horn and slammed on my brakes and watched as it crashed into the passenger side of Vince's truck.

It was like a black funnel cloud took him from me and slammed him into a pole. His truck bounced off and rocked back and forth on its axle before stopping near the side of the street.

There was a second collision—the car that hit Vince spun around and into the side of the market on the corner. Part of the building collapsed on top of the car, covering the front half of it.

And then there was nothing.

Not a sound. Not a horn blowing or a person screaming.

No sirens.

No helicopter.

No air.

I threw the gear shift in park, still in the middle of the road, and ran to him. The driver's door was bent in. The window was now a gaping hole with the remnants of glass hanging around it, and the handle was barely recognizable and no longer functioning. I ran to the other side of the truck. The passenger door was mangled and wouldn't open. I put one foot flat on the bed for leverage and tried to pry it open. I loosened my grip and ripped my calf open on the jagged metal of his wrecked vehicle. The blood poured down my leg as I ran back to Vince's side of the truck.

"Call an ambulance," I yelled to the man from the car between us. He slowly reached for his phone, still stunned. "Now! Call 911 right now!"

Vince's head hung back. I stepped up on the running board and leaned in to see him past the deployed air bag. I punched out the remaining glass from the corners of the window and climbed through. His eyes were closed, a gash above his eye was bleeding down his face, but there was no blood on his body that I could see. I straddled him, being careful not to touch him or let my weight drop to his legs.

"Colonel, talk to me." I reached behind me and turned off the ignition while I still hovered above him. My God. "Vince, can you hear me?" My words were thick with need in his ear. "Vince, open your eyes." I ran my hand down the side of his face and kissed him right in front of his ear.

His eyes flitted. He opened them and moved his head on his own, and tears ran down my face, right on top of him. He pulled me tight against him, and I let him.

"What happened?" he whispered.

"Someone blew the red light and hit you."

He ran his hands across my back and over my waist, still in a fog. He looked down at his hands on me, and blood dripped into his eye. I stopped it with my hand and searched the truck for a towel. The sight of the blood trailing down to his neck horrified me, and I took off my tank top without a word. I wrapped it around his head, using the shoulder holes to secure it.

"I'm glad you followed me," he said, never releasing my eyes. I ached to be with him. To be with this man who took care of everyone.

The sirens rang in the distance. The Chief had been in an accident. The troops would come. Questions would be asked.

Flashing lights reflected off the shiny parts of the truck's interior. "I was at the shore today. Where were you?"

Vince turned to the fire truck now blocking traffic in both directions. "I was home. Just coming to town to pick up some food." He moved his head from side to side, putting the pieces together.

"From the grocery store? Or did you place an order?"

"From the store," he lied. We now created lies together.

I leaned into him and let my lips fall to his ear again. "You scared me," I whispered before swinging my leg over him and moving into the passenger seat.

fifteen

THE CHAOS OF THE REST of the night almost obliterated my day at the shore. Had it just been me there, not a remnant would remain, but Vince's presence made it unforgettable.

I was able to kick the truck's passenger door open from the inside, and a fireman helped me out and right into an ambulance, where the gash on my leg was examined and my brain was picked for details of the accident.

I stayed close to the truth. The light turned green, the truck was hit hard.

The driver of the car between mine and Vince's was more than happy to play the role of the expert. The woman who'd run the red light was trapped in her car in critical condition. Vince was lucky.

We were lucky.

"You're going to need stitches," I was told as I watched the firemen help Vince out of his mangled truck and onto a gurney. He was looking around but didn't see me.

"I'd like to get a shirt first," I said. After watching Vince's ambulance drive away, I was given a shirt from the backseat of a junior fireman's car that read, "Sweat Orange, Bleed Blue," and allowed to drive my own car to the hospital.

I saw everything. I heard everything. There was some talk of the accident and lots of talk of Vince. Apparently he was even hotter in a hospital gown. I kept a straight face. *I barely know him. I met him once. Our daughters are in the same grade.* When my eight stitches were finished, I checked out of the emergency room and took one last glance down the hall. *Why isn't his wife here?* I never asked where his family was that day.

I forced myself to steer my car home. That wasn't normal, right? After seeing a near-death accident, mothers were supposed to rush home to their children, just thankful to be alive. But I didn't feel alive in my house. I felt alive in the courtroom. I felt alive in the ocean. I felt alive with Vince. I was selfish and immature, and I hated myself.

I opened the kitchen door, and Liv ran over hugging me. She was careful of my leg and overwhelmed with worry. She burst into tears right in the doorway.

"Hey. It's okay. Mommy's fine. Look. It's just a few stitches."

Liv examined my leg. She took my hand and led me into the kitchen, to a stool by the island. James was less distraught and more impressed with the exposed sutures. Brad asked me if I could get them wet, which I thought was an odd concern. He lost interest in the answer by the time I told him it had to stay dry for twenty-four hours.

I listened to endless stories of roller coasters, cotton candy, and a long ride home, only hiding to check my email once for word from Vince. My inbox was filled with messages from Amazon, Sephora, Nordstrom, and Wrap London, but nothing from Vince. He was fine. He was fine when I left him, and he was fine now. He'd write when he could.

❧

I WOKE UP THE NEXT morning knowing I'd dreamed of Vince. I was under water and he'd found me. I could taste his tongue in my mouth. I could feel his chest under my hands. I wondered if I'd been moaning in my sleep. I took my phone off the charger and checked my email. At 11:30 P.M. last night, Vince had written.

> V: I wanted to call you. There was so much blood on my shorts the paramedics cut them off me searching for the wound. Then I heard a fireman say it came from the woman who wrapped my head. They told me at the hospital you had stitches and were released.

> I'm sorry.

> M: Sorry for what? You haven't done anything wrong . . . yet.

I put the phone down. I needed to put myself down.

"WHY ARE YOU DYING?" I asked the plant every day for at least a month. It never answered, but its leaves continued to brown on the edges, drooping toward the floor. I'd moved it twice. Once for more sun. Once for less. I was trying. "Why can't you be happy here?"

"Why are you talking to the plant?" Liv asked as she skipped over and stuck her face in between the leaves to see if something was resting on its roots worth talking to.

"Things that are alive need attention to thrive. Imagine how sad you'd be if I never talked to you."

Liv took a leaf between her fingers and picked off the brown edges. "What does thrive mean?"

"To grow. To flourish."

"What does fl—"

"To be happy and alive," I said, ending her questions.

"You need to grow, little plant," she said, and then, bored with the lack of response, turned to me. "Where's Daddy?"

"I don't know. What time is it?"

Liv ran to the clock in the living room. "It's seven-thirty. Didn't he call you?"

"No. Maybe he's working late."

She turned and walked away.

"Grow, you motherfucker," I said to the plant under my breath. Maybe Brad was in an accident. Maybe I didn't care.

❧

THE NEXT DAY, WHILE I sat at the pool and listened to the moms discuss the "accident out on Route 40," I checked my email again.

> V: Sorry I couldn't help you. And nothing I do to you will be wrong.

He was naïve.

> M: It seems like two people together when they shouldn't be, who are then involved in a serious car accident, should consider it a warning sign.

I expected to wait. I didn't even know if he was still in the hospital. I hit refresh, and a new message from You.will.read. this.8@gmail.com came up bold.

> V: I took away two things from yesterday:

> 1—Life is short.

> 2—Me being in a car accident scared you.

And in a separate email:

> V: I need to talk to you. Use that powerful and elusive brain of yours to figure out a way for that to work.

There weren't two people more capable of a discreet relationship than the colonel and me. We both had criminal justice experience. We just needed to think like criminals. It shouldn't be a stretch; we'd taken to sinners quite smoothly.

I wrote him back:

> M: One call to thank me for helping at the accident scene seems appropriate. 856–555–1938. I'm usually alone in the late afternoon. But no promises. My time is not my own.

sixteen

"ARE YOU ALONE?" WAS THE first question out of his mouth when I answered the phone. He sounded playful, and I wished I was next to him.

"Are you?" I asked, half laughing and wanting to play, too.

"I am, and I'm guessing you are, since you answered."

I was going to be alone for a few hours. Brad had taken the kids to his annual visit to his grandmother in the nursing home. "I'm alone." *You have no idea how alone I am.*

"I'm not sure what to say. I feel a lot of pressure, because I know you're not going to give me a second phone call."

At this I laughed. As if I was giving out phone calls like gold stars in a classroom. It wasn't something he earned. Or had he? "Phone records are forever," I said, again reducing whatever *this* was to its illicit foundation.

"Tell me about the accident."

"I'm sure you've read the police report." What more could he need? Thorough was undervaluing the investigation that was completed at the scene of the Chief of Police's car accident.

"I don't remember a thing, and the police report is mostly from the man behind me's statements. Please."

I was beginning to wonder if I'd ever deny him—anything. "We were driving home from the shore. Do you remember being at The Point with me?"

"Every second of every day I remember it. I lie here healing and think of your legs around my waist in the ocean." His voice was warm and rough, and I shifted in my seat, my body responding to him without my permission. The image of my legs around him flashed through my own mind for the hundredth time.

I took a deep breath and said, "Okay," as I exhaled. "So we drove home, and when we got to the light at the bowling alley, a car came out of nowhere and T-boned you. It pushed your truck into the telephone pole. The car between us had just enough time to run off the road rather than hit you too." I lowered my eyes, as if I could hide from him through the phone. "It was a horrifying sight."

"How did you get in my truck? The police report says you kicked the door open to get out, but how did you get in?"

"I tried to open the passenger door, but it was mangled. That's how I cut my leg. I climbed through the driver's side window and spoke to you until you woke up."

"I remember you talking to me and wrapping your shirt around my head. I remember what it felt like to have you sitting on my lap."

I exhaled slowly. If I could've reached through the phone, I would have.

"How are you?" I asked. I'd stalked Facebook, but that was all I had. After a few days, the accident was old news. No one talked about it anymore. To ask would have raised a red flag. And even though I was sure this was going nowhere, I wasn't about to raise any red flags.

"Where did you grow up?" His question surprised me and delighted me at the same time. I'd worked so hard to get out of Thurmont, but the colonel asking me about it reminded me it was my hometown. Where I began.

"Thurmont, MD."

"What's it like there?"

"It's a lot like here, except farther from the ocean."

"Why did you leave?"

"Because I wanted to do something meaningful. I wanted to make a difference. Thurmont was too small." I sighed, remembering all my huge ideas from the year I graduated. "I thought I needed to be in the city where anything could happen. Not in the country where nothing was happening." As the words left my mouth, the bitterness set in. "Ironic, huh?"

"When I'm allowed out of this bed, I'm going to show you everything there is to love about a small town."

At this, I laughed. It sounded like an offer better executed while still in bed.

"What?"

"Nothing."

"What? I'm going to."

"What do you love about this town?" I could have asked every single person who lived here the same thing. What the hell was there to love about this place?

"It's a community. You're getting none of the benefits of it because you're not a part of the community. You've got to accept it for what it is and love it." His passion overflowed. This was his town, and I wanted to run from it.

"I'll give it a chance," I said, just to put him at ease.

"Why did your parents live in Thurmont?"

"Because my mother was from there."

"And your father?"

"He was from Boston. He hated Thurmont, but he said my mother was so beautiful he'd follow her to Hell."

There was a pause on the other end of the line. And then he said, "My family just pulled in, so I have to go. I'll save my thank you for when I see you again."

"Really. There's no need to thank me. You were going to be fine without my help."

"That only makes it more impressive. Can I call you again?

Or text you?"

I wanted him to text me every morning and every night. I wanted to lie down next to him and touch his chest. I wanted him to call me when he was leaving his house to steal me away, but James' backpack caught my eye. There was a blue compass hooked to the front of it, always pointing him in the right direction.

"No," I said, and there was no need for further explanation.

"Well, I'll see you soon. Until then, take care of your leg . . . of yourself." Vince was completely undaunted by my refusal.

"I will." I hung up and stared at the phone. I saved the number in my contacts under Jenna's full name, including middle initial. To the outsider, it would look like she was calling me if the number ever rang again.

seventeen

IT WAS THE FIRST FULL day of school, and I felt some free-dom sink into my bones. I went to yoga. It wasn't the ocean, but it was going to have to be close enough until next summer. If the water stayed warm, I'd sneak down a few more times while the kids were in school, but the weather and our sched-ules would have to coincide perfectly. That rarely happened for me.

I'd just gotten out of the shower and wrapped myself in my robe when the doorbell rang. I wasn't going to answer it, but I wanted to know who was there, so I peered out the upstairs window as I brushed my hair. A police cruiser was parked half-way down my driveway. With the brush in my hand, I ran down the stairs and flung open the front door. Vince was there . . . in full uniform. My breath caught. That freaking uniform was like a roofie for me. The whole get-up was Vince—honor and strength—and really tight around his biceps and shoulders. My heart raced and a smile beamed across my face even though I tried to contain it.

"Hi," I said. The joy I felt surprised even me. It must have pleased Vince, because he walked inside, grinning the entire time.

"Hi." He moved to the side and I closed the door. When I turned around he was standing still by the staircase, smiling, holding a white box with a silver ribbon around it. He seemed a bit dazed, as if the reality of us alone in my foyer was more pleasant than he'd imagined. It was a stupid foyer, one with a dying plant and a weird balcony. But Vince was here.

He handed me the box, never taking his eyes off me.

"What's this?" I asked, and he moved closer to me. He was too close, blocking the logical thoughts from my mind.

"It's a thank you present."

"You shouldn't have done that—"

"Just open it," he insisted, ending my argument and focusing my attention back on the box. I untied the ribbon and laid it on the plant stand. I opened the box and unfolded the tissue to find a white tank top, the same brand and size as the one I'd used to bandage his head.

"Impressive." I held the tank top up between us.

"I thought the same thing." Vince took another step toward me, and I backed up. In fact, I moved until my back was against the wall. Literally. This he found humorous, and the laughter in his eyes reminded me of the bus ride to Philadelphia. He closed the distance between us and rested his hand on the wall above our heads. And I stopped breathing.

A light laugh left his lips and his breath touched my ear. I fought to not close my eyes and get lost in it. I couldn't think with him that close. He was so dark. His hair, his olive skin. It made his eyes seem even more dangerous. And they were, because looking into them I wanted to run out the door with him. "I've called you the one time I was permitted to. I've replaced your shirt. I'm running out of legitimate reasons to see you."

"Yes," I eked out like an imbecile. "You are."

"I know you say you don't want any type of relationship with me."

"It's not just you," I said, and he leaned down until our eyes were at the same height. His were a deep green, silent with intensity.

"I don't want you to think I haven't been listening." His gaze fell to my mouth. Vince leaned in. His lips grazed my chin, moved up my cheek, and landed near my ear. The sensation of his touch ran from there to the tips of my bare toes. "But I need to see you again."

Each word thundered in my mind. My hands rose to his chest but lowered before they touched him. He caught me by the wrists in a tight grip and held them tight to his chest. I opened my hands and let them rest flat there. His chest was hard beneath my hands, solid and strong. I fought the urge to rest my head there, and watched as my fingers stretched over the body of the man, who was not my husband, standing with me in my strange foyer.

"This isn't possible."

"I think it is." His hands covered my own. "You're not a whore."

"Not yet," I said and moved away from him. Vince watched me place the distance between us. He watched me deny us, and then he waited.

With me settled on the other side of the foyer, he spoke. "You know everything isn't always black and white, counselor. When you're the first responder, you see all sides of a situation."

"We're on the wrong side of this. Why are you so confident about everything? It's impossible to believe you've never done this before."

"If I had, I hope I'd be a lot better at it. I have no idea what I'm doing. I want you, and I want you to see me and talk to me, and be with me, but I don't know how to convince you it's okay." He moved closer again, and before I could fully digest his words, his lips were on mine. Vince's hands in my hair guided my face to his as he towered above me. My arms stayed at my sides, unwilling to participate in this betrayal, but my lips dissented. They wanted to cover his body. To touch every inch of his skin before taking his dick into my mouth. My body left my mind behind and found Vince. There was no more hiding my need from him. I laid my head on his shoulder, rocking it back and forth in denial of what I was capable of doing to my family.

"I think you should leave." The words were slow from my mouth, but resolute. I was torn between the opposing sides of my body and mind's internal war.

He was almost laughing. As if he knew me so well, he was expecting my rejection. Vince moved toward the door and stopped at my dying plant. "You should water this plant. It's dying."

"I know."

"Literally, dying on the vine."

"I got it. I'm on it."

"Thanks again."

"You're welcome."

"I'll be waiting to hear from you." He took my chin in his hand and kissed me quickly, as if we'd been dating for years and his departure was the same as the last thousand.

I shut the door and stared at the plant.

I spent the next eight days wandering around my house and finding myself in the foyer, touching the wall, reliving every second his hands touched me. I'd close my eyes and remember his chest beneath my fingers.

I needed a hobby, or a cause. Something to fill the hole Colonel Vincent Pratt was drilling in me. Something other than exercise. Something to utilize my mind.

eighteen

I WOULD NOT SINK INTO this. I would rise above. Brad didn't beat me. He was an ass, but not a terrible person. There were moments when he wasn't even an ass. I assumed most of those moments took place when we weren't together, but I was sure they existed.

The colonel was an easy choice, but in the end it would rip the soul from my children's bodies. Liv watched every move I made. Sometimes the words coming from her mouth were the exact ones I heard from my own. She idolized me. I wouldn't let her down. I wouldn't squander her pride in me.

I pulled the double-sleepover card. I tried to save it only for events that required an overnight sitter. Weddings. Out-of-town parties. But tonight I would pull the card. Brad and I needed to reconnect, or connect, depending on which one of us you asked.

I bought his favorite beer, the heavy, dark one I could never get into. I ordered a pizza with sausage, because it was his favorite. I showered and shaved, plucked and perfumed. I was impeccable, and it would be an amazing night. I kept the pizza warm in the oven and my glass full of wine as I waited for Brad to come home. I was wearing only my robe. I thought he'd fuck me right there in the kitchen, or maybe the family room. Somewhere other than our bed. Maybe on the back deck with candles lit. Anywhere. Brad and I needed to have sex. Like, hot-lava, spine-bending, sore-muscle sex.

By 8 P.M., I knew my plan should just be abandoned, but I felt my whole marriage riding on this one sexual encounter. I texted him, asking when he'd be home. He hadn't mentioned anything he had to do after work. But he texted back that he was at a going-away happy hour for someone on his floor and he'd leave soon. I removed the now-dry pizza from the oven and put it in the trash. I kept drinking though, sure we could salvage the night. Brad would come home happy. He'd been with his work peers drinking and he'd be satisfied and jovial. It would still be a great night.

By 10:30 P.M., I turned out the lights and went to bed.

In the morning, he rolled over and reached for me. He found my stomach and then my breast, resting his hand there without even opening his eyes. "Where are your clothes?"

"I don't have any on." My voice was even. Fair, I thought. Even though he deserved to be yelled at.

Brad leaned up on his forearms, completely awake now. "Why?" He was almost laughing. When did nudity become funny?

"I thought we could have a naked dinner last night and then make love." I said it as if I was talking about another couple, completely unhurt by the outcome. In fact, I would have been more appalled had I been talking about other people. *Can you believe what an ass her husband is?*

"What?" Now he was outright laughing.

"What's so funny? I tried to arrange a romantic night for us, but you couldn't even come home."

"Well, I'm home now." Brad's hand left my breast and landed between my legs. He was rough and uncoordinated.

"How much did you drink last night?"

"Probably too much," he said, and jabbed his finger into me. The bare, unprepared skin hurt as he pulled it out. "You're so dry. Loosen up for me, baby."

"I was wet as hell last night." I rolled over and faced the wall, but Brad was ready for his morning sex and not taking no for an answer.

I was being silly. *What am I so uptight about? He's here now.* He had to *work* last night.

"You'll be wet again. Just relax." He rolled me onto my back again and raised my leg over his hip. If he noticed my zero participation, he didn't let it bother him. He nuzzled my neck and stroked me. The stench of stale liquor poured from his mouth and directly to my nostrils. I turned my head from him, and he still continued, completely wrapped up in his needs. He would fuck me whether I thought he smelled good or not.

"I'm not really in the mood," I said, hoping this would end. Like, forever.

"You will be soon. Just close your eyes and think hot thoughts."

I closed my eyes and raised my arms above my head to block his breath, and I thought of Vince. He was my only hot thought. I saw him walk into the ocean. I felt him touch me. I could feel his chest under my fingertips and his lips on mine. As I mentally fawned over every image, my insides were knotting together, intensely searching for the touch of Vincent Pratt. I was wet.

"That's it, baby."

Just like that. In Brad's hands in his bed, and in Vince's in my mind. I let it go on. I blocked Brad's voice from my thoughts and recalled the shape of the colonel's lips as he spoke. My memories fell on his mute-gray uniform and the shape of his ass in it. Brad mounted me, and I touched myself. The colonel was thrusting into me in the middle of the Atlantic Ocean, and

I pulled him further inside me with each movement. My body clenched as the motion touched the spot deep inside of me. The place that would release me. I fought for air as the rhythm consumed me, and I pressed my thighs against him.

I came, constricting around Brad and wanting him to keep fucking me until when I opened my eyes, he actually was the colonel.

"That's more like it." His voice was rough near my ear. Brad was almost finished. I was bored now. Finally he came, resting his full weight on my chest and making it difficult for me to breathe, but Brad was comfortable and that was all that mattered.

When he rolled off me, I was able to think.

This life with Brad was tolerable if the colonel was in it, too.

nineteen

I WATERED THE DYING PLANT. I watered the fucking dying plant that refused to live. I talked to it. Sometimes I even said nice things. Our realtor had sent this plant to us the day we'd closed on the house, and the fact that it refused to thrive there was an eight-hundred-pound weight of symbolism hanging over my head every day.

I dragged the plant stand closer to the window again so it would have more sunlight. *Yes. Move it into the light.* Some of the leaves were completely brown now, barely hanging from hard wooden stems jutting from the soil. It was not improving at all.

"Grow, motherfucker," I whispered to the plant, and looked up to see Liv standing on the odd balcony. She sang, "I am so awesome," as she descended the stairs in her very own Broadway number. She finished on a high note and hopped off the last step.

"Do you remember when we talked about being humble?" Liv was more about celebrating her successes than embracing humility.

"What's that?" she yelled, dramatically placing her hand near her ear, the other on her hip. "I can't hear you over the deafening sound of my awesomeness."

"I'm serious, Liv." She joined me in staring at the dying plant. "People don't often gravitate toward those who constantly tell them how awesome they are."

Liv considered my words. "What's gradivate mean?"

"Gra-vi-tate. And in this context, it means to be naturally attracted to. As in, people are *not* naturally attracted to other people who constantly say—and sing about—how awesome they are."

"No offense, but people gra-vi-tate toward awesomeness. Nothing to worry about here."

Liv skipped away, and I made us dinner. The three of us ate together as usual. Not one of us mentioned Brad.

❧

THE NEWSPAPERS STACKED UP IN our house. I rarely read them, and Brad didn't have time, what with work and all, but he still insisted we subscribe. So every day, someone tossed a paper onto our driveway, and every day I picked it up and took it to Brad's desk in his office. After a few weeks, I carried the unread papers to the recycling bin.

I removed today's paper from the plastic bag and threw the bag in the trash. The colonel's picture stopped me with the trashcan open, my foot still pressing the lever.

Chief Vincent Pratt Continues to Give Back, the headline said. I sat quietly with my paper and read every word twice. I ran my fingers across the picture of him out of uniform and helping a teenager nail drywall. The warmth I always felt near him welled up inside of me. He was a good man.

"What are you doing?" Liv asked, unfamiliar with my paper reading.

"I was just reading an article about Chief Pratt, Allison's father."

"The colonel?"

"Yes. The colonel."

Liv climbed into my lap in my chair and took the paper in her hands. She looked at the construction picture and then the small picture of the colonel in his uniform. It was only a head-shot, and his hat was on and pulled low. "Is this him, too?"

"It is."

"Why is he in the paper? Because he's the colonel?"

"He has a foundation that does repairs on the homes of elderly residents in need."

"What?"

"If an old person needs something fixed in their house, they can ask Allison's dad to fix it, and he'll come and do it. He helps people."

"All by himself?"

"According to the article, he also teaches kids and teenagers the skills to help as well."

"Wow, he's awesome."

"Yes. He is."

twenty

I FELL ASLEEP THAT NIGHT, right after emailing my birthday plans to the colonel. They were exciting plans. I was signing out and taking both kids to their yearly check-ups, and then hopefully eating out. I was sure the kids would beg for Applebee's, but I really wanted sushi. Or a beer. Or to just eat alone in a bar somewhere.

The colonel had thrown me when he'd asked about my birthday. But then I remembered he'd researched me after my trip to the police station with the Cub Scouts. And of course he hadn't forgotten it. He wanted to be my lover. Unlike the man who was my lover.

As if he could read my thoughts from London, a text was delivered from Brad, wishing me a happy birthday. The alarm on his phone must have reminded him.

> B: *Happy Birthday. We can go out to celebrate when I get home. Set it up if you want.*

Yes, please. Let me set that up. In reality, he could have put less thought into it. He could have not texted at all. And he would be sorry he sent the text, because my mind raced with ideas. I would invite Jenna and John and we'd go someplace Jenna and I would love, and Brad would have to drive us since it was my birthday. He would complain that it wouldn't be relaxing for him, since he wouldn't be able to drink, and I wouldn't give a fuck because just this one day of the year, I'd put myself before Brad. It would be uncomfortable for him.

Breakfast was rushed as usual, but both of my kids had made me a birthday card. And since I hadn't reminded them to do it, I knew they'd thought of it on their own. I wallowed in the tiny satisfaction of the evidence of thoughtful children. I put the rubber band bracelet on my wrist Liv had made me using my favorite colors and faced the next year of my life. Of this life.

I hadn't had a really kick-ass birthday since before my kids were born. One where I cared what I was wearing. I vaguely remembered years of buying something new to wear to the celebration.

Instead of caring what I was wearing, I spent the day switching the summer clothes for the winter ones in my children's closets. As I checked the sizes and inspected the clothes for stains, I recited the United States Bill of Rights. I wasn't completely bored.

And just before the end of their school day, I signed out the kids. No, they would not be returning. *We have doctors' appointments and dinner plans. It's my birthday.* As the kids climbed in the car, I saw an envelope on my windshield. I stared at it, my pulse quickening. Something different. Something out of the ordinary for this, the celebration of my birth.

"What's that, Mommy?" Liv asked as I leaned out of the car window and took it off the windshield.

"I think it's a birthday card for me."

"Oh yeah, happy birthday again," James yelled from the third-row seat.

"Thanks." I started the car and turned up the music, signaling to the kids to buckle up and settle in. As they did, I opened my card. It was a hand-drawn picture of a tree in the foreground with a bird flying away from it. The bird followed another bird into a valley in the distance. The colors were muted throughout the scene, except the birds were blue. I opened the card and inside there was no signature. Not one pen mark on the card or the envelope.

The card's text only said:

You can't be held captive
If you can't be caught

I closed the card and ran my hand over the lead bird. My gaze wandered up to the clouds, and I watched the birds fly by in the sky. Peace filled me. Peace, and the forgotten lightness of adventure. I took a deep breath and let it invade me.

Liv plopped onto the console next to me. "Why do you look like that?"

Immediately, the goofy smile drained from my face. I was swooning, or something else just as obvious even to my seven-year-old. "Why are you in the front seat?"

She rolled her eyes and buckled up behind me.

❧

AND ON SATURDAY NIGHT, I buckled into the backseat of Brad's BMW.

"Why can't Jenna or John drive?" Brad asked.

"Because it's my birthday, and you're taking us all out to celebrate. If John asked us out to celebrate Jenna's birthday, wouldn't you think it weird if you had to drive?" I resisted the urge to talk to him like a two-year-old.

"This is going to be the longest night of my life."

"It's all in what you make it. Try to have fun." *Or at least not complain.*

"I'm just tired. The jetlag from London always kills me."

"I still haven't been. I'd like to go."

"We'll get you there someday."

"You always say that, and someday never comes."

"Who'd watch the kids?" He ended the London conversation the same way he always did. It was a valid point, and probably the reason I never got to go, but I still didn't want to hear it.

Within seconds of us pulling into Jenna's driveway, she hopped in the backseat with a beer in her hand. I knew it pissed off Brad. Why should Jenna be allowed to drink even on her way to the restaurant when he could barely drink at all? If Jenna noticed Brad's annoyance, it didn't faze her. Later I knew I would answer Brad's ongoing question of what I saw in her.

John got in the front passenger seat, and Brad drove us to Riverview Inn, the restaurant on the riverbank I'd been asking Brad to take me to for three years. The view was perfection, and they usually had live music.

I'd done the best I could with what I had in my closet. My outfit wasn't new, but it was my favorite dark jeans, an old pair of snakeskin heels that would never go out of style, and a one-shoulder black shirt. It was something, and I was going somewhere. Even if Brad was miserable.

Our table was on the lawn, closest to the water and away from the safety of the patio. If a storm came up the river, we'd have to be relocated.

Brad complained about the menu.

Jenna ordered shots.

John left us all to fend for ourselves as he walked through the crowd, saying hello to every person he knew. Eventually, he called for Brad to come to the bar with him, and put me out of my misery.

"I don't think Brad likes me," Jenna said, and with no explanation of why it was funny, I started laughing. "What? He doesn't."

"Take it as a compliment. I've seen the people who really impress him." I tilted my head toward her and raised my eyebrows. Jenna understood.

"What attracted you to him in the first place? You guys are so different."

I watched Brad at the bar. He was shaking the hand of the man I recognized as the head of Cub Scouts. He was the den master or something. I'd seen him shake the hand of my father when we'd gotten engaged, and the pastor who'd married us, and his boss at the holiday party every year. "Exactly what he is right now attracted me to him."

Jenna looked at me, a little disturbed. She thought she had me figured out, but I didn't have myself figured out.

"When we were young, I wanted someone successful, someone hungry. I wanted drive and ambition and an unwillingness to let anything stand in his way."

"And now?"

"And now I'm what's standing in his way. The kids and I." The realization seeped down deep, followed by the Fireball shot, and then the shot in front of Brad's empty chair. He didn't need it. He had a life. "He hasn't changed a bit."

Jenna stared at me like I was telling her how my grandfather used to punch my grandmother in the face if she talked too much. *Is it really that bad? Are we really that bad?*

"What did Brad get you for your birthday?" Her question brought me back to our table.

"A card with cash in it." The words were a sigh in themselves. A deflated dream of romance left inside a card with five hundred dollars cash.

"God, they suck. We could do so much better."

Jenna left me alone to go to the bathroom, and I read the first of my two awaiting emails.

V: I want to see you. I could look at you all night.

I looked out at the water, wishing he was there. When I closed it, there was the other one.

V: Until you opened your eyes in the morning.

A smile spread across my face until Brad took the seat next to me.

"Are you blushing?"

"No," I said with that you're-an-idiot tone to throw him off.

Brad launched into stories of the people he was just talking to. After all, their lives were much more interesting than whatever would make his wife blush on her birthday.

John returned and suggested we move our party to the Adirondack chairs under the flag pole, away from the tables, with a perfect view of the river. I couldn't agree fast enough. Brad made us stay. He wanted to be closer to the band. It was his night, so that made sense.

And when the conversation died down between the odd group of Brad, John, and myself, I asked John the question I planned on asking every person from here. "John, what do you love about this town?" I caught him by surprise. I caught Brad by surprise, too. He studied me as if I'd suddenly spoken Arabic. My interest in my surroundings must have been more foreign than I realized.

John leaned into me making his adoration feel like a secret. "I love everything about this town. But I'm reminded of it on the late warm nights when the tractors are driving down the centers of the roads as if they own them."

I sipped my beer and sat back in my chair, pondering John. I was satisfied with his answer. He raised his beer to me and we toasted, and then he invited Brad to raise his as well.

"To Meredith. Happy birthday," John said, and for that one moment I was happy. Jenna returned, smelling of cigarettes and smiling the expression of an almost-drunk woman. Instantly the mood deepened as Brad's judgmental gaze washed over

Jenna, and John's smile faded.

"Let's go take our picture down by the water," I suggested. Jenna was out of her seat, escaping the scrutiny, before the last word left my mouth. She handed John her phone and pulled my hand toward the concrete retaining wall between the lawn and the sand. She let go and jumped down, but my shoes weren't going to survive a four-foot jump. I sat on the edge of the wall and swung my feet over the side.

John snapped a few shots with the sun falling behind us. Jenna wrapped her arms around my neck and kissed me in a liquor-filled display of affection, and I loved her. She was impossible not to love. Unless you were Brad. He cringed as Jenna's words were a little too loud, and by the end of our photo shoot he moved to the bar, returning to the people he'd rather have been with in the first place.

John hoisted me back up the retaining wall, and lifted Jenna off the sand by her wrists. She swung like a pendulum, and he placed her gently on the ground by our table. She doubled over laughing, and the sound of it was infectious. Until I saw Brad drinking shots with the people at the bar.

Men were slapping his back and patting his shoulders. When Jenna did a shot, she didn't need that much attention. I had quietly done one myself. For Brad, it was a group activity, like white water rafting. Another round was delivered, and this time all the men and women around him took one off the tray. They clinked glasses and downed the shots. I stood by our table, ignoring Jenna and John, my eyes fixed on Brad as he ordered another round for the crowd. I picked up a glass of water from the table and drank it down. I was now the driver. Anger burned inside of me, or was it disappointment. I hated both. I hated him.

Richie's dad emerged from the crowd with a shot in his hand, yelling, "Meredith, happy birthday." He toasted toward me, placed his empty glass on the bar, and made his way to the lawn. "Why aren't you doing shots?" he asked as he pulled me into a hug.

I gave Brad the middle finger/death-stare combination while Richie's dad rubbed my back. Brad laughed it off.

"Seriously, do you want a shot? Let's do a shot." Richie's dad grabbed my wrist, and I jerked my hand back, not wanting to be dragged around and not wanting to be anywhere near Brad.

"I'm actually getting ready to leave. Do you mind giving Brad a ride home?" Richie's dad stared at me, shocked. He assumed we were embarking on a fun night together. "I don't think he's ready to go yet," I added.

"But it's your birthday. You can't leave." How was it that Richie's dad felt some obligation for me to have fun on my birthday, but Brad's only obligation was to himself?

"It's been a long day," I said, and saw John kiss Jenna near the corner of the bar. I signaled the waitress for the check. It had an additional fourteen shots on it Brad had bought for his new friends at the bar. I found my birthday card in my purse and left it and all the cash inside it for the waitress. Let her enjoy my birthday, too.

I drove John and Jenna home. We rode in silence. Me pissed at Brad. Jenna piss drunk. When they got out of the car, I considered texting the colonel. Texting him and setting up a meeting. Brad wouldn't ask any questions tonight. He would have no idea I wasn't home. But instead I drove home alone.

When I pulled in, my garage door opened without my pressing the button on the receiver. Brad was waiting in the garage for me. He was resting against my car with his arms crossed against his chest.

"I'm sorry," he said as I got out of the car.

"You're sorry, or selfish?"

"I'm both, but I've always been selfish. Tonight I'm sorry,

too." I resisted the urge to slam the door of the Escalade. I walked past him and he grabbed my arm. I watched his fingers dig into my muscle and then I jerked my arm away. "Mer, I'm sorry. It's just I don't understand why you hang out with her."

"Who?"

"Jenna. She's a drunk." Brad steadied himself against the wall of the garage as he followed me into the kitchen.

"You do realize you're wasted? Like, your version of reality is not so grounded in your own spectacular existence that you can't recognize what a complete asshole drunk you sound like right now?" Brad smiled the same way he always used to when he was in trouble. That's what he used to call it when his capitalistic ideas tried to stomp out my dreams of saving the world. He would say he was in trouble. "That smile's not going to work."

"It's all I have." It was all he had. I turned away from him and walked up the back staircase to our bedroom. I closed my eyes and pretended to be asleep when Brad finally came to bed after three. His presence ushered in the loneliness.

twenty-one

IT WAS THE FIRST BIG Cub Scout camping trip of the year, and miraculously I watched Brad drive away with James and both of their sleeping bags. Liv and I were going to rent a movie until her best friend, Jill, called and asked her to sleep over. Then I was just going to watch a movie. I opened a bottle of wine. The house was so quiet. The peace seeped into me, and it surfaced an idea that would ruin my life forever. But what kind of a life was it?

I emailed Vince.

> M: *I am alone the entire night.*

I poured and drank a second glass of wine. I prayed, "God, please do not let him check his emails tonight." It was stupid, and I was stupid. I picked up my phone to email something intelligent back, like, "Just kidding," and saw he'd already responded.

> V: *Follow these directions.*

Below was a list of stops and turns at rural landmarks. No road names were mentioned. I stared out the window. There were no stars visible. The moon was hidden behind a drenching rain that continued to pour on the side of my house. Brad had lucked out that they were camping in cabins. He was lucky, alright.

I threw my yoga pants—always a symbol of my lack of contribution to this life—in the hamper and pulled a simple jersey dress over my head. It was short, with long sleeves, and comfortable. I left the television on. A rented on-demand movie I'd seen ten times continued to play as I walked out the door. If they came home unexpectedly, I'd say I went to the grocery store for ice cream. That would disgust Brad, but I was pretty sure less so than the truth.

I left the radio off as I followed the directions to the other side of town. The rolling fields surrounded the road, but I couldn't see a thing. I watched for eyes of deer, the evidence of a car accident more daunting than the actual collision. I followed the directions precisely, using my odometer for the "After 6.3 miles, bear left onto a small lane with an open gate" part. Without the exact mileage, I would never have even seen the gate. The Escalade stomped over the gravel path through the woods, dipping into several larger grooves in the ground, making me fear I'd get stuck. At the end of the lane, deep in the woods and far out of sight from the road, I parked next to Vince's truck.

This would be just once. I ran the idea in my head over and over again. Just once. The sex could not live up to what I had in my mind. He couldn't be as great in bed as he was on a school bus. We would have sex. It would be average, and then I could put this whole thing to rest.

Just once.

I sat in the Escalade in the rain.

I put the car in REVERSE and then in PARK again.

I wrung my hands and bit my lip.

I let my head fall back on the seat behind me as the rain assaulted the sunroof above me. It was loud enough to drown out my thoughts. And then I jumped at the knock on my window.

It was Vince, standing in the rain with an umbrella for me to step under. He didn't look torn at all. *How can that be?*

I unlocked the door, and he opened it. I took his hand and slid off my car seat and under the umbrella. He was close, and rather than walking into the tiny wood cabin in front of us, I kissed him right next to my car. I rose on my tiptoes in my rain boots and wrapped my arms around his neck, pulling him down to me. I let my greed take over and quiet my mind.

Vince had no hesitation. He turned my back to the vehicle and pushed me against it, grinding his body against mine as he held the umbrella above us. There was so much that needed to be said, and I wasn't going to speak a word of it. I was there for a reason, and it wasn't to do the right thing. What I lacked in loyalty, I made up for in follow-through.

"I'm glad you came," he said, barely audible over the rain drops hitting the leaves around us. I could see in his eyes how glad he was, how much he wanted me there, and I kissed him again, leaving no question of my own gratitude. "Come inside."

He took my hand, and I followed him under the umbrella to a small cabin in front of his truck. He opened the door to a room lit only by candlelight. I let my eyes adjust and focus on the simple kitchen area with an old wooden table and chairs, a wood burning stove, and a sink near the corner. Through the doorway, I saw a small couch and a half-dozen mismatched chairs. Three sets of bunk beds lined the walls.

"What is this place?" I asked as Vince shook the umbrella outside and set it open just inside the door.

"It's my hunting cabin."

"How fitting." I slipped out of my rain boots. Vince watched me from the center of the room as I placed my boots near the door. I stood up straight, facing him, facing *this*.

"I just lost power." He was still watching me as if I might disappear. "Luckily, I had some candles."

I nodded, again surveying the stark décor.

"Meredith—"

I took two long steps and interrupted him with my hands on his stomach. The fabric of his T-shirt was thin, and damp from the rain. His chest heaved as his hot breath swept across my face. Everything about him was warm and inviting. I rested my forehead on his chest and let the scent that was distinctly his flow through me. It took me back to the school bus to Philadelphia. To where I first inhaled the perfect mix of mahogany and strength.

"Meredith," he started again, and I wished he wouldn't. I raised my lips to his neck and inhaled again. I wouldn't let myself think. He hadn't shaved, and I let his beard scrape against the side of my face, anything to touch him. I didn't want to consider this, I wanted to feel it. "This can be whatever we want it to be. It doesn't have to be an affair. It doesn't have to be what everyone else has done before us. We're not them."

His argument against *typical* did nothing to sway me to our union's merits, but the expression on his face, his determination to make this work, moved me.

"Tell me what you want." His voice was gentle near my ear, and I wanted to stay in this cabin, in the storm, forever.

"I don't know what I want anymore." The tension rose in my chest. All the schooling, all the money, and I didn't know what I wanted. How was that possible? I could have anything, but I couldn't name one thing. "Since I stopped working, I'm lost." I lowered my eyes to his chest. I was ashamed.

"No, you're not." His arms wrapped around my shoulders, his hands moved my hair away from my neck, and he leaned down, letting his lips rest there. I shivered before a heat spread through me. "I found you," he said, and tilted my face to his. Vince kissed me without waiting for an answer.

He kissed me, right there in the middle of the room, until a heat sank down my spine, anchoring me to the ground in front of him, assuring me against every reasonable argument that *this* was going to be okay.

The rain was a mix of a washed-out deluge hitting the walls of the cabin and a metallic pinging as it assaulted tiny pieces of the flashings and the roof. It was a constant hum around us, and it blocked every thought but the ones craving Vince's body. I pulled him toward me, wanting him inside of me. I was selfish and unapologetic, and he responded to every need I had without me voicing a word.

I reached my hand down between us. I felt him hard behind the zipper of his jeans, and I stroked him through the fabric. I inhaled deeply at the size of him and the anticipation spread through me, a heavy demand that could only be satisfied by him. I unzipped his jeans, and he let go of me to lower them to the floor. For a split second I clung to the idea this was going to be terrible, average at best. This was a huge mistake, and my punishment would be a below-par sexual experience to relive in my mind in the coming weeks and solidify the universe's thoughts on the righteousness of an affair.

Vince took the hem of my dress in his hands. He watched me as I raised my hands high in the air above us. He lifted the dress up and off of me, leaving me naked in front of him. I burned from the urge for him. I could feel it just under my skin, a heat spreading through me, anticipating his hands on me.

I tilted my head to the sound of the rain. It thrust us forward, protected us from reality. It was a cushion from the pain we would inflict on each other, and it succeeded. When I turned back to Vince, his eyes were wandering over every inch of me, and I braced myself for his proclamation of my beauty. The one *they* said to everyone. But it never came.

I realized Vince was waiting for me to give myself to him. He was waiting for my consent. He wouldn't take *this* from me. He wouldn't seduce me any more than he would purposely hurt me. He was a gentleman. But there was nothing he could do or say in this dimly-lit cabin that would turn me away from him. I needed him to breathe. I needed him to live. I just hadn't known it until that moment in front of him, with my dress still hanging from his hand at his side.

I took two steps to him and ran my hands up his shirt. I pushed it over his head and leaned into him. The touch of his skin on my breasts forced my lips upon him. I wrapped my arms around his neck, pushing myself toward him until he lifted me, and I straddled him. Right there in the center of his hunting cabin. He walked to the wall, pressed my back against it, and fucked me until I didn't care if my legs would ever move again.

He held me in the air, the muscles in his chest and arms locked beneath my legs, and I pressed the back of my head to the wall behind me, trying to breathe. Trying to hold off the release I'd sought since his thigh had touched mine on the school bus to Philadelphia. It was a thick drumming inside of me, coming closer to my core with every thrust into me. I pressed myself against him, against the pulsing, but he held me tight against the wall. I was trapped. I came and crumbled around him. And then he fucked me some more.

And right there, in a cabin deep in the woods, I let myself be found by Colonel Vincent Pratt. It was an unearthly feeling. I knew I could fly, and with Vince's dick in me, I rose above all the rest and floated away. I listened to the rain as he pulled out. It was slowing, giving me room for my thoughts. And the only ones I had were of Vince, the way his body felt on mine.

He carried me to the couch and sat down with me still on top of him. I waited for him to say something. He was always so thoughtful, which gave me the sense that he would know what to say, what to do now. But instead he kissed me again, and when his lips released mine, I silently told myself, *you do not love him.* Vince paused, watching me, and for a split second I feared I'd said it out loud.

"We should have talked about protection," Vince said as

I straddled him on the small couch. We were naked, his dick resting against his stomach, and a sense of wholeness filled me, along with his sperm.

"You should have talked about protection. I had my tubes tied after Liv was born." I moved closer to him, resting my chin on his shoulder. I wanted to climb inside him. Live his life with him, and not my own.

Sensing my need, Vince threaded his hands in my hair and leaned me back to face him. "I know you feel comfortable never answering a question, but since we can make this whatever we want it to be, let's start with being completely honest with one another. Don't hold anything back."

It was a foreign concept. Not in any relationship, not even with my father or Liv, had I been completely open, but whatever this was, it was already different than anything I'd ever known. I looked up into his eyes wanting me, needing me.

"After the accident, you said it scared you." The car hitting him at the traffic light flashed in my mind again, and it hurt inside me. "What scared you?"

The pain of the memory sank to the bottom of my stomach. I moved closer to him, wanting every inch of me to touch him. "I thought you were dead. And it was the first time I'd felt alive in years. If you died in that accident, I thought you'd take me with you." I stared at him, letting the words sink between us. Tears filled my eyes.

"Hey. Are you okay?"

I leaned down, ignoring his question, and kissed his neck. I thought I'd never be able to verbalize what I was. Vince pulled me back again. "I'm more than okay." I lowered my eyes to my chest and continued, "Just saying those words brought me back to life." My nipples were hard, my breasts stood at attention. "I've stopped time and have you all to myself, and in the moments I'm quiet, I'm trying to figure out how to never start it again."

Vince was speechless. He'd become so accustomed to holding up both ends of the conversation, my contribution threw him.

I ran my hands up and down his chest, and then landed on his dick. I stroked it until it hardened between us. "But more than anything, I want you again."

twenty-two

BRAD RETURNED FROM CAMPING PISSED off. James was exhausted. Liv looked like I should put her right back in bed when I picked her up at 10 A.M.

I was exquisite.

Every time I walked past a mirror, I was shocked. Like a fairy godmother had blown magic dust on me that illuminated my skin and put a twinkle in each eye. I was shimmer and sparkle and seduction all combined in the morning after a betrayal. I was lovely. I stopped and rolled my eyes at myself in the hall mirror. *Seriously?* This was exactly what happened to the others when they started having an affair. It injected its fantasy into every corner of their lives. The whores . . .

I shook out my hair, pushed it behind my ears, and finally pulled it back into a messy ponytail. It still didn't help. One night of the colonel's dick in me couldn't be erased with bad hair. The feel of him between my legs raced through my mind, and I put my hand on the wall to brace myself as the waves of orgasm washed over me again through memories that would never fade.

"So how was it?" I asked Brad after the kids had snuggled onto couches far from earshot.

"Horrible. It was a cold Saturday night, and I was in a cabin. There was no television, no internet, and no alcohol. It was as close to Hell as I ever want to be."

"Then you should be a good person while you're here on Earth."

"How biblical of you," he said and finally smiled. "What did you do last night?"

"Watched a movie," I said too fast, and then quickly recovered, "Well, I rented a movie. I slept through most of it. I really caught up on my sleep last night. I feel great today."

"How about we not talk about it. I think I slept twenty minutes. I just lay there on my bunk listening to many, many people breathe."

"It does sound like fun," I sympathized with him. James was the only one in our family who ever considered camping an activity. I'd been once before, but it had involved alcohol and lots of it. Brad had never been before and would be happy to never go again.

"Hey, what do you think about Matt Thompson?" Brad asked nonchalantly. Like, too nonchalantly. He was watching my reaction, which was hilarious, since I'd just spent time trying to seem like I hadn't had sex with someone else, but it wasn't someone named Matt Thompson.

"I don't know him."

"Yes, you do." Brad was impatient. He liked immediate answers.

"Who is he?" I watched Brad stare into the refrigerator for far too long. I finally moved him aside and reached in for the soda I knew he was searching for. It was behind the hummus.

"He's that kid's dad who's in James' Cub Scout den."

I shook my head. "Not really narrowing it down for me. What's his son's name?"

"I don't know. Matt's tall, kind of burly. Actually, he's a bit of a fat ass if you ask me."

"That's nice."

"His kid is the one who always eats the donuts right before he wrestles."

"Richie?"

He clapped his hands together triumphantly. "Richie, that's it. What do you think about his dad?"

"Nothing. I think nothing about him. Richie seems fine."

Brad took a sip of his soda and sat on an island stool, watching me. I wasn't sure if I was supposed to walk away or say something. I had an email I wanted to compose. "He seems to like you."

"Who?"

"Matt Thompson."

"Oh, Richie's dad. Well, I'm pretty likable."

"Yeah," he said and took another sip. I did walk away because I had no time for jealousy. Especially when it was so unfounded. I obviously wasn't with the man last night. He'd slept with Brad.

I hid in our room and folded laundry. Brad was rarely jealous. And when there was the tiniest hint of it, he was usually jealous of me, not another man. I folded towels and sheets and baskets full of the kids' clothes, and I thought about Brad and his questions.

Brad knew nothing about me. But something was bothering him. I wondered what he was up to, or what Richie's dad was up to. Suddenly it seemed like the whole world was cheating.

twenty-three

"WHY DO YOU LOOK SO . . ." Jenna stopped walking through the crowd and inspected me.

"So what?" Could I possibly look like I'd fucked a man other than my husband for the first time in over a decade? My hand reached up to my face, searching for the evidence of an orgasm.

"So serene. You hate this shit. Why do you look so happy?" I watched the children running and laughing in the center of the closed street.

"Did you get high without me?"

"No!" Brad was talking to some of the dads from James' soccer team. The Fall Festival brought out everyone from this town and the neighboring ones. It was forced gaiety, and typically I'd want no part of it, but lately—well, since the night at Vince's cabin—nothing bothered me. I watched James get paint all over his shirt as he decorated a pumpkin, and the unicorn with her ladies in waiting sneering as they whispered about someone, and Brad talking to everyone as if he was their best friend, and none of it mattered as long as the colonel would fuck me again.

And then he walked up . . . in his uniform. I squeezed my thighs together and closed my eyes, remembering the sound of the rain on the cabin's walls as I came with him inside me.

"Mommy." Liv yanked me back to Earth. "Mommy, it's

time for the costume contest." Liv was wearing the swim fins she'd been wearing around our house for weeks. On the pavement, the slapping of each exaggerated step was less violent than on the Brazilian cherry floors of our home. When she'd come downstairs in a bathing suit, a homemade tutu, and the swim fins, I'd tried to talk her out of it, but she'd explained the costume was, in fact, awesome.

"Okay, I'll walk you over there, but I don't want you to be disappointed if they don't share your vision of a . . ." I tried to remember what she said.

"A scuba-diving ballerina." She pulled a mouth piece and goggles from her candy bag. "It'll be fine. I'm awesome. Come on."

I tried.

I walked her to the stage and offered to help her up the stairs, but the fins were as good as shoes after weeks of walking in them on land.

There were seven girls entered. Three were Disney princesses, and two were homemade princesses. The colonel's daughter was next to Liv. She was dressed as a butterfly. And then there was my little scuba-diving ballerina with her goggles covering half her face and her mouth piece inserted.

"James," I half yelled over the people next to me. When he turned to me, I said, "Go tell Daddy to come here and watch Liv." I pointed to Brad, and James went to get him. The parents filled in around me, the colonel just behind my right shoulder. His wife was next to him, videotaping the stage. I could feel him there. I could feel the heat from his body, and it spread its warmth through me. Suddenly, the cool fall day felt hot. I raised my hair off my neck and let the breeze try to soothe me. It was impossible.

"What the hell is she?" Brad asked as soon as he walked up. "Why did you let her wear that?"

I kept my composure and again reminded myself he wasn't

trying to be an ass. "It's the costume she made. From her imagination. It's awesome, like her."

Brad's scowl settled in as his need for Liv and me and James and him to fit in perfectly became so clear. She should have been yet another princess up there.

Each girl held the microphone and said their full names and costume. Liv was just "Olivia," like Madonna, or Jesus. When she said her costume, half the crowd laughed and the other half looked at me for some explanation. Instead of feeding into it, I kept my eyes on Liv. I winked and gave her the thumbs-up sign.

And then she won.

Because she was awesome.

The other mothers gathered the princesses together for a picture. Liv didn't mind being excluded. She was being interviewed for the paper. God help me.

I found Jenna in the crowd, and she tipped her plastic cup to me and smiled. She should have had a daughter. She was better equipped to handle one. Brad busied himself again with "his people," so I let the kids run wild in the Kid Zone and went to talk to Jenna. "Hey, are your boys in the chorus?"

"No." Her sour tone told me she already knew what I was suggesting. "Only John, Jr."

The colonel and his wife gravitated toward the conversation. Their movement was natural, and led by his wife. We were, after all, parents of children in the same grade.

"Oh," I said weakly, barely able to focus on Jenna.

"Just tell me what you're doing while they're all at the Statue of Liberty until 8 P.M. next Thursday."

I started laughing, and the colonel stopped on his way to the exit.

"Are you guys talking about the chorus field trip?" Lynn Pratt chimed in. She was actually *in* our conversation.

"Yes. Meredith was just about to tell me what wonderful plans she has for her twelve hours alone."

"How did you get out of going?" Lynn asked, obviously scheduled to have a seat on the long bus ride.

"I put my name in but I didn't get picked," I said honestly, and then acted disappointed.

"Tell me. Just go ahead and tell me what you're doing."

"I'm going to the shore if it's nice, but it'll probably rain."

Jenna took a long sip from her plastic cup. The colonel cast an eye over the crowd, watching something or someone.

"Oh, no. I'm sure it'll be gorgeous. The last gorgeous day of the fucking year." Jenna was too loud. We were in the Kid Zone. I shushed her through my laughter. Lynn thought Jenna was funny, too.

"If it makes you feel any better," I said, "this is probably my only year. James is hating choir."

"No. No better. If I were you, I'd stay in bed all day," Jenna said.

The colonel caught my eye and quickly looked away. It wasn't a bad idea.

twenty-four

I DROVE DIRECTLY TO THE cabin. I was invited. He'd sent an email, but it wasn't necessary. I knew by the look in his eyes when Jenna had suggested I spend the day in bed that I was invited to the colonel's hunting cabin.

It was different in the daylight, without the rain pounding on the walls and the candles flickering on the tables. It was stark, filled only with the idea of touching the man standing behind me. I waited for the guilt. I waited for the images of Brad and my children to fill my mind and stop me, but they never came. They couldn't penetrate the adrenalin racing through me, willing me to take something for myself.

I would take it from the colonel. From his wife and his children. I would steal today and as many other days as I could, to feel the way I did when he touched me. *Just once*, I thought, and a smile lit up my face.

"What's so funny?" He moved closer to me and pushed my hair to the side. He bent down a few inches and caressed the back of my neck with his lips. My spine responded to his touch. It straightened and arched, and my head fell forward. "Hmm?"

"I was just remembering the last time I was here."

He paused on my neck. "Was that funny?"

"The entire ride here, I told myself it would be just once. That having sex with you couldn't possibly live up to the expectation created in my mind. You wouldn't feel the way I imagined. You wouldn't be the way you are."

Vince's hands moved up my shirt to the back of my bathing suit, which he untied. He slipped both hands under the triangles of fabric and grabbed my breasts firmly in his hands, pulling me closer to him. I let my head fall back, inhaled deeply, and my need for him filled me. It coursed through me, stealing every thought but the touch of his hands on my skin. A throbbing began deep inside of me, and my breath echoed it. I could feel him hard behind me. "What were you going to say to me?" he asked, but I could barely concentrate on his words.

"I don't know. I didn't get that far."

I reached behind me, wanting him inside me. I grinded against him, and his hands reached down between my legs. One lifted my leg and the other dove into my suit bottoms, finding the already wet area wanting him. "What did you expect?" I eked out as I lowered myself further onto his finger. I was shameless with my need. My body found it easier to be honest with Vince than my mind. It told him everything—loose lips.

"I expected nothing." His breath was hot near my ear, his words barely above a whisper. "I just wanted you." He took his finger from me, leaving me with the emotion of want to ponder. He ran his hands up my back, slowing over my waist, and then landing on my neck. "I wanted you on top of me, and under me, and next to me."

Vince turned me around to face him. He bent down, taking my suit bottoms with him. And lifted me, setting me down on the back of the couch. "I needed to see your face when I touched you." He spread my legs and slowly guided himself into me, and I caught my breath. Half a moan escaped when I remembered to breathe again. He pulled out slowly. "I wanted to know what you looked like when you came."

He kissed me, and I forced him inside me. I wrapped my legs around him, unwilling to let him all the way out again.

Vince held me on top of the couch as he pounded into me, stealing the air from my lungs and replacing it with an urgency building between my legs and throbbing with impatience. I fisted his hair in my hands and brought his face down to mine, and stared at him as I came.

"I wanted all of you. Every bit. And I'm not letting go," he said, and I closed my eyes and let my head fall back.

~

"WE'LL NEED TO ESTABLISH SOME rules," I said as we walked over the dune. We left the cabin and followed each other to the shore. It was October. These days were ending, in every way.

"Rules?" he asked, and laughed. The colonel didn't seem to take this seriously. He was enjoying every minute of our new relationship, and I was determined to manage it somehow. I would not be reckless with him or my children.

"Yes. Rules. We need to both understand exactly what is expected of the other. You can call it "expectations" if that sounds better to you."

"Both are very hot."

"This isn't supposed to be hot. This is the calm, rational part of whatever *this* is." I walked to the beach where the water curved around to the inlet and grabbed the sheet from my bag. I snapped it up into the air and watched as the wind billowed it from underneath. The colonel grabbed a corner and helped me lower it to the ground and lay it flat between us.

"What if we have no rules? What if we do exactly what feels right and not worry about the rest of it?"

"If that's the way you feel, you should go home now. This is never going to work out." I stopped moving. He was serene as he lay on the sheet, the sun lavishing his dark skin. "Aren't you worried in the least?"

"I'm not." He said it as if I was crazy to worry. As if nothing could penetrate what we had together. And all I could think of was the thousands of things that could ruin it, and ruin James' and Liv's lives.

"Do you know anyone who's ever had an affair?"

"Like, personally?"

"Yeah. Personal enough to know the details." I lay down next to him, close enough for our legs to touch.

"A guy I work with repairing houses is having one."

"Right now?" My eyes bulged. I couldn't reconcile in my head the idea of cheating, with people living in my town who were actually cheating.

"Yes. I think he's going to leave his wife."

I rolled onto my stomach and buried my face in my arms. Affairs ended in divorce. *How typical.*

Vince moved closer to me, his head next to mine. "I told you, this is going to be whatever we make it. Whatever we want it to be."

"It's going to be an affair, regardless of what we call it." I raised my head to face him. He was smiling at me. He really found me ridiculous. "And it's going to end in a fiery crash. Something awful, like James walks in on us having sex, or your wife follows you to the cabin and watches us through the window, or Brad finds out and shoots you from behind. We're going to be on Dateline."

The laughter stopped. The corners of his lips shot down and the tiny lines on his forehead deepened into grooves. Vince's eyes were filled with horror. "What is wrong with you? Seriously, what happened to you that made you this way?" Relief flowed through me. I was finally getting through to him. This was serious. And life-changing. And God help me, so, so wrong. "When your parents were alive, were they still together?"

"They separated when I was eleven, but they didn't divorce until I was fourteen."

"Interesting. Now we're getting somewhere." He lightened, happy to dispute my feelings with diagnosed Daddy issues. "Tell me more about that."

"No." I wasn't there for his entertainment.

"Yes. I need to know everything about you. I need to know why your parents split."

"I don't know why."

"Tell." He ran his fingertips down my side, and tiny trembles originated under his touch and flowed through me. I'd never thought much about the reasons for my parents' break-up. I'd always just blamed my mother. My memories were a series of moments watching my mother chastise my father for dreaming big, and my father shielding me from her tiny thoughts.

"My mother was old school. She believed women should stay home with their children."

"And your father?"

"He believed I was invincible. That there was nothing I couldn't do, and that I should try all of it." I sighed. I missed him. *What would he say about my life now? About my lack of a life?*

"He sounds amazing."

"He was. I worshipped him until I had children."

"And then?"

"Then I thought I should have listened to my mother more. Look at me now. I'm invincible, and I'm wasting away because I believe it to be true."

Vince ran his fingertips down my back. "We get one life, and you didn't leave yours in a courtroom. You live every day as your invincible self whether you're an attorney or not." He kissed my cheek, and his breath hot there made me believe him. "It wasn't who you were, it was what you did for a living."

"That's interesting, coming from the man who dressed like a police officer every year for Halloween."

"I've had a shift in perspective recently."

I paused, letting my gaze rest on Vince's lips. I didn't ask for more information. I didn't want to know if I had anything to do with it. My instincts told me with information came guilt. "Are your parents still together?"

"Married forty-eight years next month."

I shook my head. "You are such a black sheep." Vince pushed the hair off my face and kissed me again. He stood up straight, every bit the police officer, except his uniform had been replaced by swim trunks. "When we ruin our lives, your parents are going to turn to me for answers to how I ruined you. How I seduced their sacred son. You should have run from me when I told you to."

"Is that what you wanted?"

I lifted some sand in my hand and let it cascade back to the beach. Vince was standing in front of me with the entire ocean behind him.

"What *do* you want from me?" His question laid between us. What did I want from him? "More than anything else, what do you want from me?"

I considered being coy and saying I wanted him to fuck me. It was entirely true, but anyone could fuck me. I could say I wanted him to hear me, and that was true, too, but there was more to it. "I want you to keep this secret with me."

I realized, with the salt air filling my lungs and the sound of the ocean surrounding me, that what I loved about Vince was he was working with me. We were a team, and I was no longer alone.

"What did you think I was going to say?" I asked.

"That you wanted me to love you."

"Never that," I said and looked out to the horizon.

twenty-five

LIV WAS A SUBMERGED BALLERINA, or whatever she called it. James was a ninja, and the three of us walked our development ringing door bells and asking for candy. Many houses had fire pits lit and drinks flowing. It was nice in our neighborhood. We were cut off from the world, and we felt safe with our kids roaming the streets after dark. The little boy from across the street who'd seen me in the shower was a policeman for Halloween. He was now one of two who'd seen me naked.

Brad came home just as we were finishing trick or treating. He changed, made a big deal out of the kids' hauls, and went next door to sit by the fire pit and drink. I got the rest of my family ready for bed and ready for school the next day. And then I read my email and told myself it wasn't my favorite part of day.

> *V: I promised I'd show you what there is to love about a small town.*

> *M: That shouldn't take long. Do you have a picture you can email me?*

> *V: Very funny. You have to give it a chance.*

M: For you, I will.

It was quickly becoming clear I would do anything for him. Almost anything. I needed a reason to be out of the house. Vince had said, "An excuse to disappear with me for a few hours."

❧

TWO DAYS HAD PASSED BEFORE I spoke to Brad. His personal Halloween party left him hungover and miserable, so I stayed away. But silence was a waste of time. By the second day in November, I needed things to get back to normal. I called Brad and asked if he wanted to meet me at the mall for dinner.

"What?" was his answer. The idea was clearly absurd. He *worked.*

"I want to buy the kids Christmas outfits. Everything, especially the shoes, sells out so quickly."

"I can't. I'm working. Maybe if you want to try this weekend."

"No. No. That's fine. I think I'm going to have someone watch the kids so I don't have to drag them around with me. Make sure you have some cash to pay her in case you get home before me."

"I always have cash. And I won't be home before you."

"Okay."

He was tired. He probably should have not partied at the neighbors on Halloween, but he worked so hard. He needed an outlet.

With everyone and everything ready for school the following day, I welcomed my babysitter to my house and drove to the truck stop the next town over. I'd never been to one before, and I was a little overwhelmed with the enormous eighteen-wheelers until I saw Vince's truck parked toward the back of the lot, way behind the restaurant with the blinking "Open 24 Hours" sign.

I parked next to his driver's side and watched him exit his truck and climb into my Escalade.

Vince sat on the leather seat beside me, silently looking me up and down before finally smiling the same easy way he had at the Phillies game and saying, "Thanks for coming."

"I couldn't stay away." The immense trucks were lined up in a long row toward the highway. "But is this what you plan on showing me? Because you can't be seen in my car."

"No one's going to see me but you." He leaned over the console between us, lying on his side. He rested his head on his left arm on top the console and reached his right hand between my legs. His shoulders and back took up every inch of space between our seats, and I inhaled deeply the scent of him in my car. He pulled my right thigh toward him, and I wasn't sure I needed to see anything else. I already knew what I loved about this town. I watched as his hand gripped my thigh tighter, and a heat rose inside of me.

"Hmm. I love it already."

"I told you. Now take a right out of the truck stop."

I followed Vince's directions back toward our town. He kept his head down, his hand between my legs. I tried to stay focused.

"There should be a shopping center on your right. Park in the middle row, away from other cars if there's a spot."

I did as I was told. We were in a strip mall, facing a salon, a gymnastics school, a diner, and a carwash. I recognized it from a birthday party Liv had gone to at the gym.

"Do you see Latteria? It's an ice cream shop in the middle."

"I do. You want ice cream?"

"I do. Do you mind getting it?" He reached into his back pocket and pulled out his wallet.

"I'll buy it."

"Here, take money." He was now rushing.

"I have money. What flavor do you want?"

"What are you getting?" he asked and took out a ten-dollar bill.

"Whatever you are. There's only one of us, remember?"

The colonel took a deep breath. His chest rose, the fabric of his T-shirt stretching against it, and I watched. "Surprise me. Nothing with nuts, though." He handed me the ten, and I took it because I wanted him to be happy more than I wanted to make a point about who paid for what in *this*.

"Got it." I hopped out of the car.

Latteria wasn't just an ice cream shop. It was ice cream heaven. The flavors were listed on a large chalkboard behind the counter, and each one made my mouth water. Black Cherry Vanilla, Peanut Butter Oreo, Vermont Maple Walnut, what the hell? I might leave Vince in the car and just eat here. Like, everything. How did I not know about this place? How did I not know about Vince? It was as if that giant house Brad had deposited me in was an actual rock.

I bought a large Bourbon Cookies and Cream and returned to the Escalade. He was still spread across the front seat, exactly where I'd left him. To the outsider, it appeared like I put the ice cream in my cup holder. In reality, Vince held it for me. "Now where to?"

"Take a right onto the Swedesboro Road and follow it until you see the abandoned farmhouse a few acres off the road. Make a right there."

I rolled through the stop sign at the exit of the parking lot.

"Was that a stop?" The colonel popped his head up to see if there was a sign.

"Down, boy," I said and kept driving.

Vince fed me a spoonful of ice cream. It spoiled me for all

other foods in my future.

The right turn dropped me onto a dirt lane that passed the farmhouse and went into the woods. We bounced as the Escalade dipped into the bumps.

"Is this right?" I asked.

"Yes, but feel free to slow down," Vince said and laughed before taking a spoonful of the ice cream for himself. "There should be a clearing soon."

The road ended at the tree line and broke into a clearing at the top of a hill overlooking a pasture with a small lake in the center of it. I parked at the fence. It was as far as we could go. Vince sat up.

"Here." He put the spoon in my mouth and removed it out slowly. My eyes locked with his and the familiar longing, the ever-present need to touch him seared through me. The ice cream melted on my tongue before I could process the cold. All that was left was a hint of sweet bourbon.

Cattle caught my eye. They were each some hue between brown and black, and moseyed across the grass. The herd walked away from us, following each other to a destination blocked from my sight by the hill.

"Where are they going?"

"It's dinner time. The ranch hands just put out the hay. Sometimes when I'm on patrol, I come out here to watch the sunset."

I just looked at him. I could watch him for hours. Whenever we were in public, I felt as if I had. Each minute we were separated by the truth felt like hours as I observed him with other people. The other people we were allowed to be with; the ones who weren't a secret.

The orange sky in front of us blazed on his skin. He was still a light olive-brown from the summer.

"Are you Italian?" I asked.

"I should be offended. I'm Greek. At least on my mother's

side."

"No wonder you're so beautiful," I said, and I meant it. Vince leaned his head on the cushion behind it. I dragged my gaze away from him and turned the key in the ignition. I put the Escalade in REVERSE.

"Are we leaving?"

"I'm turning us around so we can properly watch the sunset." I pulled out and backed into the spot. I pressed the button above us to open the lift gate and shut off the engine.

Vince opened his door and paused as he watched the running boards automatically come out from the side of the vehicle. "Fancy."

"That's one word for it," I said, and got out myself. We met at the back, the pasture in front of us. We sat in the back of the Escalade, and Vince fed me our ice cream. We finished as the last moments of light disappeared, and then we were alone in the dark. And we were outside, the night air touching me everywhere Vince's hands were not.

We climbed into the car and had sex in the third row. The one I'd always found useless. It was roomy and comfortable, and suddenly I liked my car a whole lot more.

"Do you still have time?" he asked as I tied my wrap dress.

"I have a babysitter until eight."

"Okay, there are a couple more things I want to show you. Go back the way you came on this road."

"Road?"

"It's serviceable if you don't try to do sixty miles per hour on it. You can slow down, you know?"

"What fun would that be?"

Vince directed me to the YMCA on the outskirts of town, by the bank of the river that was nearly forgotten. He had me park at the liquor store across the street. There were bars on the windows of the store, and the Y was surrounded by fence topped with barbed wire.

"This is nice," I said, and watched as people, young and old, walked into the Y. There were cars filling the small adjacent lot and more on the side streets surrounding it. Vince sat up in the darkness in time to see a bus drop off more people. "What are they all doing here?" I'd never been to the Y. Not in the three years I'd lived in the town.

"They're having dinner together."

"Who is?" The people were white and black and Hispanic and waved hello to each other and hung their heads and moved at all different speeds. Some held a child's hand, some held the elbow of another to steady them on their tired legs. There was no unifying characteristic.

"The hungry. Some for food, some for human interaction."

I watched as the door to the Y was held for each person in line. They were all greeted with a smile by a man who was familiar. I'd seen him around town before. "How many of them come?" *Had I really been making fun of my automatic running boards earlier?* My belly was full of Bourbon Cookies and Cream.

"Each month between one hundred fifty and two hundred."

"It's remarkable." I turned to Vince. Hallmark-type thoughts of community and human kindness filled me. And because Vince was the faucet that had turned them on, my appreciation landed squarely on him. I stared at him through eyes overflowing with emotion, or something more devastating to consider.

"It's why I love a small town. All these people volunteer to host and serve the meal. All the food is donated by local restaurants. Mrs. Steen and Mrs. Moore bake forty dozen cookies each month. The Hitchner farm sends twenty gallons of iced tea and tomatoes when they're in season. The high school baseball team cooks the chicken in the fall, the football team cooks in the spring. The rest of the year is covered by a list of organizations. We take care of our own."

My eyes moved to Vince's lips and back to his eyes. He was satisfied with my silence, as if he'd gotten through to me and before tonight, I'd been impossible to reach.

"These are the saints, now let's go check on the sinners."

"Aren't we the sinners?"

Vince bent over again in my car and returned his hand to my thigh, and I forgot what we were talking about. "Head back into town. To the Catholic Church."

Vince told me to park in the back of the church lot, but before I even reached the driveway, I saw what we came to see. I inhaled sharply at the sight.

"We're here?" Vince was still hidden for me. The cemetery glowed a warm light as each gravestone had a lit candle upon it. It was breathtaking.

"What is it?"

"It's All Souls Day. The day Catholics pray for the dead who haven't made it to heaven yet. For those still in purgatory."

I looked down at him. All Souls Day could be added to the list of religious rituals I'd never taken part in, and probably never would, but the vision of the cemetery twinkling in the November night made me believe in God. "Are you Catholic?"

"Not anymore. Every year, the women of the church come out for All Souls Day and light these candles."

I turned back to the stones. *They take care of their own.*

"And they pray."

My chest rose and fell as I watched the tiny white lights illuminate the tops of the stones. *Who will light a candle for me when I'm gone? When I am more lost than I am alive?*

"A person can change the world in big ways and in small ways. They do it with every interaction, every day."

I DROVE HOME AND LEFT the windows cracked in the Escalade parked in the garage. I paid the babysitter and kissed my sleeping children in their beds. And then I went to sleep in my bed . . . alone.

twenty-six

"WE WILL NEVER LIE TO each other," Vince read off the paper in front of him, and then watched me and waited.

"And?"

"And nothing. That's all I need."

I grabbed the paper from his hands. "That can't be it. We were supposed to make a list of what we needed from *this*. How this is going to exist, *exactly*. And you have one thing?"

"I want you, and I want you to be honest with me. The rest is up to you. I told you that before."

I handed him back the paper, feeling an odd mix of defeat and regret. I took my list from my purse. "Well, I have a few others."

"I figured." His easy smile and his naked body next to me in my car put me at ease.

"Never call my house, or my cell phone.

No texting.

We are only acquaintances, having met briefly a few times.

Do not ask anyone about me.

Never complain about your wife. God knows she's a saint to put up with you.

No gifts.

No cards.

Nothing that can later be found.

No arguments about money. We are not dating. I'll pay for whatever I want.

No love declaring, no needy emails, no begging."

I looked over, and he was smiling.

"If I ever send you an email with no subject line, and nothing in it, you are to delete your account immediately and not contact me. At best, it means questions are being asked." At the suggestion of these events, the smile drained from his face. "And never call me by my name," I added. "Think of something else."

"Why?"

"In case you ever talk in your sleep. You're not sleeping with me."

"How about 'eros'? It's the Greek work for love."

"The root of erotica?" I asked, and Vince kissed me. "What's the Greek word for harlot?"

He shook his head. "I'll keep working on it."

He kissed me again and lifted me on top of him, my legs straddling him the exact way they had after his accident. His hands rested on my thighs, and his eyes begged for the truth from me. "What if I fall in love with you?"

"You won't. Save your love for your wife."

"What if I'm already in love with you?"

I stopped breathing. A chill skipped across my breasts. "This won't work if you're in love with me. A mistake will be made."

He reached up and pulled my lips to his. I fell into him, letting him support me with his kiss. He wrapped his hands around my ass and moved me closer. I pressed myself against him, wanting him.

"It isn't a mistake," he said, and took my lip between his teeth.

"It's worse. We're a tragedy." I waited for his denial, for his insistence that I was not a whore, but he only kissed me instead.

twenty-seven

I WASN'T AN IDIOT. I knew several women who'd had affairs. "The Whores," as Brad called them. It never ended well. They were all lonelier than they'd been before the affair started. Most were without the financial security they'd enjoyed while married, and dropped their children off at their ex-husband's house Christmas morning every other year. I was going to risk all of that. But I was not going to be stupid about it.

One Saturday night, while enduring the endless winter weekends of Brad's history channel on the television, I broached the subject of joining a book club in Philadelphia.

"Why wouldn't you just join one around here? I'm sure Jenna knows of one."

Why he cared, I couldn't imagine. A thought occurred to me immediately. "Why don't you join it with me? It's usually the first Thursday of the month, and they meet at restaurants and bars to discuss the book. It might be fun."

"I don't have time." Brad shook his head, dismissing the idea immediately. Which of course, I knew he would. The predictability of these conversations was less painful now that the colonel was involved.

"Well, if we don't do the book club together, maybe we can do something else. Golf or tennis or something," I said, still enjoying myself.

His reaction was so foreseeable, I almost felt bad toying with him. "Look, I know you're a little bored." *A little.* "But I'm not. I have more on my plate than I can handle at the moment. You forget what it's like to work."

But that was the problem. I hadn't forgotten. I couldn't forget. How it felt to have a deadline, or people needing me to understand information and explain it to them. How fast I'd had to shower to get out the door and contribute to society.

"Alright. I understand. You won't mind if I join, though. Will you? I can get a sitter to put the kids to bed before you get home." And just like that, I started asking permission to do things. "It's only twelve nights the whole year." Seeking permission would have angered me, but the things I was actually going to do were all to Vince's body.

"Whatever makes you happy," Brad said, and the smile spread across my face.

"Great! This month's book is *A Farewell to Arms* by Hemingway. One of my favorites."

The next day I sent an email to the colonel, letting him know I'd joined a book club and the date of our next meeting. He was much more excited about my new hobby than Brad. Go figure.

⁂

MY FIRST BOOK CLUB MEETING was at Fado Irish Pub in Center City. The bar was forty minutes away, and about two blocks from the Hyatt Bellevue. The crowds of the city streets and the Bellevue's old world elegance almost had me forgetting I was a whore.

I was a smart whore, though. I'd siphoned twenties off Brad's nightstand when he came home after happy hour, or from business dinners half lit. I overcharged him for school lunches, field trips, and fundraisers. I told him our cleaning lady asked for a raise. Anything that required cash. And I did it with a smile on my face. Until I had enough money to purchase a two hundred fifty dollar Visa gift card from the grocery store. Once I had it in my hand, I used it to reserve my room. Our room.

I drove to Philly, parked by the pub, and used Brad's credit card to pay for the parking. I walked to the Bellevue and used my gift card to pay for the room. I paused for a second, considering the term "gift card" and its perfect meaning. Once I had my room key, I walked back to the pub and waited for Vince. I kept a low profile. I watched as the book club filed in and gathered at a table in a small area in the back. I went to the bathroom and listened to their conversation until I had a good feel for the tone of the meeting. If there was ever a question asked about this book club, I would have an answer. I watched, I listened, and I waited for my lover at the bar.

Anticipation coursed through my thighs and dampened my underpants at the mere thought of him in my hands. By the time Vince arrived, I was ready to crawl out of my skin. I watched as he took the stool next to me and ordered a beer. He smelled of some cologne he'd probably received as a Christmas present from his wife last year. He drank his beer fast, my hand slipping between his generous thighs, my eyes closing at the feel of him. And when he placed his empty glass on the bar, I was already halfway out the door with my copy of *A Farewell to Arms* trapped safely in my bag.

It'd been weeks of emails he addressed to Maris, a Greek name meaning "of the sea." Maris was more me than love, and he gave it to me, so of course I did love it. Something I would never tell him. We would never speak of love. My emails I addressed to the colonel. Some relived the night in his cabin or our day at the shore, but most exchanged information about our younger lives. We both steered clear of discussing spouses and children for the most part. Vince and I were separate from them, and as much as I always knew it was impossible to separate something like that, for a little while I did. Brad separated us from his life. The colonel was now my career.

His favorite color was blue. The very gray-blue, military blue.

He broke his leg once on a high school skiing trip.

The only laws he'd ever broken were under-age drinking and driving without a license.

He only danced when he drank a lot, and he rarely drank that much.

He was a republican, but from the Left.

He had two older sisters.

He was a Pisces, his birthday was March fifth.

He loved the idea of pesto, but was allergic to pine nuts.

He believed I was a mermaid, that I enchanted him.

He told me about his day. Every day. And I felt life coursing through my veins with every new email that popped up on my phone screen. The emails were long and eloquent and encouraging in a familiar way. They convinced me it was only us involved, and I clung to them. Until I permanently deleted each one.

But as the elevator doors opened on the third floor of the Bellevue, there were no more words that needed to be said. Vince grabbed my hand and we walked the hall together. Not like husband and wife. Not like young lovers. Like two people who'd lost the urge to rip the clothes off their lover and finally felt it again. We savored every touch, every word, every breath the other took until he slipped the key card in the door, and then there was no other. We were one.

twenty-eight

JENNA DIDN'T NEED ME TO help her. She helped herself to my purse and dug through it the same way my kids would have. "What's with all this cash?" She held up the wad of twenties I was saving for my next Visa gift card.

"I'm saving for Brad's Christmas present." That could not have been further from the truth, but it must have sufficed, because Jenna continued her search.

This was why I never saved matches or key cards or any other memento from my meetings with Vince. I wanted to. I longed for the keycard on the coffee table in the room at the Bellevue. I had run my fingers over it, tapped it on the glass top of the table, and finally tossed it into the trash can. He—we—could only exist in my mind.

"Are you sure you have a lighter in here?"

"I think so. Here, give it to me."

Jenna handed the bag over our high-top bar table. We were trapped inside the waterpark of the Poconos hotel we were staying at with our five kids. This was how I spent the kids' fall break. At an indoor waterpark, completely dry, drinking with Jenna and watching them float by in the lazy river or careen down the two-story slide. Living the dream.

"Have you ever thought about having an affair?" I blurted out and finished my beer, waiting for Jenna's answer as I searched my bag.

"No." She laughed. And then she stopped laughing. She leaned toward me and examined my eyes as if searching for signs of drug use. "Why are you not laughing?"

"Not sure."

"As in, not sure you haven't had an affair?" Jenna asked and sucked on the straw of her cup. It was filled with Jack Daniels from the jug in her purse and soda from the concession stand.

"Not sure I'm happy. Fulfilled."

"That's a different story. You didn't ask if I was fulfilled." She took another sip and sat back in her chair. "I know it must seem that way. The way John fawns all over me and constantly asks how we can explore my interests." My shoulders shook as I laughed, too. "But I'm actually not fulfilled."

"No? That is hard to believe. Are you difficult to satisfy?"

Jenna's oldest ran over and handed her a wrapper from a lollipop he'd fished out of the water.

"Apparently, I'm a trash receptacle. That's satisfying." She threw the wrapper on the table and took another sip from her cup. Jenna and I looked out into the indoor waterpark abyss. "My sister had an affair once."

"She did?" I lowered my voice. These things were secrets.

"It's over now. She was fucking her boss. Her husband found out. They went to marriage counseling, and now it's over."

"Gloria? The sister I met?"

"Yeah. She had to quit her job, but otherwise I think things are fine." Jenna shrugged as if we were talking about her having her car repaired after a minor fender bender. This was news to me. In my head, affairs equaled divorce equaled no one ever being fine again. *Does anyone ever come out of this situation unscathed?*

"Why did she decide to stay?"

"Her marriage counselor told her if she divorced her husband, it would fuck up her family for generations to come."

Jenna raised her eyebrows and nodded. "He worded it differently, but you get the point."

"So she stayed?"

"She stayed."

"Does she ever talk to her boss?" The thought of never
talking to Vince again was more terrifying than never having
sex with him again.

"Not that I know of. We all act like it never happened. Her
kids don't know."

"How could it have never happened? How could they stay
married?"

"Her husband's a great guy."

I leaned back in my chair. "Brad would be a complete dick
about it."

"You think?" Jenna's sarcasm overflowed. Brad was a lot of
things—powerful, strong, competitive, intelligent—but no one
ever said he was a great guy.

"My first year out of law school I worked for a woman going through a divorce," I said, thinking back to the year my boss
almost withered away. She had missed a ton of work, was always on edge, and was exhausted throughout the entire process. "She said her ex was the nicest guy when she married him.
She must have told me ten times, 'You never really know someone until you divorce them.'" I stood up to get another beer.

"I believe it. Get me another soda?"

I looked around the dripping mega park that housed hun-
dreds of kids. "Man, I am thankful for the years of swim lessons
I endured. Have you seen the kids?"

"Liv floated by a few minutes ago. She looked awesome."

"Of course."

twenty-nine

"I'M THANKFUL FOR YOU," I said, counting my blessings in my head. "You are my day off, my birthday surprise, a rainbow, a full moon, a four-leaf clover, and a lucky penny all rolled into one."

"A lucky penny, huh? Are you happy you found me?" He was naked, lying next to me with his head propped up on his hand. We'd made it to another secret day at his cabin. "Be honest."

"I thought I always had to be honest with you." I leaned over and kissed his lips and pressed my whole body against his. Vince wrapped his arms around my shoulders, and I hid there in his arms.

"Does that bother you?"

"No. Yes. Sometimes."

He laughed at me. "Why is it so hard for you?"

I considered the question. I'd always thought it was hard for everyone, but Vince just said whatever he was thinking. He was the most non-conniving person I'd ever met. Maybe it had to do with our different roles in law enforcement. "I have a lot of thoughts I'd prefer to keep in my head."

"But those are all the ones I want to hear." He held me tighter. "Not today, though. Not unless you want to tell me."

"No thank you," I sweetly said, letting my eyes stay closed against his chest.

I wanted to ask him so many questions, but I was afraid of his answers. They scared me almost as much as the thoughts in my head. I wanted to know why he was here. *Why me?* Why not some other woman from the stay-at-home mom pool? Why he was cheating in the first place? My reasons seemed so insignificant and illegitimate. I needed this to mean something, but that would make it into something it wasn't—which was an affair.

"Vince?" His fingers stopped moving, and his chin pointed down to my head. "Do you think we're bad people?" I was an ass for asking. Why couldn't I just lie there and enjoy the feel of his chest beneath my face?

"I don't know," he said, and it was worse than him denying it. He was always so sure that we were fine. That *this* was fine, but that was all to put me at ease, and if we were being honest, neither of us knew who we were anymore.

He reached down and caressed my lower back, letting his fingertips drag up again, and then he pulled me up to face him. He was magnificent. A souvenir I hadn't paid for, the vacation I didn't earn. He was stolen goods, and I never wanted to return them, but I also knew I wouldn't do the time to keep him. The cost was too high.

"Let's just enjoy right now. Okay?" he said, and I kissed him. His tongue told me not to think too much, to not be honest with myself or anyone else.

"YOU HAVE TO DO ME a favor." The fact that Jenna had called rather than just texted meant I really did have to do it. Whatever it was.

"Are you okay?"

"I'm so hung over. I cannot tell you how fun yesterday was, because no happy thoughts can penetrate the throbbing over the entire top of my head." Her voice was rough, that of a man forty years older than her.

"You sound horrible."

"I am horrible," she croaked out, and I could feel her headache in my own mind.

"What do you need?" Jenna knew before she called that I would help her.

"Today is the Veteran's Day celebration at school. I need you to take my place as a greeter."

"Really?"

"Molly's mom is the other one, and I cannot deal with her and this headache. Please. I am begging you." She sounded like she might die at any minute.

"Okay."

"All you have to do is say hello to each veteran that walks in, thank them for their service, and pin a boutonniere on them."

"Okay."

"And wear something patriotic."

"What?" I immediately regretted agreeing to help.

"Yeah. You've got something in that closet of yours. Something red, white, and-or blue."

"What were you going to wear?"

"A red dress."

"Seriously?"

"Yes! This town takes Veteran's Day very seriously."

"I know. I know. I was at the Fourth of July Parade. Okay, what time?"

"You need to be there in an hour." Jenna sounded relieved. I was searching my mind for something to wear and wondering if I had time to flatiron my hair.

"I'm trying to still love you."

"I still love you. In case that helps. It's really not a big deal. Just saying hello to people."

"You know me. That's a big deal."

THEY FILED IN. EVERY SINGLE one of them on time. They were, after all, our military, and they were glorious. So thankful to be recognized; happy to be alive. They wore hats and shirts from their branches of service. A few young men and women were in uniform, still active duty members, but the majority were older than me.

And then there was Vince.

I struggled to affix the boutonniere to the gentlemen in front of him. The veteran kept talking, putting me at ease as I forced the pin through the fabric of his sports jacket. He was seventy-three and had served in the Air Force. When I finally finished, I stepped back to admire my work. *Whew.*

"Thank you for your service," I said, and the man pulled me to him and hugged me. I wasn't used to this much human interaction on a Monday, let alone hugging, but I hugged him back because I *was* thankful for his service.

He finally released me after the man next to us made a joke that he was only supposed to get a flower. We both laughed and he walked away, leaving me with Vince to greet.

"Good morning," I said without a hint of familiarity.

"Good morning."

I bent down and selected a red flower from the box on the chair beside me. I thought it would look best on his police uniform. With my heels on, we were closer to the same height. I could speak softly, and he could hear me without bending down.

"Thank you for your service," I said, and started to sweat a little. I wasn't used to being this close to him with anyone else around.

"You're welcome." His voice was strong. We'd done nothing wrong. *We barely know each other.* For the first time, Vince was more on top of our lies than I was. His eyes never left me as I fumbled with his flower, finally forcing the pin into the back of the carnation. I took a deep breath and let it out, moving away from him.

"What? No hug?" the man behind Vince asked, and we both froze, staring at each other.

"I'll give him a hug," Molly's mom said and pulled Vince over to her. The crowd laughed, and Vince hugged her back, and I couldn't help but laugh at all of us, Molly's mom included. When she let him go, Vince walked to the cafeteria to meet up with his daughter for lunch, and I moved on to the next veteran. I was grateful Jenna couldn't make it.

thirty

THE ANNUAL CHRISTMAS PARTY AT Brad's boss's house in North Jersey was always the first Thursday of December. The problem was *this* year I was also supposed to be lying about a book club I'd never joined, while I was fucking the colonel on the first Thursday of December.

The email I sent Vince was logical and rational and laid out the valid reasons why I couldn't miss Brad's work holiday party to meet him in the city. I was trying to convince us both. His reply back was one word: Unacceptable.

I SMILED AS THE OTHER parents filed into the auditorium, and I showed Vince some pictures on my phone. They were of Liv and his daughter from Halloween, and I'd saved them for just this type of covert conversation. He watched as I scrolled through them.

"How can I make it up to you? Book club is out." I smiled up at him fakely and pointed back at my phone.

"I want to spend the night with you."

"No," I answered too quickly.

He kept the smile plastered on his face, but I could see the lines of frustration in his jaw. "I want to open my eyes in the morning and feel your skin against mine." His fingertips brushed across my arm as he took the phone from my hand and examined a picture closer. "I want to fall asleep with my hand on your breast. I want to hear you breathe until sleep takes me."

I let the words sink in, contemplating the unthinkable he was suggesting. My eyes wanted to close and stop time for the moment, but instead I made light of it. "You're very dramatic."

"You're making me this way. You spending the night with me would be a tremendous gift."

I nodded at the unicorn as she came through the door, and I leaned back from Vince. "We're not exchanging gifts. Ever."

"Then think of it as a payback for taking book club away during the holidays."

"I can't pull that off."

"Can't or won't? Because I think you can do anything you put your mind to."

Jenna came in and walked over. She took the phone from Vince's hand and looked at the picture of Liv and Allison standing together on the stage. "Wrong holiday," she said and handed the phone back to me.

"I haven't seen the Pratts since the festival. I've had these pictures on my phone for weeks."

"Why not just put them on Facebook?"

"Are you on Facebook?" I asked the colonel, still playing the game.

"I am, but I rarely go on there."

"Your wife's on there all the time. Tag her," Jenna said as if this was an obvious solution.

"We're not friends," I said, and Jenna grabbed my phone from my hand. She went into Facebook and friended the colonel's wife from my account. I smiled like a lunatic at both the colonel and Jenna.

With that settled, I followed Jenna to seats in the middle of the auditorium. The first and second grade holiday music program was about to begin. I fired off an email to Vince, who was now sitting—in his uniform—two rows in front of me, so I could stare at his shoulders instead of the stage.

> M: *We've been together only two months and whatever this is keeps growing. If I spend the night with you now, then what?*

> *Vacation together?*

> *Valentine's Day dinner?*

> *I think we should stick with the original plan.*

I tore my eyes away from Vince's shoulders to see Liv do a Swedish dance during her class's number. When I was safely buckled in the driver's seat of my car, I opened my email and found Vince's response.

> V: *Then find a way to get out of his party and come to book club. THAT was the original plan.*

Suddenly, my priorities weren't as clear.

thirty-one

WE WERE LATE. BRAD'S FANCY car's GPS directed us to an abandoned convenience store, rather than the hotel. Brad was a dick. Things weren't going his way. I searched the hotel on my phone and used the directions on their website to get us there.

The woman at the front desk didn't know what she was doing and she was unlucky enough to encounter Brad in a bad mood. Incompetence turned him into an even bigger dick. I thought I'd give him a blowjob when we got to the room. It would settle his nerves and hopefully keep his hands off me later. But the check-in took so long, all he cared about was not being late. He rushed me through my makeup and practically tapped his foot as I put my dress on.

It was simple. A tailored, column maxi dress. The top was jersey, the bottom more structured, and it was all black. Conservative.

"I sent you the email it was business casual, right? Did I tell you his assistant told me most of the women would be in pants?"

"I got the email. I'm not most women." I put on my coat and pulled my hair out of the back of it. "Ready, Mr. Executive?"

Brad motioned toward the door, and I led the way.

It was a small group of some of the most powerful people in the company. The CEO showed up in jeans; it was the business equivalent of Jesus actually doing some carpentry work. Brad left me immediately. He had lots of people to talk to. Not one picture was posted on Facebook. Not one person commented on another's attire. These people worked, goddammit. They had things to say. They had no time for nonsense.

I tried his female coworkers. They tolerated me. The conversations were short after I told them I didn't work. About an hour into the wine, one actually asked what I did all day. She had two nannies. The morning nanny put the clothes in the washer, the afternoon nanny folded them. She had a cleaning lady, an "extra" who came twice a week and straightened up. She commuted to the city and was never home before seven. My existence was completely foreign to her, somewhere defined by the roles of the four women running her house.

"It's busy," I said.

Before I could elaborate, she proclaimed, "There are days when I wish I could just lie around at home."

So . . . then I tried the spouses. The wives of Brad's coworkers complained about their husbands. The husbands were as bored as I was.

By the time our host called our attention to the middle of the room and made a toast, I was ready to announce to the entire party that I was fucking the Chief of Police in my town, and his cock was a thing of beauty.

THAT, is what I am doing all day.

Brad was in the corner, hysterically laughing at something the man next to him said. He was practically slapping his knee, and I gravitated toward him, desperately seeking some joy.

"Hi," I said to both of them. Brad just stood there. "I'm Meredith. Brad's wife."

The man shared a warm smile and took my hand. I waited for Brad to say something.

"Rob," the man offered. "It's nice to meet you. Where have you been all night? I thought Brad was here alone."

So did he. "I've been mingling. What a great crowd."

"Yes. Jack always throws a great party."

Both men looked at me, unsure of what to do with me. I excused myself to get a drink and emailed the colonel from the bathroom. I only wrote one sentence: I miss you.

But I missed me, too.

thirty-two

EARLY SNOW BEFORE THE HOLIDAYS kept us from the cabin. Even with the Escalade, the fresh twenty inches were too great a risk. Vince's emails begged me to arrange another meeting spot. We had the book club and one day at the cabin. Brad's work Christmas party ruined book club this month. Without the cabin, there just wasn't enough time. The kids would be off from school soon. I already missed him.

But no matter how hard I tried, I couldn't come up with a way to see him. Jenna would help, but I held Vince and me too deep. A secret buried so far down that guilt couldn't touch it. Before I went to bed, I emailed him I couldn't figure it out. There was no other way to safely see him, and we'd have to wait until book club in January.

Around eight-thirty the next morning, the police cruiser pulled in my driveway. I looked out the window twice to be sure I was seeing what I thought I saw. I opened the front door and yanked him inside before he rang the bell.

"What are you doing here?"

He pressed me against the wall and kissed me, threading his hands in my hair and making me forget where we were. "Official business," he said. His words were rough from his lips and crushed me with the weight of his body and the depth of his need.

I reached down and grabbed him. He was already hard, wanting me more than anything else, and I would let him have me every time he asked. I stroked him, kissing him at the same time. I could feel the inside of my body coming alive while my hands touched him.

Vince reached down and unhooked his holster. He placed it on the table next to my dying plant. I dropped to my knees in front of him and unzipped his pants. I lowered them over his hips, and his dick fell out, pointing straight to me.

Vince ran his hands through my hair as I played with his balls and continued to stroke him. My need for him, for his body, was somewhere near worship, and yet he gave it to me so willingly it bordered on obsession. I took him in my hand and then into my mouth as far back as it would go. I released him slowly, letting my lips linger on the tip, and Vince tightened his fists in my hair as his head dropped back.

His ecstasy was my drug. I licked and teased and finally fell into a rhythm that would swallow us both whole if we let it. Vince's hand rested on the back of my head, and when he finally came, he left his hand there as if he was unable to control the movements of his muscles. He stayed still with his head still hanging, and inhaled deeply into his chest. I kissed his inner thigh, and a jolt spread through his body, and I was satisfied.

I stood in front of him.

"Thank you."

"You're welcome," I said and blushed, and then just to ruin the sentiment, I added, "I could suck your dick all day."

He laughed, knowing I couldn't leave it a sensual encounter. I had to reduce it somehow. He watched as I straightened my T-shirt and fixed my hair. He pulled his pants up and picked up his holster. He moved through the foyer as he put it back on. Vince wouldn't have sex with me here. We'd already gone too far. Too far in my family's house. Too far in their lives.

"This is awkward," Vince said as he regarded my wedding portrait on the top of the hall table.

"It's this foyer. And that strange balcony." I pointed at the top of the stairs to the half-moon overhang which still made no sense to me.

He looked up at it, too. "That is strange."

"I know. What is the point of it?" Vince's eyes came back to me. "I want to paint a mural on the staircase to draw the eye away from it." He stayed watching me, drinking me down, and I stopped talking. I was unable to think with him looking at me that way.

"You're lovely, you know."

"Perhaps a mural of my head then."

Vince laughed, his spell broken. "I mean it," he argued, but I already knew he did. "Have you looked on Pinterest?"

The word from his mouth sent a shocked laugh from my lips. "No. I have not."

Vince kissed me again, and I wanted him to climb in bed with me. "Now I have to go knock on some of your neighbors' doors and ask them if they've seen anything suspicious. Anyone stealing out of parked cars around here. You know, official business."

"Maybe you'll get another blow job."

"Maybe I'll have some follow-up questions for you."

My back was to the wall again, and I pulled him even closer to me. "About blow jobs?"

Vince didn't answer. He didn't have to. "How do I have you?"

"It's your giant cock." I could feel the lov—affection, it wasn't love—in my stare. I couldn't turn away. I couldn't deny him it.

"I'm serious," he said through his laughter. "How many lovers have you had?"

"I like to say three."

Vince grabbed me by the chin and kissed me again. "Tell me about each one."

"What?" Surely this was a joke.

"I'm trying to figure out how we ended up here together. I need to know your past. Not in a creepy way. Just who you've been with and why you're no longer with them."

"Oh, like a sexual outline, a resume of sorts?" I loved watching him laugh. "Okay. But you'll need to do the same."

He kissed my lips lightly, making me want him to throw me down on the floor. He moved back, giving me a chance to breathe, and a shy smile fell upon his lips. "You have to be honest."

"Always."

"Write them in an email and send it to me at seven."

"Why seven?"

"I don't know, but I'll send you mine then, too. It'll give me some time to work on the list."

I blushed at the thought of the women Vince had been with. I could almost see him riding his Spanish teacher in high school as she rambled off obscenities in español. The thought of the list made me want his clothes off him again.

"I have to go. Are you going to Sarah's Christmas party?"

"I don't know. Brad's out of town. I can't decide whether I'll be talked about more if I'm not there, or if I'm there alone."

"Depends on what you're wearing."

"What am I supposed to wear? The invitation said something crazy like—"

"Holiday Cocktail."

"Yes. What is that?"

"I wear a suit every year."

"A suit? I've never seen you in a suit." I'd imagined it though. Vince in a suit. Vince in his uniform. Vince in a swimsuit. Vince in cargo shorts. Vince standing in front of me completely naked. The temperature in the foyer rose. I pulled my T-shirt away from my skin seeking cool air. I took a deep breath and steadied myself.

"I've got to go." He quickly kissed my cheek, which was hot from the images of him floating through my mind.

"Yes. You do."

"Email me." He opened the door and stepped into the cold wind. With the front door open, I watched him walk to his police car.

thirty-three

THE LIST WAS MORE DIFFICULT to write than I originally thought it would be. And longer than I'd remembered. I'd
always told Brad I'd been with three people. It was a nice number, and I think we both found it to be respectable, yet not uptight. But Vince wanted the truth, and his insistence on honesty,
while uncomfortable almost one hundred percent of the time it
was invoked, was one of my favorite parts of our relationship.
It was everything but typical. I sat down at the kids' computer
in the kitchen, signed into my spam email account, and drafted
the requested email to the colonel.

Those Who Have Come Before You

#1—Was my boyfriend and my senior prom date. We'd
already had sex, of course. Eventually he cheated on me,
and I was okay with it because even back then I knew
neither of us had the emotional capacity for an honest
conversation about what we needed from each other, or
our relationship.

#2—Was #1's friend. Because although I was "okay with
it," I was going through an eye-for-an-eye phase.

#3—Gave me my first orgasm, so I'm still obsessed with
him. In fact, your hair reminds me of his.

Kidding.

Not totally.

#4—Was a guy (friend) who lived two floors below me in my dorm. One night he decided we should have sex and was so relentless, I fucked him so he would finally shut up and I could go to sleep.

#5—Was a highly intelligent, bit of an outsider, who picked me up at the library. He had the biggest dick I'd ever seen. It was awkward. Not only trying to fit it in me, but even more so because I never got his last name and felt weird asking after we'd had sex a few times. So I call him John Richardson because he lived on Richardson Street. Sometimes, my roommates and I called him Big Stick John, but mostly John Richardson. I'd love to see him again, but without a name . . .

#6—Was a bodybuilder I met on the beach. Nice guy. Small penis. Didn't eat bacon.

#7—Coworker. We're still friends. He wanted to fuck everyone. I didn't blame him.

#8—Brad. I made him wait a month because I knew within a few hours that we'd marry. I told him so, and he didn't run, which only fueled the idea.

#9—My dalliance into law enforcement.

It will take years of therapy to truly know why I made it to Lucky #9, but if I had to self-diagnose, I'd blame it on my search for structure and discipline during a foreign period in my life. And the fact that when you sat next to me on the school bus, I knew you'd be amazing in bed.

I closed the email. It would be saved in my drafts until 7 P.M., and then I would send it to the colonel. And I would open his email and drink a glass of wine while I read about the women he'd fucked before me. This was a brilliant idea. I closed my spam account. Went to three more websites to drop the email provider in my web history, then cleared the history completely. I shut down and restarted the computer, and opened our web browser with the address of the kids' favorite site. *What? Mommy was never even here.*

∽

AT SEVEN, MY PHONE ALARM went off as I was examining my plant. It was showing some signs of life. Its leaves had strength. They were holding their own and more green than brown. It was far from thriving, but who wasn't? I found my phone and shut off the alarm. *Right on time.* I uncorked a bottle of cabernet and navigated into my spam account on my phone. I found the draft and sent it to the colonel. The email from him, already in my inbox, was no surprise. He was dependable. I poured my wine and peered into the family room. James and Liv were in their PJs, lounging under blankets on the couches and watching the original *Star Wars* movies. I was free.

The wine tasted like an open fire at a ski lodge. I was someplace far away from here. I was glorious, in a crowd, with an oversized turtleneck sweater, and the colonel sitting next to me. We were vacationing together. I sat down at my kitchen island and opened his email, of which the subject was, "People I Have Blessed with my Nakedness." There was so much to love about this man. I opened it and found:

> *V: I had sex with my wife in high school, my junior year. We attended Penn State together and I continued to date her there. After graduation, we married. She's the only other person I've been with.*
> *Until You.*

I put the phone on the counter and let the oxygen return to my head.

I picked it up and read the email again.

What. The. Fuck.

I closed the email. I opened the email. I read it again. I wanted to call Jenna and ask her if this was normal. How could he have only been with one woman? How could he have been with one woman and then be with me? Thoughts were screaming in my head. This email was a horrible idea. I thought of the one I sent him. *I am a whore.*

I replied to his email:

M: *We need to talk about this.*

V: *Don't freak out.*

M: *Too late.*

V: *I'll be over after my shift. Around eleven.*

M: *No. Someone is going to see you.*

V: *I'll make sure they don't. Leave the back door unlocked.*

M: *Footprints.*

V: *Have a little faith.*

M: *Has your wife ever been with anyone else?*

V: *No.*

BY THE TIME THE MOVIE ended and the kids were asleep in their beds, I was putting the empty bottle of wine in the recycling bin and opening a beer. I was going to drink until the contents of his email were forgotten. One lover.

One person . . . his wife . . . he was practically a virgin. They'd been virgins together, then they'd gotten married, and *then* there was me. The whore from out of town who would ruin everything because she was bored.

He came through the back door, and even the words in my head were slurring a little. My eyes darted to every window in the room and across the side lawn at my neighbors' house, wondering if they could see in. Vince gently closed the door behind him and turned out the kitchen lights. And then we were alone, and in the dark.

"What are you doing?" I asked, and he knew I didn't mean with the lights. What the hell was he doing with me?

He walked toward me, and I put my hands up to halt him. I wanted to hear what he had to say without his body blocking my thoughts. I pointed my finger at him and said, "Stay right where you are, you adulterer." My words were slow, and I stumbled over the last syllable in adulterer. Even in the dark, I knew he was about to comment on my drinking.

"You're taking this harder than I thought."

"You think I'm taking this hard? Wait until your wife finds out." I dropped my voice to a whisper as if someone might hear us. "Women who marry men they give their virginity to carry it like a sword. She will kill you. And this will kill her. What have you done? Why? Tell me why, Colonel?" The word colonel dripped with contempt, and I steadied myself with a hand on the countertop.

"I'm going to walk over to you. Hold still." He was talking to me like he'd just pulled over a crazy person. I was drunk. Not crazy. Maybe.

"Whatever."

Vince came and stood in front of me. He took my face in his hands and pointed it toward the hallway, where a tiny light was shining into the kitchen. He was examining me, because he was always a cop.

"I'm fine. It was just a little—bottle—of wine."

"Mar—"

"Don't 'Mar' me, Colonel Pratt. What the hell are you doing with me?"

He took a deep breath and kissed me on the lips, and even with the wine, I didn't forget the explanation I needed from him, but I wanted him. I wanted him the same way I had since I'd first met him.

"I spent my entire life knowing I was going to be a police officer. I worked at the station answering phones and cleaning up when I was in high school. I studied criminal justice in college. I was ROTC. I interned. I prepared. I served as an MP in the Army. It is my passion." My jealousy over his passion stung my throat. I vaguely remembered what that felt like. "It *was* my passion."

"She must have been, too."

Vince's head dropped. *She* was never a part of us. "I was so focused on the law, I let everything else just naturally move forward. Including my relationship. We're together because I never stopped to think about not being together."

"You're making a mistake with me because of a mistake you made with her. You can't just let your life happen. You have to choose to live it."

"That's interesting, coming from you." He looked at me again. He was determined, but his intentions were unfathomable. "I'm a good man. And even though I don't always do the right thing, I'm still a good man." *The best,* I thought. He was staring at me, but far away in his mind. "Have any of your friends died?"

I ran through the corners of loss in my mind. *Only my father.*

"No."

"Last year, I lost a buddy from the Army. He was a year younger than me and *died* while running down a country road. Fell over and died." I watched Vince, the horror trapped in his eyes. "I swore, from that moment on, I would live purposefully. I would actively live my life. I started the foundation. I volunteered at the school and spent more time with my kids. I thought those were the things I *should* be doing." He ran his hands down my arms, warming me with his touch. "But the moment I sat with you on that school bus, I wanted something more. *Someone* even more than I wanted to be a police officer. I wanted you. And it scared me, because nothing has ever felt that way to me." He threaded his hands in my hair and lifted his face to the ceiling. He inhaled deeply and blew it out his mouth in frustration . . . and I waited.

"I'm not proud of what I've done, but I'm not ashamed either. Every minute you're awake, you exude an 'I don't give a fuck' attitude, and it's intoxicating. That's why women don't like you, and men can't get enough of you."

"Women don't like me?"

Why the fuck do I care about this? Wine makes me weepy.

"Women don't know what to make of you. They prefer women who care about everything, but you don't, and that's somehow threatening." He lifted my chin and ran his lips across my neck, and I trembled from his touch. I pulled him closer to warm me, not caring anymore who hated me. "I'm with you because I can't figure out how to be without you. And to be honest, I haven't tried very hard. You are intelligent, and funny, and a challenge at all times. And if I didn't spend half my day hating your husband for living with you, I'd almost pity him for having to deal with you. You're too smart for your own good. And I don't care what you think about my past love life. This is the one I'm not giving up."

"Vince." His name from my lips let us both know the

conversation was about to change.

"Whether I had a hundred lovers before you, or just one, it doesn't change a thing between us." He kissed me again and stepped back. An ache shot through my body and a moan slipped from my lips. I wanted so much more of him. "I have to go. I'll email you tomorrow."

I dropped my face in my hands, and he walked out of my kitchen and into the darkness.

The next day, I searched for footprints in the snow and there were none.

❧

"DO YOU EVER THINK WE should add at least one more day?" Vince asked, and I just stared at him. "Or maybe twice a week instead of twice a month."

I pulled the sandwich out of the bag. It was a classic size. Enough for Vince to eat on his own, but I'd refused to buy two in case I saw someone I knew. So he was on a bit of a diet . . . and we'd had to agree on a sandwich. We'd negotiated naked.

It was turkey on wheat for me. With mayo, tomatoes, and lettuce for Vince. And hot and sweet peppers.

"No response?"

"Is this a serious question? I'm thankful we haven't been caught on our twice-monthly visits."

"Visits?"

"What do you call them? Call *this*?" I waved my hand across the coffee table picnic we were sharing while our clothes laid in a pile on the floor next to us.

"This I call heaven. Except the wheat roll. That I call a huge concession."

Vince was usually so serious. He was quiet strong. Whenever he joked with me, no matter how insignificant, he melted me a little more. I picked up my phone and snapped a picture of him.

"Did you just take a picture of me?"

"I did. I deleted the one of your ass from the shore. But it almost killed me to do so. That's right around the time I got this fancy new phone with its 'private mode.'"

"What's that?"

"I can save photos or videos to a place in the phone that can only be accessed with my fingerprint."

"What?"

"I know. It's a cheater's phone." I'd spent hours on the internet researching the private mode. The idea of having photos saved anywhere violated every rule I had about Vince's and my relationship. I had promised myself I'd only look at them sober, and completely alone. I always left my phone unlocked and available for Brad to use. There was never a reason for suspicion, because I would never have an affair. But even with the security code, he couldn't see the photographs without my fingerprint. "Thanks for having lunch with me." I leaned over and kissed Vince.

"What was that for? Compromising on a roll making you love me? Cause I'll eat more bread."

I knew the look in my eyes was confusing him, but I couldn't stop. I loved him over that wheat roll. But this couldn't be about love. And then his question scared me, because I didn't want to—no, I couldn't—answer it honestly. I put my sandwich down and climbed onto his lap. I took his sandwich and put it on the coffee table in front of us. I kissed him again. A kiss capable of ending the conversation.

❦

THAT NIGHT I DREAMED BRAD left me. Not in blaze of glory, but just calmly told me he knew I was whore, and that I'd never see the children again.

"You fucked with the wrong guy, Meredith," he said. The hatred in his eyes tore through me. "And now, you're going to have to face the consequences of that poor decision." Brad walked to the front door. He was whistling as he opened it and walked out into the sunshine. I awoke frantic with fear.

Brad was sleeping next to me. I rolled over and leaned on him. I needed his assurance he knew nothing of who I truly was. He wrapped his arm around my shoulders and pulled me closer. Without even fully waking up, he kissed the top of my head, and I fell back asleep.

thirty-four

"IT'S GOING TO LIVE," LIV said, and touched the green leaves of my plant. It did appear like it might survive. "I think it's because it wants to live with me. It doesn't want to leave me."

"That's probably it." I kept moving, throwing stuff in our bag. This family couldn't go ten minutes down the road without a car full of stuff.

"Did you put the beer in the car?" Brad asked as he came down the front stairs.

"No. It's still in the garage. I need the kids' sleeping bags, too."

"Why?"

"Because John is going to put on a movie for them when it gets late, and they'll be more comfortable in their sleeping bags." For some reason, this pissed Brad off.

"God forbid they not be comfortable."

"Why can't they be comfortable?"

Brad scoffed and walked away, and I was glad to see him go. *Why can't they be happy?*

We piled in the Escalade and drove to Jenna's and John's. Partying at their house was becoming a monthly thing. Even Brad was getting used to it. He didn't hunt, and he didn't own a tractor, but he was making inroads with the local men. I'd forgotten how likable he could be. I probably forgot it when I stopped liking him myself. Watching him at the parties reminded me of how things used to be. I relaxed, letting the tension of our current relationship fall away.

The car was barely in PARK before it was engulfed by a dozen kids opening the doors and pulling mine out. They would remember these parties the rest of their lives. These were the moments of their childhood they'd talk about when they came home for the holidays with their own children.

I helped Brad carry what seemed like everything we owned into Jenna's house and was handed a beer by John as soon as my hands were free.

"You guys movin' in?" he asked and handed a beer to Brad.

"Should we have asked first?" Brad joked, and then fell into an easy banter that flowed into the backyard, where a bunch of men were smoking cigars and standing around a fire pit. Something about fire; men always had to stand around, and poke it.

I left my purse on the front table and made my way to Jenna's kitchen, sure she would be there. She was mixing a drink and talking to four other women I recognized immediately. They were my team. The same women I spent the summer with at the pool and the winters with at kids' birthday parties.

They were talking about unique finds on Pinterest and stopped abruptly when they noticed me.

I shook my head at them. "Don't let me interrupt."

They all said hello, asked me how Thanksgiving was, if I was ready for Christmas, and then, unable to help themselves, returned to Pinterest.

"I have a confession to make," I said.

Silence. This group loved confessions. They'd have been priests, but they couldn't keep a secret.

"I went on Pinterest the other day and actually found some good stuff."

"Of course you did. There is nothing *but* good stuff on Pinterest. What the hell have you been waiting for?" Molly's mom asked.

"'Hell'? Are you drunk?" I made fun of her cursing.

She laughed, and then everyone joined in. Molly's mom never cursed. Once, she'd been telling me a story and had spelled the word "freaking." I'd figured that was the last time we needed to speak. But hell? Next she'd be dropping the F-bomb and asking couples to swing.

"What did you find?" Richie's mom asked as the laughter died down.

"Stair murals. I'm thinking of painting my staircase."

"Oh. Lynn did that," Molly's mom said.

"No, she had words painted on her stairs," Richie's mom said.

"She did? I thought it was a picture." The two women went back and forth about a staircase I hoped to never see. "Are you sure? I thought it was a mountain scene."

"I'm sure. Lynn's not creative enough to do a landscape. She's boring as hell. It was just a bunch of words."

I was pissed. I didn't want to hear any criticism of the colonel's wife. Lynn had somehow become like a mother in my mind. You know, how only you could say something bad about your mother.

"Sounds creative to me," I retorted without a hint of banter, and the conversation became uncomfortable. I'd recently become protective of Lynn. Her and her virginity.

I would never get over it.

After I ruined that moment, Jenna fixed it by mixing everyone another drink. The kids were outside in the cold making a snowman and rolling in the snow. Jenna's house would soon be filled with snow pants, boots, and gloves.

I bundled up and joined Jenna outside while she smoked a cigarette. The night air was a mix of cold and fire. The wind shifted and blew the smoke toward us, and Jenna and I took cover behind the corner of the house. She lit her cigarette, inhaling and brightening the red tip, and smiled as she exhaled the smoke above us.

"Can I ask you a personal question?" I asked. Jenna took a big sip of her drink.

"Anything." I heard her answer her boys the same way. She was taking care of me.

"How many people have you had sex with?"

Jenna kept a straight face. "Today?"

We both laughed, and I wished I could tell her about Vince. I could tell her anything I wanted about Brad. He was mine to share information about, but Vince was someone else's business. Not mine.

"I've had sex with John."

"You're kidding." I shook my head, begging her to deny it. "Please tell me you're kidding."

"I'm not." Jenna took another drag of her cigarette and a sip of her drink.

"Is that normal around here? Is that normal anywhere?"

"It's not normal. At least I don't think it is. But John and I fell in love in high school, and it's been the same ever since."

"Have you ever thought about it?"

Jenna practically spit out the last sip of alcohol. "With who? His brothers? There's no one in this town who can keep a secret." Jenna put her cigarette out on the brick ledge of the kitchen window. "You've been asking a lot of strange questions lately. What's going on?"

"Nothing." She raised her eyebrows, still questioning me. "I just heard the other day about a couple who'd only been with each other, and it made me feel like a whore. Brad wasn't exactly my 'first.'"

"Oh, well, that's different. You're a total whore."

"Thanks. Can I ask you something else?"

"No. I will not hook up with you. God . . ." I loved her.

"What do you love about this town?"

Jenna studied me again. She peered through the smoky air at the frozen moon, and then returned her gaze to me. "I love how we're all a little fucked up, a bunch of idiots trying not to raise bigger idiots, and this town keeps us from falling off the Earth in the process. It's the tie that binds." I looked up at the moon. "Ask me again later. After we get high." She put her arm around me, and we started walking to the back door. "I'll tell you some divine story about how the trees flower in the spring and the snow geese land in the winter."

thirty-five

I DROVE THROUGH THE TOWN. The houses were lit with Christmas lights everywhere, and I was at peace for the first time since I'd stopped working. With Vince in it, this felt like the life I was meant to live. I didn't let myself focus on the fact that I was stealing it from another family.

I handed my bottle of wine with the fabric ribbon bow over to the unicorn just inside her front door. The garland on the stairs was hung at precise intervals with glittered leaves and poinsettias dotting the greens. It almost looked real.

"Your house is beautiful," I said and started taking off my coat.

"You've never been here?" Sarah was shocked. I wasn't. "That's impossible."

"No. I haven't been. It's lovely, though." I switched my purse to my right hand and felt the weight of my coat lift off my arm. Richie's dad surprised me. I hadn't seen him when I'd first come in and then he was right there, helping with my coat.

"Merry Christmas, Meredith," he said, and began joking with Sarah about Santa bringing them vodka and grapefruit juice for Christmas. I paused, wondering if I might not like this crowd more without their children. And with vodka.

Richie's dad handed my coat to Sarah, and I took a second to smooth my dress. I'd tried to be conservative when I'd chosen it. It was black. The universal conservative color. I wasn't going to be the woman who showed up in red to this hen house. It was tight, but the neck was high and the hem was to my knees. The only noteworthy style element was the crossed straps at my back. Most of my back was bare, which I did accent with side-swept hair. Because apparently I can't behave even when I try.

Richie's dad's fingers touched my back, and I arched at the chill.

"Sorry, my hands are cold." He put a card face down on the table next to us and rubbed his hands together, breathing on them. His eyes were mischievous over his hands, and I wondered where Richie's mom was. "Okay. Turn around."

"Why?"

He put a hand on each hip and twisted me, and just to not make a scene, I let him. "It's a game. There's a famous person's name written on the card I'm about to tape to your back."

"Oh." I started scanning the room for the vodka. Surely this game had a drinking component.

"You'll have to mingle with the crowd and ask people questions about yourself to figure out your name." He rubbed the tape in, having chosen to affix it directly to my skin. "See?" he said, and turned his back to me and displayed his three-by-five card with "Clint Eastwood" written on it. I looked over my shoulder to see mine. "No cheating."

I took a deep breath as the colonel appeared in the foyer in front of me. "Right. No cheating."

Vince smiled at me. He'd been waiting for me to arrive.

"What do I get when I figure it out?"

"You get to remove the card," Richie's dad said, ignoring the colonel and I staring at each other. I waited to hear the colonel's wife's voice, but the party seemed void of her.

I played along.

"Am I a female?"

"Am I an actress?"

"Am I a politician?"

And in between, I drank my wine and answered the others' questions about their names. I was interviewing the head of the PTO when Vince walked by, and she stopped him.

"Hey! Where's Lynn?" His wife's name spoken between us was intrusive and still sensitive. I stood still, waiting to hear his answer.

"Home. Allison has an ear infection, and she didn't want to leave her with a sitter."

"Poor thing! And she let you come here alone?" *What is all this letting?*

Vince laughed a little, and I hung on his words like they gave me some vital element of life. I should have walked away. His wife was none of my business. I liked it that way. I'd already heard enough about her. "Well, she was out last night, and she made all of these this morning, so it would have killed her to not have them at the party." Vince waved past a tray of what appeared to be round brownies with white icing, topped with strawberries to look like Santa hats. I raised my eyebrows at them.

"They're adorable. I'm taking a picture to put on Facebook and tagging her. I can't wait to eat one." The head of the PTO left Vince and me alone. She was calling someone else over to see the Santa-hatted brownies.

"Pinterest?" I asked him once we were out of earshot.

"Of course." I took a bite of one, and the chocolate and strawberry mixed with the wine was heaven. I closed my eyes to only focus on the wonderfulness in my mouth. It was a large bite that I split into two, and icing covered my top lip. When I opened my eyes, Vince's were fixed there.

"Watch yourself," I said, my voice low as I licked the icing off.

"Am I starting to look like Richie's dad?" Richie's dad was not his concern.

"You're starting to *sound* like my boyfriend."

"Watching him practically knock me down to get to you when you came through the front door made me feel like your boyfriend."

I smiled. This conversation would have to seem light to anyone watching. *We're ready for the holidays, and family is coming to town. Yes, we love the snow. Well, as long as we don't have to drive in it. And no, we can't believe it's December. Where has the time gone?* "You're not, you know?"

"I know," he said, resolute with our situation. I kept the smile on my face as Vince and I had a silent conversation about our roles and what we owed each other, and ourselves, and the people we loved. It had all been said before. I could argue it with my eyes and never speak a word.

"I'm going to go mingle." I found the trashcan under the sink and dropped my napkin in it. When I leaned up, Vince was standing even closer to me, and my heart jumped at his closeness.

"Do me a favor?" he asked.

"Anything . . . probably."

"Stay away from Richie's dad."

"I was going to do that for myself, so it shouldn't be a problem."

His fingers brushed against my back as I walked by, and I stopped, frozen by the tiny pulses darting to my breasts and between my legs. Vince's breathy chuckle behind me reminded me to keep walking, that I was on my way somewhere. To someone, anyone else.

Jenna and John arrived. While I'd worked hard to find an

irreproachable dress, Jenna had obviously shopped with a look-at-me-now take on the whole thing. Hers was green, with a plunging neckline, a high hem, and a tight silhouette. She was gorgeous, and John seemed to notice. I watched as he helped with her coat and then leaned down to kiss her. It seemed no matter what Jenna did; he loved her. She was the mother of his children, after all. Didn't she deserve his adoration?

Her presence was perfect. If I could have Jenna and Vince with me, I could fall in love with this town. Maybe even with the brownie Santa hats. None of it mattered as long as they were around. Jenna entertained everyone. She could easily switch from bitching about the school buses to her favorite Christmas carol. She did it all with a glass in her hand and a smile on her face. Jealousy crept into my reverence. She was meant to be here. I was not.

Pictures were taken. I downloaded one from Facebook and cropped the colonel and me out of it. I saved it in my "private mode." The hidden files were becoming a source of constant humor between us. The first two couples left, and I eyed the colonel as I began to say goodnight to the guests around me. I walked to the office to dig through the coats piled high on the desk, but before I reached the doorway, Richie's father caught me.

"Oh, no. You are not leaving so early. I feel like everywhere you go, you leave early. We're about to play a game."

"We already played a game," I said and moved closer to the door. After about an hour of questioning people I barely knew about my identity, a woman finally took pity on me and whispered, "Cleopatra," in my ear. The unicorn made a comment eluding to the fact my own identity was almost as mysterious as my game one, and I pretended she never spoke.

"New game. Now that the pastor went home, we can play

the fun games."

"Why? Is the pastor no fun?"

"You'll see." I found Vince with my eyes, asking him for some direction, but he just angrily watched Richie's dad.

"I'm heading out," Vince said and proceeded to say goodbye to everyone but me. I wasn't sure what to do. I was led to a spot on the corner of the giant island in the kitchen. The remaining guests gathered around it. It was like an enormous craps table. The desserts were moved to the side counters, and our drinks were pushed closer to the center of the island.

Richie's dad pounded the island with open hands, and the crowd responded with hoots and hollers, obviously aware of the game. It might have been twenty years since I'd played.

"Thumper?" I said incredulously.

"Not just Thumper," Jenna answered.

"Sexual Thumper," John yelled, and everyone started drumming their hands on the island except the PTO president, who'd obviously never heard of the game.

"What's the point of the game?" she asked, not realizing the firestorm she set off.

"What's the name of the game?" Richie's dad yelled over the thunder of our hands.

"Thumper!" we shouted.

"Why do we play?"

"To get fucked up!" we yelled, and I doubled over laughing. Richie's dad was in his glory.

The pounding continued as we went around the circle and each of us took turns making a sexual gesture. They were a diverse bunch, and I tried to memorize each one. The woman next to me had a double boob grab, the man across the island had an awesome orgasm face, Jenna licked her lips wildly, John gave the cunnilingus sign, and I made the blow job gesture, complete with my tongue pushing my cheek out. I could barely breathe by the time Richie's dad acted like he was stroking a thirty-inch-wide penis attached to him. And then the unicorn made the fisting motion, and my eyes couldn't find Jenna fast enough. We lost it. What the hell was going on in the unicorn's bedroom, and was this on Pinterest?

The game began with lots of banging and plenty of laughing. Like, bent-over, lips-hurting-from-smiling, cracking-up laughing, and I could barely believe whose company I was in. I liked them! The image of Sarah fisting would forever replace the Pinterest crown in my head. By the time we were done, we had no place to go but home.

The PTO president spilled her drink, and Jenna yelled, "Amateur!" The president then declared it was time to go, and Jenna called her a quitter. But it was time for all us to go. John convinced Jenna to leave, and I followed them to the door.

I held my own while Sarah's husband asked me questions to confirm I was safe to drive. John watched from behind and laughed as I recited the alphabet. Someone made a joke about the chief leaving before he had to administer sobriety tests to all of us. At the mention of the chief, I felt alone, and I wished he hadn't left without me.

It was eleven thirty. My kids were at my brother's until tomorrow, and Brad was in London until next weekend. I was as free as I could be. Vince coming alone to the party was a surprise. He was supposed to torture me all night in his role as a husband, but instead, he was as single as I was.

And when I pulled out of the unicorn's neighborhood, Vince's truck turned onto the road in front of me. He'd been waiting for at least an hour, and now he'd wait to see where I went. When he made a left at the lake and drove out of town in the opposite direction of my house, I followed him to the cabin. I wished I could leave my car somewhere. I'd love to drive together for once. I'd taken for granted sitting in the passenger seat next to someone as we traveled together in the public's eye.

thirty-six

VINCE PULLED TO THE SIDE of the lane, parked by the open gate, and waited for me to drive through so he could lock it behind us. Locking us away from the world. I parked in my usual spot and waited outside my car until he pulled in next to me. When he stopped the truck, I opened his passenger door.

"Do you mind if I come in?" I asked.

"My truck?"

"I'm not wearing any perfume. We'll just need to be careful of stray hairs." I looked around the gleaming, and still new, black interior. Maybe this was a bad idea.

"I wasn't even thinking that. Come in." He motioned toward the interior of the warm truck. "It's freezing out."

I climbed in, and Vince raised the center console, leaving us with one long bench seat. I closed the door behind me and moved across the seat. My coat was a straitjacket, gathering around my thighs and restricting my movements even more than the vehicle's size. I pushed it off my shoulders, hiked up my dress, and climbed onto Vince's lap.

His hands moved to me, and over me, and into me, and I was swallowed whole by the honorable Colonel Pratt. A desperate longing strummed through me, as if this was the last time we'd ever be together. The feeling frightened me. And Vince must have sensed it, too. He didn't just fuck me, he made love to me. He held my face in his hands when he kissed me; he was urgent, as if he realized someday I'd be gone. And with every touch of his hand, every thrust of his hips, he took another piece of me for his own. In that moment I knew I would never stop wanting him, never stop needing him, and I was okay with the knowledge. I let myself disappear.

"I have something for you."

"Is it your dick?"

Vince laughed. He liked it when I verbalized how much I wanted him. "Let it rest for a few minutes." He reached behind his seat and brought back a ring box wrapped in silver paper with a tiny red pre-made bow stuck to the top of it. The image of his wife using the same paper to wrap his mother's Christmas present flashed through my mind.

My head shook from side to side, not letting the vision sink in. And then I raised up to my knees to climb off him. He was infuriating.

"Wait. Don't move." He pulled me down against his naked thighs. He held the present between us. I didn't know whether to scream or cry. "Talk to me."

"We said no gifts."

"You said no gifts. I wanted you to have this. Just open it."

"No. We said no gifts. I've always been honest. That was your rule." My hands fell to my sides, as far away from the little silver box as possible. "For a man who's spent his life enforcing rules, you seem to be struggling with these."

"Aren't you even the tiniest bit curious what it is?"

"Honestly?"

"Always."

"I'm sickened. All I can picture is a ring with a colored gemstone that has a secret meaning to us. Some ridiculous romantic token of our union dangling from a chain. Something—"

"Typical." Vince took my face in his hands and pulled me toward him. He uttered some sound, a heavy, frustrated breath, and kissed me. He leaned back and said, "Sometimes it's like you don't know me at all."

"If there's a gift in that box, you don't know me either."

Vince grabbed the little silver box and tore open the paper. My chest tightened. His biceps flexed as he crumpled the paper and threw it on the floor of the truck.

"Make sure you don't—"

"Shhh . . ." He kissed me, silencing my directives on secrets. Vince put the box on his stomach, resting it there between us, and I stayed still. My cheeks flushed, the heat rising up my neck and settling below my eyes.

"I'll open it for you."

Vince lifted the lid, moved a flat piece of cotton to the side, and took out a penny. It had a heart carved out of the center of it and looked like one you could make at a highway rest stop. The machines always stood somewhere between the restrooms and the Roy Rogers.

I held out my hand, and he dropped the penny into it. Relief spread through me as I turned Vince's gift over and over again. "A lucky penny." It took my breath away. I closed my palm around it and shut my eyes. It wasn't a silly piece of jewelry. It wasn't flowers. It wasn't typical in any way. It was a tiny secret I could drop in my wallet and know he was with me everywhere I went. I wished we could stay like this forever. Vince kissed my forehead, leaving his lips there, willing me to accept him. To accept us.

"Now that we made it through that," Vince began, and I kissed him before he could fully chastise me. I pulled him close, cherishing his understanding of what I needed. He was my savior.

"I love you, Mar." My chest tightened at his words. I shook my head, and Vince kissed me again. He held my face in his hands, halting my denial.

"You don't love me." I stroked his dick, my nipples hardened from the feel of him beneath my hand. "You love how this makes you feel." A smile spread across Vince's face. He was expecting my reaction. "This is fun and young and wholly ours. It has nothing to do with me. You would love whoever made you feel this way."

His smile faded, and his frustration returned. "You are one of the smartest people I know, but you're wrong about this."

I leaned into him, my lips by his ear. I felt him harden beneath me, and my body immediately demanded he fuck me again. "Do you love this?" I whispered in his ear.

"I love you."

I sat back and kept my hands to myself. "There are a million things that can ruin this. Love is the most destructive."

"You have all these reasons for why you're here. You were lost and ignored and bored. I have only one, and it's you. From the moment Sarah put that ridiculous nametag around your neck, I wanted you, and I haven't been able to stay away since."

"This can't happen."

"It already has."

Tears filled my eyes. The loss, and the ugly feeling of being lost, sank down my chest and dragged my heart down with it. His words would only ruin us. We were a horrible mistake, even if some part of me knew it all along . . . and wanted it. His love was the nail in the coffin. We were having an affair.

"Hey. Don't cry. It won't change a thing. I promise."

I just stared at him, thinking of all the dumb women before me who mistook their lover for their soulmate. I knew the declaration of his love set off the countdown of the minutes until we parted, and I hated him for ruining it. And I hated myself for starting this in the first place.

"I'm going to go."

"Tell me," he said, holding my face in his hands, not letting me escape him. "Tell me exactly what you're thinking." His eyes could make me do anything, which was what scared me the most. The anything I would do.

"I'm mourning us. When people like us delude themselves into thinking this dirty little secret is anywhere near love, they start to make the mistakes that ultimately rip them apart. All in the name of love."

"How is it that me loving you somehow makes this dirtier in your mind? You're fucked up." His voice thundered through the truck and out into the woods. For the first time, Vince was angry at me.

"I know." I climbed off him and found my shoes. I put one on each foot, grabbed my coat and underwear, and opened the door.

"Wait. Don't go."

"It's okay. I am fucked up. I don't deserve you any more than I deserve any of them." I slammed the door, and then opened it again and picked up the crumpled wrapping paper off the floor and put it in my coat pocket. I didn't even look at him, couldn't even look at him. Even in this ugly moment, when he'd declared his love for me, all I could do was cover the evidence.

thirty-seven

THE HOLIDAYS CAME AND WENT, and so did another foot of snow, making it impossible to get to the cabin. We waited for the first Thursday of the month the way our children had waited for Santa the month before.

Brad gave me five hundred dollars for Christmas. Cash. Not even in a card. Just took it off his nightstand with the tired explanation of how he had no idea what to buy me, and I should take myself shopping. I used sixty dollars to buy a purse I claimed was three hundred, and gave him a blow job as thanks. Then I hid the remaining four hundred and forty dollars in the bottom of a tampon box under my vanity. Nothing repulsed Brad more than menstruation.

Vince and I had six to eight hours a month. It was an acute attraction. Every breath, every sigh, every word meant so much. He would have given me more. I wanted to take it, but this tiny sliver of time was all I would allow either of us to have. He never told me he loved me again, and I loved him even more for keeping it to himself. He never voiced the words because of my reaction, the way I'd hurt him. And I never said the words because they weren't mine to give him. We couldn't be in love. And yet, he was becoming a huge part of my life, a huge part of me. We didn't see each other much, but we wrote every day. And with each email, I wanted to respond "I love you," or "you're a good man," but I couldn't love him, and the circumstances which kept me from loving him were why he wasn't a good man.

I PARKED BY FADO'S AND walked to the hotel. This month I'd booked our room at the Ritz. I hoped with the higher room rate, there was less of a chance of seeing someone we knew. Each hotel always had a bar, an easy explanation of why one of us might be there. *I was just meeting an old friend who was traveling through Philly.* The bar at the Ritz seemed like an easy choice. The hotel was impressive, built in the early 1900's and modeled after the Pantheon in Rome. It was originally a bank, and the vault staircase was still intact. The hotel was an attraction in its own right, but we weren't there as tourists.

Because of the frigid January temperatures, I skipped Fado's altogether, leaving the book club alone and, for the first time, deviated from my lie. I checked into the Ritz with my Visa gift card and took the elevator to my room. I let the bar lock keep the room door from shutting completely, allowing the colonel to slide in without detection, not waiting in the hall for me to answer. City Hall's spire grabbed my attention and pulled me to the window as soon as I entered the room. Willy Penn stood atop it, the founder of Philadelphia, the believer in liberty. I wondered how many lovers he'd had.

I went straight to Google on my phone. Because that was what I always told James and Liv to do whenever they had a question we couldn't answer. But before I read all the results of my search, I felt him enter the room behind me.

When I turned around he was standing just inside the door in his police uniform. I gasped, fighting for air against the rest of my body that just wanted him. The heavy hotel door closed behind him, but our eyes never left each other.

"You wore this for me, right? A belated Christmas present?"

"Actually, there's a flu going around, and I need to work a double. I'm on my dinner break. We don't have much time." We never had much time.

"Shouldn't be a problem. I almost came at the sight of you."

Vince chuckled. Amusing him was my second favorite thing to do to him. "How have you been?" he asked. He always asked.

"Since I emailed you last night?"

"Yes."

"Needy, lonely." My feet moved toward him. My hands found his chest, my tongue his mouth. I ran my hands down the fabric of his shirt and over his dick, already hard in his pants. "Leave this on."

Vince unbuckled his holster and laid it on the table next to the bed. "Really?"

"Yes. Leave it on and show me how to get out of a ticket."

Vince feigned he was appalled. "Can you ever behave?" I couldn't. My heart was racing and a deep ache between my legs forced my thighs tight together. A tiny tremble accompanied my exhale.

I unbuttoned his pants and lowered his zipper. "Will you cuff me if I don't? You'd literally bring my dreams to life."

He kissed me and lifted my sweater over my head. The closet door caught my eye and the mirror hanging on it.

"Fuck me in front of the mirror so I can watch."

"What has gotten into you?"

"It's the uniform . . . and you." I unzipped my riding boots and tossed them across the room, climbing out of my jeans and underwear before they landed.

I turned to Vince. My needs were savage. *What has gotten into me?* I reached into his pants, lowering the waistband and releasing him. He watched me; the intensity of his eyes burning through me as I stroked him. I wanted him in my hand and my mouth and between my legs. I was insatiable.

Vince grabbed my wrist and spun me around. He pushed

my hair over my shoulder and with one finger, traced my spine to my waist. He looked at me in the mirror in front of us, and then bent me over in front of him. He was rough, matching my need with his own, and he pressed two fingers inside me. His chest heaved as he pulled his fingers out and replaced them with his dick. He thrust into me, and I watched as he lifted his uniform shirt, letting more of our skin touch.

I wanted him to ram me right through the mirror, and he knew it. He always knew exactly what I wanted, what I needed. With one hand on my hip, the other gripping my hair in a ponytail, Vince thrust into me again. He tightened his grip and moved my body by my hair, pulling me toward him as the muscles in my groin constricted around him. He could have ripped the hair from my scalp and I wouldn't have cared as long as he kept fucking me.

And I watched.

Vince pulled out and took two steps to the side, exposing our profile to the mirror. To us. He fingered me again and leaned over my back. His lips near my ear, he said, "Touch yourself."

And I did.

From this angle I could see Vince's whole body as he pounded into me, and I touched myself, and within seconds I couldn't watch anymore. I couldn't see anything. I closed my eyes and came, reaching for the nightstand in front of me to stay on my feet. Vince took my arm back and held me up as he fucked me until he came, and then I looked in the mirror, and his eyes met mine.

"That was amazing."

You are amazing.

I love fucking you.

I love you.

I could barely speak as my body attempted to recover, and Vince let me go. I fell backward onto the bed, and he climbed on beside me, still almost fully dressed. I stared at the ceiling, fearful he could read my mind or see the love written all over my face.

"I like the Ritz," he said, and I turned toward him, still breathing hard.

"Yes. It's nice here."

He laughed, and I closed my eyes, enjoying the sound of it. "Do you think if we were married to each other, sex would always be like this?" he asked, and I rolled onto my side, and faced him. Faced *this*.

"No. I think that's the biggest lie of the affair."

"What is?"

"The one cheaters tell each other of how different their lives would be if they were together. But they're never actually together. They're hidden in time."

"I disagree."

I ran my hand down the side of Vince's face and kissed him. "You're such a romantic. But this isn't real life. We can be whatever we want to be because we're stealing time. There are no appointments, no disagreements, no nasty relatives or annoying neighbors to deal with. We have no bills, no decisions. We have each other for a few minutes a month. There's not a bit of this that's real."

"You sell us short."

"You refuse to see the truth in front of you. We're not together. We're not part of each other's lives. We're a fantasy. A play with an opening night and a curtain call."

"We're perfect together."

"We're a secret."

The playfulness drained from his face. I'd hurt him. He hated when I reduced us to something lewd. But if I let him keep seeing this as a fairy tale, we'd never survive. I had to be the voice of reason, and sometimes that voice was an ugly one.

I rolled on top of him. Even though I knew I was right, I

didn't want to hurt him. "But I love us. You make me feel alive, and I need you more than I need to be right about what this is."

Vince rolled us over, him now on top of me. His triumphant smile lit up his face. He kissed my neck, letting his lips caress the skin right below my ear.

"I love us, too," he said, and kissed me, making me forget I had another life. A life. He studied me and I braced myself for his thoughts. "I'll never ask you to divorce. I know you'll never break up your family." It wasn't a statement, he wanted a response, but I didn't have one for him. "But why? This fear you have of divorce is unfounded. They'll be happy, and they'll know you as happy."

"My children are happy right now. Their world is intact. Their mother is not cheating on their father. Their father hasn't been awarded joint custody, and then ignored them or shipped them off with a nanny. They're not miserable at the hands of the step-monster Brad married."

"None of that will happen."

"The first part already has."

"You are impossible."

"I know."

thirty-eight

SCOUT SUNDAY MEANT LITTLE TO me except that we were all attending church that morning. I made sure we were ironed. We looked good. Respectable. I couldn't wait to see Vince.

"Lono, mai tu lo?" Liv came up and asked in her own language.

"It's on the coffee table. Where you left it."

Brad just stared at us as Liv skipped away. "What the hell was that?"

"It's Liv's language."

"How did you know what she was saying?"

"Because I spend every minute with them, and their lives are fairly predictable. Once she's dressed, she brushes her hair."

"How long has she had her own language?"

"I don't know. Ask her, but make sure you translate it into Livism when you do." I zipped my boots. They were tall, unseen under my long dress, and probably unnecessary to keep me warm if the colonel was coming to worship.

James leaped off the bottom of the staircase and picked up a box of crackers off the kitchen table. He read the box, and Liv stood in the center of the room, spinning. She kept spinning until Brad yelled at her to stop, and then she took two dizzied steps backward, almost falling down on her way out of the room.

"You know, there are three hundred and ninety-six crackers in this box," James said, and Brad glared at me as if there was something I should be fixing.

"What?" he asked James.

"Three hundred and ninety-six. Eleven servings of thirty-six crackers."

I beamed proudly at James. We were finally getting somewhere with math facts. I'd say we'd surpassed them. Brad was not beaming.

"Get over here," my husband said, pointing at the island stools. "You, too, Liv. Get in here and have a seat."

"Cooka?" Liv poked her head into the kitchen, beckoning in her own language for some clarification.

"Yes, you," I said to her, and she walked in and hopped up on a stool.

"Look. I know Dr. Seuss, and maybe even your teachers at school, are encouraging you to be . . . individuals, but I really want us to shoot for normal today. Do you guys understand?"

"What do you mean indiliduals?" Liv asked.

"What do you mean, 'normal'?" James asked, and Brad lowered his forehead into his hand. He turned to me for assistance, but I was enjoying this rare moment of parenting from him, or maybe it was his frustration.

"Meredith!"

"Cooka?" I asked, pointing to myself.

"It's not funny."

Both kids laughed.

"It's a little funny," I said.

"I'm serious. I would love to spend the next hour in church appearing normal."

"What do they do there? Do they dance?" Liv asked, and Brad was outraged.

"You don't know what they do in church?"

"No. How would I know?"

"How would I know?" Brad mocked, and then looked at me.

"What? We can go to church if you want. I haven't been keeping it a secret or anything."

We settled into chairs toward the back. James was in the hall with the other scouts, preparing to be presented to the church. Liv was kicking the chair in front of her, and Brad was sweating. His perfect family was not normal.

By the time the service was over, I thought he was going to run out of the building screaming, but he made it. The kids attacked the pastries during fellowship time, and Brad settled into playing mayor with any adult who would talk to him. I watched Vince from Brad's side. He was as magnificent in church as he was sprawled naked across the rickety couch in his hunting cabin.

"I keep telling Meredith that," Brad said, and I started listening to his conversation with the unicorn.

"We should do it," she responded, and I was scared. *Do what?*

"I'm sorry. I was off in space. What are we talking about?"

"Starting a book club in town," Brad said. "I keep telling you not to drive to Philly every month."

No, you don't. Disbelief, mixed with anger, rose from my chest to my eyes, and I worked hard to hide it. We hadn't spoken a word about the book club since I'd first asked him about it. He didn't even ask me how it went every month. But I played along with him now. "I know, but now I really like all the people in my club. I would hate to leave them."

"Maybe I'll just come to yours . . . with you," the unicorn said. "If that's okay."

I was paralyzed by the thought of the unicorn anywhere

near me in Philadelphia. Vince and Lynn were moving closer to us, and I caught Vince's eye right before Lynn joined the group. His easy-going smile was replaced by a tight jaw. He was worried, and he should be.

"Good morning," Lynn said. Her bloodshot eyes had dark circles beneath them and her hair was sticking up in the back. I waited for her to tell us a story of a sick child, or too much caffeine, but she kept smiling as if that was just her appearance, poorly rested and oblivious.

"Morning. Cold out there, huh?" I would say anything to change this subject. If I had to, I would have stripped naked right there in church, because none of these bitches were coming to book club with me next month. The sight of Vince fucking me from behind—in his uniform—flashed through my mind and solidified my commitment to it *not* happening.

"We were just talking about starting a book club in town," the unicorn piped in, and I just stared at Vince, who quickly caught on to the severity of the topic.

"Oh, I would love that," Lynn said.

"See?" Brad turned to me, and I wanted to kill him. My eyes avoided him and I noticed Liv with chocolate all over her face. Brad wouldn't want that.

"I'll be right back," I said, leaving and hopefully ending this entire conversation.

On the way home, Brad was happy. We did it! We were normal in church. He suggested going back again. I didn't respond.

"What's wrong?"

I wasn't sure if I was more surprised he asked, or that he'd noticed at all. "I don't want to go to book club with the women of this town."

"What's wrong with the 'women of this town'?" His tone made it clear he was unwilling to consider my feelings, but I continued anyway.

"I have a book club. It's full of thoughtful, intelligent, articulate members and we are doing fine. Why must you take every ounce of joy I've found for myself and give it to the unicorn?"

"You are so ridiculous. Do you hear yourself?"

"Maybe we should move." That I said just to be a bitch.

thirty-nine

THE DOZEN WHITE ROSES ARRIVED midday on February fourteenth. White roses always made me think of funerals, but that was just me. How could Brad have known? I was grateful the card was made out to me and not mixed up with one addressed to another woman he probably sent flowers to. I knew an unwarranted assumption your partner was cheating was a common byproduct of an affair. *Well, if I'm over here doing this, what must he be doing?* I tried to keep it in check. But if I could find a way to have Vince with Liv and James always with me, surely Brad had something on the side. His life was made for two women. Hell, even two families. These thoughts should have upset me. I should have some bitter, sinking feeling in my stomach, a dull pain at the back of my head, but I'd become accustomed to multiple families being in my personal relationships.

It would have to be someone from work. His assistant, maybe. He was rarely in the same place long enough, but she often traveled with him. I smelled the morbid roses and tried to remember if she'd recently gotten engaged. I thought Brad had mentioned we'd be invited to her wedding. Unmarried people didn't get engaged while they were fucking their boss, so maybe not. Yet.

I texted Brad in Miami, wishing him a Happy Valentine's

Day and thanking him for the "beautiful" flowers. I promised him we'd "celebrate" when he got home. My eyes rolled, but he seemed pleased. Brad responded immediately—which for him was rare—that he couldn't wait. He must've needed to get laid. He certainly wasn't getting much from me.

It was supposed to be like any other school day. After I picked up the kids, we had homework, dinner, wrestling for James, tennis for Liv, showers, lunches, notes, bed. As I ate with the kids, I endured another conversation that killed more of my brain cells. The crux of it whether Liv pronounced pollo correctly in Spanish. It was a debate, just short of an argument, because no one cared enough to be passionate about it. I didn't even tell them to stop. I was becoming immune to the ramblings of the under-ten crowd.

Once I insisted they use their silverware.

Twice I told one of them to get their feet off the other's chair.

At least three times I asked them to chew with their mouths shut.

For fun, I chewed all my food with my mouth wide open. They laughed and yelled it was gross, but kept doing it themselves.

And when I thought I couldn't sink any lower, my romantic meal ended, and I signed into Facebook. My timeline was flooded with pictures of the colonel and his wife on their "date night." Everyone was commenting on what a great couple they were and wishing them a "fun night" and "Happy Valentine's Day." *Gag.* I pored over the pictures. His wife had posted six of them.

Six.

I got the point after the first one. This was how the other woman spent Valentine's Day. How the whore he slept with in cars spent all holidays. I deserved sixty pictures of them.

Before I went to bed, I opened my spam email account and found one email from him.

V: Leave the back door open.

"Why? So you can come spend some time with your other Valentine?" I muttered under my breath, hating myself for having feelings of jealousy for my lover and a mere curiosity for how Brad might manage another whole family. I would let Vince in the back door and let him know this had to end. I should not feel jealous about him having dinner with his wife. I was not having an affair.

He walked in around eleven, hours after the kids fell asleep. He was giddy, almost laughing as he took off his coat and turned off the lights in the kitchen. Brad was only this type of happy when something had gone his way . . . or after he came. I squeezed my lips together, afraid of what I might say.

His jeans were the same dark blue as he'd had on in the pictures, but instead of a button down, he wore only a T-shirt. It was a police shirt, a symbol of all the rules we broke together. The laws of relationships. His chest in a T-shirt disarmed my anger and left me trying to remember what had pissed me off so much earlier.

Vince walked over and leaned into me, pressing me against the counter behind me. "I figured you saw the pictures online," he said, threading his fingers in my hair and reminding me of why I was angry to begin with. "And I figured you felt like a whore and never wanted to see me again."

"So you thought you'd stop by and assure me I'm not a whore." The words reeked of contempt. For him, for us, for everyone.

"I thought I'd stop by and make the way you're feeling at least worth it."

His lips found mine, and it was worth it. I would feel like

a whore every day of my life for him to kiss me. I arched my back, wanting him inside me. Vince lifted me and with my legs wrapped around his waist, his tongue in my mouth, he turned and sat me on the island in the middle of the room.

I ran my hands up his neck and down his shoulders, wanting to touch every inch of him and knowing our time together was limited, as usual. I squeezed my thighs together, pulling him toward the pulsing that ached for him. Vince took my hands and placed them behind me, leaning me back. He untied my robe and ran his hands roughly up my hips as he raised my night shirt, exposing me to the cool February air filling the house. My skin was on fire. My nipples, as hard as rocks, would only be satisfied with his tongue on them. He yanked me to the edge of the countertop, jerking me forward, taking what was his, and all I wanted was for him to plunge his dick into me until I screamed. But instead he kissed me again, and I forced my tongue into his mouth, mimicking the attention I craved.

"I know what you want," he said, and his words made the muscles in my stomach and groin clench together, fighting for him to be inside me. He pushed my robe off my shoulders and lifted my night shirt over my head. I was completely exposed, in every way. Vince's lips found my nipple and he played with it as I watched. The warmth of his mouth and the chill of the air combined and held me captive. I wanted to feel him, but I couldn't move; the touch of his tongue on me my divine paralysis.

His lips trailed down my stomach and his hands spread my legs wide as Vince's tongue tickled my clit. My eyes followed his finger in and out. Again and again. I was mesmerized. Vince leaned up and kissed me one more time before laying me on my back. The rich scent of mahogany filled my lungs as I fought for air. His finger, his tongue, his breath continued to focus and my body responded with a wet heat I couldn't, wouldn't control.

"If you are the whore you claim to be, you're my whore,"

he said, and returned his tongue to ripping my core from my body. A throbbing centered on his tongue. He played with me, his fingers teasing me while his tongue owned me, and my orgasm lifted me off the counter, my chest heaving toward the pendants hanging above me. Vince continued, unwilling to let my body recover, and I jolted again, losing all voluntary control.

"Stop," I managed, and gasped for air. Vince pulled his finger out, and I laid my head on the counter, fighting for air. I inhaled deeply the heavy morbidity of the roses in the hall. I felt more alive than I ever had before.

"Happy Valentine's Day," he said and covered me with my robe. He kissed my cheek. If I could've managed the use of my arms, I would have pulled him down to me, but I was still lost somewhere outside my body. "You own me when you come."

He walked out the back door and, without sitting up, I knew he was navigating the woods behind my house. Walking a quarter of a mile to his truck parked nowhere near here. If there were ever questions, they wouldn't include me. I walked on shaky legs to my bed and curled up. I fell asleep before Vince had a chance to email me that night. I was content, finally happy with what I had, but it wasn't mine to have.

☙

THE NEXT MORNING, I TALKED to the kids about whether a dinosaur or a dragon would win in a fight as I poured their Cocoa Puffs into a bowl. Brad loathed the sugary cereals I let them choose at the grocery store. As if that wasn't bad enough, the milk I added wasn't organic. The lone box of cereal was fought over, ripped from the hands of the other, until I took a second box out of the pantry and set it between them. I sipped my coffee and ran my hand over the countertop, closing my eyes to see Vince.

When I opened them, Liv had stopped reading the box and was watching me.

"What are you doing?" she asked, her critical eye engaged.

"This countertop is quartz. It's nice, huh?"

"It's not that nice."

"I must appreciate a good countertop more than you," I said, and watched Liv scrutinize me. I took another sip of my coffee, raising my eyebrows and challenging her. Not in her wildest dreams could she come up with this.

forty

IT WAS THE LAST EVENING herding of the school year. I hoped. The parents' meeting for the Spring Fair. I usually went alone, sat through the presentations, and signed up to paint kids' faces on the day of the fair.

Tonight Brad was with me. It was pouring. He parked three blocks away, and we huddled together under my umbrella to make it inside. I'd given up the hope he'd become chivalrous over a decade ago. My mother would never have walked, even in the bright sunshine. She would have been dropped at the door, but then again, she hadn't liked my dad very much.

We reached the auditorium's entrance at the exact time Vince dropped Lynn off at the door. I caught his eye as she climbed out of the truck. She looked up, and I smiled and waved. Lynn, Brad, and I walked into the auditorium together. Brad took the seat on the end of the aisle. I followed him in with Lynn behind me. We took off our damp coats and spread them across the backs of our chairs.

Lynn had on pants that were not sweatpants and not yoga pants. They were perplexing. Perhaps part of a track suit. *Do they make tracksuits anymore?* She was wearing a police shirt. Of that, the bitter taste of jealousy rose in my throat. Whenever Vince wore one, I'd put it on and lie in bed. It smelled like him. It was him. I leaned toward her and inhaled subtly, but this shirt fit her. It smelled like her. It was hers. I was in jeans, wedge sandals, and a cute top. After the meeting, we were all going to the bar. They should have the meeting *at* the bar. More people would volunteer.

"Oh, I almost forgot. My husband had me put this in my bag for you." She took out an envelope with the town hall's address in the left-hand corner. "Mrs. Walsh" was written in the center of it. "He said you were an attorney. I had no idea." She was . . . genuine.

"It was a thousand years ago."

"Well, you'd be perfect for the job. If you don't mind making *no* money."

"Job?"

"It's a posting for the receptionist position at the police station."

"Oh." I opened the envelope and read the top half of the posting.

Clerical. Part-time. H.S. Diploma. 20–30 hours/week. $10/ hour. My mind raced at the idea of a job. A real place to be where I needed to shower before I got there. Adult humans wanting to discuss things with me bounced around in my head. Just the posting in my hand was satisfying. Someone handed me a piece of paper to read.

"What's that?" Brad asked, hovering over the papers in my hand.

"A job posting for a part-time job at the police station."

"Oh. Now you're going to work?" He continued looking at the papers. "For ten dollars an hour?"

"It's not about the money," I whispered as the meeting began.

The PTO president droned on about how important our children's memories are and how the Spring Fair was a cherished event, decades old, and always the highlight of the school year. The entire speech, I pictured her Sexual Thumper sign—the double middle finger jabbing upward.

And then Vince walked into the room. Soaking wet . . . dripping . . . stopping my heartbeat. Lynn was annoyed. I was in rapture. My mind drifted to the first night we were together, in his cabin, in the rain. I squeezed my thighs together as I savored every detail of his body in my mind. Lynn waved to him, and he came and sat in the seat Lynn had saved between us.

"Sorry," she whispered over him, apologizing for him making me wet. I smiled back. It was no problem. *Happens all the time.*

I inhaled until I couldn't fit any more of his scent inside my body. Brad's movement next to me reminded me to breathe.

"How long is this thing?" Brad was inconvenienced. He was trapped in my world for twenty minutes because it was on the way to the bar, and he was already annoyed. Vince was quiet next to me. Serene as usual. He calmed everyone around him, especially me.

The PTO president continued with her pleas, listing the numerous volunteers we needed to host a fair for five hundred kids on the high school's football field. When she finally finished, the room was silent.

"So if we could at least confirm a chairman, or woman, before we convene, we could all sign up for volunteer opportunities and provide that person with the information tonight."

No one said a word. I wasn't even sure I heard her right. *Who usually chaired this thing?* "Just a chairperson. That's all we need to get the ball rolling."

Silence.

Even the unicorn stayed still in her seat right in front of us. It sounded right up her alley to me. Brad checked his watch. Vince leaned ever so slightly toward me, and our shoulders touched, and then he readjusted and moved away.

And then . . . I raised my hand.

The PTO President saw my hand and looked to see if there

was an emergency I was alerting her to. Finally, I stood.

"I'll chair the committee," I said, and the unicorn turned in her chair. She flung her hair to the side to see me better. "What?" I challenged my mythological creature friend, and held my ground.

From the other side of the auditorium, a slow clap began, followed by a healthy applause of the joyous parents who'd escaped the position. Jenna cheered and winked at me from across the room. This would give us something new to complain about over cocktails.

I turned to sit. Brad was lost in shock. The colonel was proud. He was satisfied with my action and that satisfied me, more than anything.

"Mrs. Walsh, can you stay after for a few minutes?"

"No. Say no," Brad whispered beside me.

"Sure." I didn't even try to hide my pleasure at his inconvenience.

The meeting adjourned. I collected my wet coat.

"How long are you going to be here?"

"Get a ride," I said to Brad and turned to the Pratts. "Would you mind giving Brad a ride to the bar?"

"I have to stay, too. Security for the fair," the colonel said, and I looked past them to see Jenna and John already walking outside.

"I'll take Lynn to the bar with me, and you two can come after the meeting," Brad suggested, collecting the umbrella from the floor next to us.

"You have to go get the car. Don't make her walk in the storm."

"I'll get the car." He said it as if I was an ass to suggest he might make her walk. "Have fun, you two." He was so pompous, telling Vince and I to have fun.

It was a mere twenty minutes later we filed out of the school. The only person left was the PTO president. We watched her lock up and get in her car in the side lot. The clouds were circling above. The rain was steady, but not nearly as bad as when we'd arrived. Vince's truck was barely visible a quarter mile down the road. Everywhere was darkness, and then the president waved as she drove away.

"I'll get the truck."

"No. I want to go with you."

"What? It'll just take a minute."

"I don't want to lose a minute."

Vince studied my face, and finally he took my hand and we ran down the center of the street, avoiding the pools of water on the shoulders. We were out in the open, running in the rain and holding hands. Together. In public. And Brad had given that to me.

forty-one

IT WAS AS IF THE colonel was the one enchanting me. Within weeks, I stopped fighting the idea of us together and I stopped calling myself a whore. I started to see Brad differently, too. His mere existence no longer annoyed me; his success wasn't at the expense of my own. Somehow, letting Vince in quieted the internal struggles of my marriage. He was absolutely the wrong answer, but the solution I'd chosen, and everything seemed to run smoother with his inclusion in our lives.

I was unwilling to seduce myself into thinking Vince and I were ours alone. I tried. Every day I tried to keep him separate, not letting our relationship influence any decision made with regards to my family, but my relaxed demeanor, my ease with Brad, my increased patience with my children's mind-numbing stories, even the plant's thriving green leaves were because Vincent Pratt was a part of my life.

Jenna drove up as I was lacing Liv's roller skates. I tugged on each string, tightening them until she winced, and crossed the laces behind her ankle twice before double knotting them high on her ankle.

"You know, when you invited me over to do something 'girly,' I had a pedicure in mind," Jenna said as she got out of her car, reached through the open backdoor window, and pulled out a pair of roller blades. "Not roller skating."

"But roller skating is so fun!" Liv said and rolled away from me on wobbly legs.

I slipped my feet into my roller blades. They weren't extravagant, even when I'd first bought them almost twenty years ago. The hard plastic under the insufficient cushioning brought back memories of skating through the streets instead of studying for exams. We would do anything to avoid our responsibilities, especially on a warm day. I watched Liv skate. It was the first warm day of the year.

"I was purposely vague. I wasn't sure you'd say yes."

"I shouldn't have. I live with four boys. I should be sipping drinks and getting a facial as we speak." Jenna sat next to me and untied her shoes. "But I'm here, so we may as well skate." Liv rolled backward in front of us, unable to stop herself. "Looking good, Miss Olivia."

"I think roller skating is the relaxation equivalent of a facial," I tried.

"Really? Did you read that somewhere?"

"Not sure." I shook my head and stood up, holding on to the railing next to me. I took a deep breath and hoped it was like riding a bike. Liv had on a helmet and elbow and knee pads, and I had on jeans and a T-shirt. Breaking my arm would make it more difficult to see Vince.

"You can paint your toes anytime. In the middle of the night, in the freezing cold," Liv said and skated in front of us. She raised her face and her arms to the sky and spun in a circle. "Only in the sunshine can you float through space like this."

Jenna and I just watched her. She was already sure again on her wheels, rolling with long strides and then finishing with circles, sometimes on only one foot.

"You sure she's not getting high?"

"I'm not sure she'll ever have to," I said, and we watched as Liv closed her eyes and skated with her hands out in front of her. "Eyes open, Liv."

"Come on, you two. We have to go. The wind is calling us."

"She talks to me a lot," Jenna said and balanced on her skates. Within seconds, she lunged forward in complete comfort. "This morning she told me not to go too fast, that casts aren't pretty on old women."

And for once, I loved my neighborhood. Jenna, Liv, and I skated around the one street that formed it. It was a giant circle with a steep hill at the top of the arch. The first time we went around, we were going uphill for it; then we got smart. When we reached our house, Liv told us to switch directions, and our next pass, we were careening down the hill and around the bend.

By the third lap, my thighs were aching and my feet were screaming to be released from the ancient roller blades. We collapsed on our front lawn. Liv rested her feet on my thighs so I could untie her skates first. As I slipped the second one off her heel, Brad and James pulled in the driveway. He waved and continued driving to his garage bay. Liv was on her feet running after him, and Jenna and I watched as he met her just outside of the garage. He lifted her up and over his shoulder, spinning her around and making her laugh. The sound of it traveled through the trees and sang to the wind.

Brad placed her back on the ground, and she begged for him to lift her up again.

"I've got things to do," I heard him say, but he lifted her again, and again her laughter rang through time. It was the way it should be. A father should return home to his daughter. To the place they lived together with the rest of their family. The two of them reminded me of the moment before my father had walked me down the aisle. He'd told me that no matter who I married, I would always be "his girl." And then he'd given my hand to Brad, who'd looked like he'd just won the lottery. He'd wanted me so much back then, and I'd wanted him to have me.

I just hadn't realized how much he would take.

forty-two

SINGAPORE WAS THE REASON BRAD was gone for three weeks. Three glorious weeks alone in Singapore.

"I've got things covered here. Go. Have fun," I told him. Vince really was meat on a stick, because I meant it. I really wanted Brad to have fun, knowing his fun couldn't touch the fun I'd been having; I was generous with my good wishes. So much so, I feared Brad would become suspicious, so I started bitching about him leaving me just for good measure. I made a point to ask him the time difference and what time he thought he might call, but I didn't care if he called.

My excitement dampened dramatically when the email came about the Cub Scout campout. It had a long list of items that needed to be brought to the campsite, as well as the reminder that no child was allowed to attend without a parent or guardian. The day it landed in my inbox, I picked the kids up from school to hear the entire way home about who was going on the camping trip and what they were going to do and how excited James was. And I wondered if I could talk Jenna into going. Probably not, since there was a strict no-alcohol policy at all Cub Scout events.

Jenna actually laughed when I asked her. Funny, because

she'd had the same reaction to the book club in Philadelphia. Although I technically had never invited her to that one, I'd let her believe I had as she'd laughed and said there was no way in hell she was reading the "boring-ass books" I was assigned each month. The book club was perfect. I'd replaced challenging my mind with challenging my body with Vince's cock.

"John is responsible for all scouting events," Jenna said with great satisfaction. "He told me the other day they need to learn how to hold a gun."

I wasn't surprised. Nine was not too young in this town. The town where Youth Hunting Day was celebrated every year.

"I told him to teach them how to hold their dicks straight while they're peeing first. Once they master that, you can take them hunting." Poor Jenna really was immersed in man-mess. "I should just give up, though. I don't think John can hit the target himself," she added and took a sip from her plastic cup. "Do you want me to keep Liv?" she asked, but I'd already arranged for her to sleep at her friend Jill's.

I tried to convince my brother to go camping, but he conveniently had plane tickets to Disney. I was all James had, and I was going camping.

❧

WITH THE CASE OF BOTTLED water I'd signed up for, our sleeping bags and our tent, James and I drove to the Sportsmen's Club for our scouting adventure from hell. The guard at the gate pointed toward the gravel lane through the woods I was to follow to the parking area. From there, I carried my case of water—without complaining—to our campsite in the middle of a grassy field. I could hear the gunshots in the distance and see the lake at the bottom of the hill. Thank God it was too cold to go swimming. I guessed. What else were we going to do?

It took about ten minutes to realize I was going to watch sixteen boys run wild most of the night. There was fire lighting, hot dog cooking, and flashlight tag once the sun went down. I was wrapped in a blanket over my yoga pants and sweatshirt. It was cold. It was dark. And I had to use the bathroom. I asked one of the dads to keep an eye on James while I traversed the grassy plain in the direction Richie's dad and another father had just walked. About thirty feet from the building, the other man emerged and pointed me toward the side of the building with the ladies' room.

It was dimly lit, and the outside door didn't close completely, but for some reason that was preferable. There was a door on the stall, and I hurried to get out of there as soon as possible. I washed my hands and dried them on the hem of my sweatshirt before opening the broken door and enduring the freezing night air.

"What a pleasant surprise it is you're here. Is Brad away?" Richie's dad asked as I hopped off the sidewalk patio in front of the bathroom doors. I hadn't seen him in the dark.

"You scared me."

"Sorry. I didn't mean to." He came closer to me. Close enough to smell the tequila on his breath, and then a disgusting grin spread across his lips. I moved back, my heart beating closer to my chest, feeling his want before he showed his cards. "I was thrilled when I saw you get out of your car. I'm just really, really glad you're here."

"You mentioned that." I smiled and took another step backward. "I'm going to head back before James sends out a search party."

"Why so soon?" He grabbed my wrists and drug me toward him in a revolting display of his strength's superiority to my own. He leaned his face toward mine, and I bent backward until I fell to the ground with Richie's dad on top of me. His full weight crushed my skin against the gravel as he raised up to see me, but before he could, he was yanked off me and punched in the face . . . by the colonel.

Vince grabbed his shirt and pulled his head off the ground and hit him again.

"Vince!" I hissed, and he stopped. It was long enough for both of us to realize Richie's dad was unconscious. "What are you doing?" I'd never seen Vince anything but calm.

"Deciding whether to kill him or arrest him." His chest heaved as my glare darted from him to Richie's dad; I was repulsed by both sights. Vince for being here when he never should have been, and Richie's dad because he was an ass. "Are you okay?" Vince came to me and ran his hands over my shoulders and hips. He turned me around and lifted my ripped pant legs, exposing the patches of scraped skin underneath. "I'm going to kill him," he said under his breath.

I moved back. "We're at the Sportsmen's Club."

Vince was hurt, and then understanding spread across his face. He removed his handcuffs from the side of his uniform and walked toward Richie's dad.

"What are you going to arrest him for?"

Vince stopped and looked back at me. He was unable to reconcile he was the one with cuffed hands. He shouldn't have been here in the first place. Protocol didn't warrant him beating the man unconscious. And arresting Richie's dad on any charge that was running through Vince's head would only bring questions neither of us wanted.

"How about you let me handle this?" I said and walked past him to examine our mutual friend. Richie's dad rolled onto his side, still groggy, and closed his hands around his now-bleeding head. "Go. I'll email you as soon as I can."

Vince stood still, not giving an inch. Not taking his eyes off Richie's dad. With utter despair filling his eyes, his jaw locked in anger, he didn't move a muscle. "If you're not home in an hour," he finally said to me, "I'm coming back and arresting you."

For the first time since I'd parked today, I smiled. "I'll be fine.

Now go, please. Before someone else has to go the bathroom."

I watched as Vince walked back to his police cruiser. He turned to me as he opened the driver's door, and silently begged me to leave. When he drove away, I ran back to our camp, yelling for help. Help for Richie's dad. I tried to make it seem non-critical. I didn't want to upset Richie. John and a few of the dads ran to the bathrooms to take care of him, and I stayed behind with James and the rest of our group.

"What happened?" The other dads looked at me, wanting answers. Really they wanted to go to the bathrooms, too, and see the situation for themselves, but they couldn't leave me there with sixteen boys.

"I don't know. He wasn't there when I went in the bathroom. When I came out, he was on the ground holding his face. I thought maybe he fell . . . I rolled him over to see if I could help him, and I smelled tequila. I think he might have been drinking . . ." I mouthed the last part with an air of regret. The other dads caught on that this was not a conversation to have in front of the kids and no more questions were asked.

But there were questions. John returned from the bathrooms with lots of them.

"He looks like somebody beat the shit out of him," he said, accusing me of something.

I rose from my chair, leaving my blanket behind and displaying my meek frame to all those who thought for one second I had something to do with it.

"You didn't hear anything while you were in the bathroom?"

"No. I didn't hear a thing, and the door wouldn't shut completely. When I came out, he was lying on the ground." I wrapped back up in my blanket to cover my ripped pant leg.

"I think we should call the police."

"Are you sure about that?" I leaned in so none of the scouts could hear me. "I thought I smelled tequila on him." I raised my eyebrows at him, and he took a deep breath and blew it out his mouth. John was used to covering for a drinker. He would understand.

In the end, they got Richie's dad back on his feet, and John drove them home. The rest of us took down our tents and went home, too. The "accident" had ruined the jovial mood of the campout, and the looming questions of what had actually happened had left everyone feeling a bit unsafe.

James wasn't even that disappointed. He was exhausted, and begged me to carry him to his bed. By the last of the steps, I thought I'd fall over, but I got him tucked in and went downstairs to find Vincent Pratt standing in my kitchen.

"What are you doing here?" I whispered and turned out the lights.

"Are you kidding? Where else would I be?" He closed the distance between us and pulled me to him with steel arms wrapped around my waist. "Are you alright? Did he hurt you?"

"I'm fine. You didn't have to punch him. I could have handled it." My tone overflowed with frustration. He'd risked exposing us. And over what? Richie's idiot dad.

"You were on the ground, and he was on top of you." Vince's lips touched the top of my head, and I inhaled him deeply, unable to maintain frustration when he was so close.

"What were you even doing there?"

"I was checking on you. I'm always wherever you are."

I leaned back, not sure whether to believe him or not. "Are you serious?" This was bordering on Richie's dad's overzealousness. Vince was better than that. We were better than that.

He held me tight to his chest, but I kept my eyes on him in the dim light of the kitchen. "Yes. If I know you're out someplace I can get to, I'll drive by and check on you." He must have realized how crazy it sounded, because he added, "I'm a police officer. I'm supposed to keep people safe." He was losing perspective, and as a result losing me. My chest trembled as my breath caught.

"You could have ruined everything tonight," I said, and started to cry. "Even right now. You're taking too many risks. Someone is going to find out."

"No one is going to find out." Vince wiped a tear from my face and kissed my cheek. "You worry too much."

"You don't worry enough." I moved toward the door and wiped my face with the back of my hand. "You have to go."

I could feel his disappointment. He didn't say a word but never took his eyes off me. With every breath, I said goodbye to him a little more. *This won't end like the others.* I would not be exposed because we stopped being smart. I was never going to drop James and Liv off at their father's house for Christmas.

"I think we should be apart for a little while."

"Mar . . ."

"I do. I need some time to recalibrate."

"Don't do this." The horror in his eyes was beating me down until I finally looked away. "He was all over you."

"Give it a few days. You'll see the same thing I do."

"What do you see?"

"Two people throwing their lives away."

"Mar, don't." He came to me and kissed me, and I tasted him for the final time. The tremendous weight of loss sunk down my body, and threatened to drop me to my knees. How could I ever let him go? The tears streamed down my face as James' voice yelling "Mommy" set the house on fire.

My head dropped, and he took one step back and let go of my hand. He turned toward the back door and disappeared into the night.

forty-three

THE COLONEL EMAILED ME AT least once a day. I never responded, but I read his emails. Until it became torture. I could hear his words. I could taste them on his lips. I could feel him inside me, and the absence of him nearly crippled me. After six weeks, I shut down the account.

I started going to book club for real. I managed to finish my first book for the club, Junot Diaz's *This is How You Lose Her*, without committing suicide. It was touch and go for a while, though. I drank my way through the conversation and cried the entire drive home, but I was faithful to my husband and faithful to my children. And there was nothing to cry about that.

I threw myself into my children's lives. If I was going to give my entire life to them, I'd make it seem more like that. I leaned on Jenna, although she was unsteady herself. I spent every Tuesday with her watching the latest reality television and sipping cocktails, and if I didn't let myself think, I was okay.

My plant nearly died. I only remembered to water it when Liv told me to. Its leaves hung low to the ground, mirroring my shoulders when no one was watching. *Maybe I'll repot it. Maybe I'll move and leave it here.*

The Spring Music program at the school arrived like a corroded knife to my heart. I was beyond wounded. I got there early, hoping to be in the front row. I figured I'd sit and never look back, but because this town *loved* their elementary school music programs, the first eight rows were already filled, and I was squarely in the middle. Worse, the colonel's wife was saving him a seat two rows up from me. I read the program resting on my lap thirty times. Liv had a speaking part. She was listed as Olivia Walsh, and the sight of her name gave me the strength to watch her. I smiled and waved and videotaped it because Brad was in London, and she'd want his praise. And when the show was over, and my children returned back to their class-rooms, I kept my head down and sat in my seat until the rows ahead of me filed out, and then I sat in my car and cried until I couldn't breathe.

And on my way home, he pulled me over.

I was almost out of town, just before the township line, and his lights flashed behind me. My head rested on the steering wheel when he reached my window and knocked on it.

"Open the window," he said. His voice was on the verge of breaking. I pressed the button, and the window dropped, leaving no barrier between us. My cheeks were still damp from my tears, and I didn't care. There was nothing to hide. Even if I tried he knew without seeing me I was devastated without him.

"It doesn't have to be like this." His voice was filled with kindness. The only thing saving me was the traffic that passed us on the country road before me.

"I think it does."

"You're wrong. Please, just say the word and this will be over."

"What word? Whore? Tramp? Liar?" My anger at myself for so desperately needing him, I directed squarely at him. Him in his ridiculously hot uniform. "What word are we talking about?"

"I'm about to rip you out of this vehicle, and I don't care who sees me!"

"Which is why we don't work." He calmed, instantly

recognizing the truth in my words. "Don't turn us into everyone else. I won't hurt my children that way."

"How about you? How much will you hurt yourself?"

The tears ran down my face again without my permission. They were loneliness streaking the face of a sinner, and I tasted them as they fell.

"Please, just say the word."

I put the Escalade in DRIVE, and when he stepped back, I pulled away and drove home. I parked in one of my three garage bays and walked into my enormous empty house, and I thought of disappearing. But the pictures of Liv and James were everywhere, reminding me of the only reason I wasn't with Vince. I wouldn't live without them, and I wouldn't let them live without me if I could help it.

And with the strength of their love, I didn't reopen the junk email account to read the words I knew he'd send. The plea to see him. In the rare moment of clarity, I realized how lucky I'd been that no one had seen us in Philadelphia. It wasn't that far away. Lots of people worked there, went out there. We could have run into a dozen people in the corners of dark bars, or the well-lit hallways of the city's finest hotels. Yes. We were very lucky.

I SMILED JUST ENOUGH. I complained just enough. I was just enough. And for Liv and James, I was everything. Their homework consultant, their meal maker, their cheerleader, their sounding board. I tucked them in at night and woke them every morning, and Brad never questioned a thing, since his life was perfectly designed with him at the center of it.

He surprised me with tickets to a Beef 'N Beer at the Moose Lodge. It was a fundraiser for the middle school. Certainly a good cause, but the Moose Lodge seemed like a stretch for fancy-pants Brad. I tried to say no, tried to wiggle out of it. I was afraid the colonel would be there, but in the end, Brad made it impossible not to go.

We were assigned a table with the colonel's wife and six other couples. The colonel was on duty, and I was on a tour of my own. I discussed the new math curriculum. I joined in the moans of the half-day conference schedule. I nodded when they called the new young teacher a whore for wearing a short skirt. Basically, the tiny group of cells still operating in my body let go and died while I consumed beef with my beer.

We returned to our house and paid the babysitter. When I undressed, my drunk husband grabbed me from behind, bent me over our bed, and shoved his dick in me.

"How's that, baby? You like that, don't you?" Liking was an emotion never to be experienced again. This was perfunctory and boring, but I was his wife.

"It's great," I said, and buried my face in Brad's pillow until he finished. I could have cried out, but the only person who would have cared, I'd stopped speaking to months ago.

I fell asleep to the sound of Brad's heavy breathing. His chest lifted as I watched, the moonlight just enough to see his body still alive in every way. I rolled onto my back and let sleep take me. It was the only place the colonel still touched me.

I dreamed Brad took all of our money and the kids to Singapore, and when the phone rang, I woke up ready to kill him. When it rang again, I realized it was only a dream and grabbed the phone off my nightstand. The number flashed on the screen as Jenna's full name, including middle initial, and I ran with the phone out of the room. I was furious.

"What?" I answered.

"There's been an accident." My heart dropped, first for him and the familiar need his voice invoked. "It's Jenna."

"What? How? Where?" I couldn't piece thoughts together. "Where is she?"

"They're airlifting her to Cooper Hospital now."

Airlifting . . . I hung up the phone and grabbed clothes from my closet. I tried to wake Brad, but he was incoherent. I left a note on my pillow and ran out the door to Cooper.

The hospital was basically three roads from my house but thirty miles away. I made it in twenty-five minutes. I hoped the helicopter made it in five. I searched my mind for stories of others airlifted. Cooper was a trauma center, so I knew it was bad, but she was alive. She had to be alive.

I parked in the deck and ran into the elevator. I pressed the floor with the star next to it frantically until the doors shut and opened to a catwalk connecting the main building. I found the signs for emergency and saw Vince standing beneath it. I ran to him and launched myself into his arms, not caring who saw me. He held me tight to him, pulling me back to the safety of Vincent Pratt. When I'd taken enough from him to stand, I stepped back, out of his arms.

"How is she?"

"We don't know. She was unconscious, and there was a lot of blood. But she's alive."

"Did you call John?"

"Right after I called you. He's on his way." I wondered who was watching the boys. I should have called him before I came up here. But I couldn't have stayed away.

"What happened?"

"She wrapped her car around a tree on Marlton Road."

"What was she doing there?"

"From what I've pieced together, she left the Beef N' Beer and went to the bar." Vince leaned into me, and his voice lowered to barely above a whisper. "There was an empty bottle of vodka in the car."

My eyes searched his for answers. Jenna had been drunk. This was his way of telling me she'd been drunk when she'd hit the tree.

"Oh."

forty-four

SHE WAS SO PALE. ALMOST lifeless. John and the boys had been there earlier; they must have exhausted her. Jenna always had so much to give them, more than I ever thought I could muster, but now she appeared empty.

Her leg was in a contraption, slightly lifted off her bed, and her arm was in a sling. She was bruised. There were stiches across her forehead. Her face was foreign without a smile. But most of all, she was pale.

"Hey," I said and walked to the side of her bed. She didn't smile at me, didn't make a joke. Jenna's humor had been silenced by a tree on a country road. "How are you doing?"

"Shitty." She barely acknowledged me. Jenna always made everyone, including me, feel like the center of her happy universe, and now she locked me out of it, unable to enter herself. "You shouldn't have come."

"I couldn't stay away." This was foreign territory for us. I couldn't make a joke. Nothing seemed funny now. "I should have driven you home. I didn't know you were in trouble. I didn't know you needed help."

"I didn't need help. I don't need help." Her words were filled with hatred. "What do *you* need, though?"

My head shot up. She wasn't talking about the accident. I leaned back, putting a foot between her bed and me, not letting her so close. "What are you talking about?"

"I don't know. The last few weeks, you've been depressed and completely withdrawn, but you never said a word to me about it. Is Brad sleeping around?" Jenna looked right through me. "Are you?" There was nothing left of my best friend in this hospital bed. She was distraught and taking it out on me, or maybe I deserved it.

"Where is this coming from?"

"You seem so worried about me. I thought we should talk about you for a while." Her words were filled with venom.

"I'm not here to talk about either of us. I'm here because I love you."

"I don't need your love, or your pity." Jenna turned her head toward the wall, leaving me cold and alone standing next to her.

"I'm sorry."

"What do you have to be sorry about?" Her voice was like a fist around my heart, squeezing the life from me.

Without an idea of what else to say, I turned and walked out of her room. I leaned against the wall and let the tears fall down my face.

"You okay?" John walked up and stood in front of me.

"Why is she so angry?" I wiped my tears, not wanting John to have someone else to deal with.

"She's detoxing. It's making her miserable. I should have warned you."

"Detoxing?"

"She's an alcoholic." Every cup she'd ever held in her hand flashed through my mind. Every hiccup, every hangover. I thought she was a mother, not an alcoholic. There was little difference in my mind.

"She's one of my favorite people in the whole world."

"She loves you, too," he said, and walked into Jenna's room. I thought I heard crying, but I wasn't sure if it was her or John.

I left the hospital and cried the whole way home. I cried for Jenna, and I cried for myself, and I cried for Liv if she ever thought being a mother was different than it actually was.

forty-five

JENNA'S ANGER HELD STRONG FOR two weeks. She hated everyone, but her children. I knew how she felt, and I wasn't detoxing . . . exactly. I opened the door to the police station and behind the front desk was a younger officer. Late twenties, perhaps. He looked up as soon as the door opened. He was on alert. "Can I help you?"

"Yes. I'd like to speak with Officer Pratt."

"Oh, the chief." The young officer and I both turned toward a door that opened, and Vince emerged from it.

"I've got this, Daniels. Come in, Mrs. Walsh."

I nodded thank you to the officer at the desk and followed Vince into his office. It hadn't been included on the Cub Scout tour. It was small with wood paneling covering the bottom halves of the walls. There was a credenza on one side with stacks of files and books on top, next to a wedding picture of him and his wife. On the windowsill behind his desk were school pictures of each of his children. Quite the family man.

Vince motioned for me to take a seat in the chair in front of his desk. He leaned on the credenza, blocking my view of his wedding. I watched his chest rise with every breath and remembered the anger that led me here.

"You gave her a DUI?" I kept my voice even, not letting my emotions get the best of me.

"It's good to see you." His eyes shot liquid heat through my body.

"You gave her a DUI?" I repeated, there for only one reason.

"She gave herself a DUI. I just wrote up the paperwork."

"How could you?" After everything between us . . . she didn't deserve it.

"How could I not? If I let everyone I know in this town drive drunk, we'll all be dead."

I sat silently. The thought of Jenna given the news about her arrest while still in her hospital bed swirled furiously in my head.

"I'm a police officer. You, better than anyone, know what that means."

I used to know what it meant. There was a time when I believed so wholeheartedly in the law, I'd have given my own mother a DUI. Now I smoked pot and dreamed of running away.

"It was all in the hospital records. She had no way to avoid a DUI. And quite frankly, I think the accident was her wakeup call, and the DUI will force her to follow through."

"Follow through on what?"

"Mar, I know you love her, but surely you can see she needs to make some changes."

The same outrage from John's call telling me about the DUI seared through me again. "Are you calling her a drunk?"

"No." His eyes pleaded with me. "I'm saying she needs help. She wrapped her car around a tree. Her blood alcohol was over two times the legal limit. She's lucky she didn't kill someone."

My anger at Vince moved to Jenna. She could have died. She could have left those three little boys here without her and they'd be lost forever. At the thought of it, my eyes filled with tears, spilling over and running down my cheeks. Vince stood from the credenza and walked toward me. I threw my hand in the air, halting him. I was out of my chair and moving toward the door before he could come close to me.

"There's still a job opening here," he said, and I turned toward him. If me working at the police station had been a bad idea when we'd been together, it was a painful thought now.

"Thanks for seeing me."

"Wait. Just give me a minute." He held his hands in the air, surrendering, promising to not touch me. I couldn't look away. My eyes were frozen with my heart, waiting for him to cure me. I let them move over every inch of his body. He watched me longing for him. He waited, letting me suffer through my sight. I wanted to throw myself on the floor and sob.

I wanted him.

"I understand why you stopped 'talking' to me. I was in over my head with you. Too invested in your wellbeing. I let my emotions overrule my mind, and I put you in jeopardy. I'm sorry."

"You owe me nothing. There's no need to apologize."

"You're lying. To me and yourself. And you promised to always tell me the truth. That shouldn't have changed."

I took a deep breath, and as I exhaled, the tears came back. I was trapped by him. I could barely deny him my body, and never deny him the truth. "I accept your apology."

"I want you back. I want all of it back. I miss you, Mar."

"Why? So we can end either in a public scandal or with our hearts torn out?"

"It won't end. I get it. I know all too well what you're unwilling to risk, and I won't cross that line again."

I wanted to believe him. I wanted to believe it was possible. I wanted to fold into his arms and finally, after months away from him, feel alive. "The truth?" I asked, and Vince nodded, confirming he knew what he was asking for.

"Yes."

"I was hanging on by a thread before I met you. But once I left you, I realized how much closer to the edge I could get.

I've been in misery since the moment you walked out of my kitchen." Vince took a step toward me, and I held my hand up, touching his stomach. The feel of it beneath my fingers almost launched me into his arms. "But I told you before, I'm not the kind of woman who has an affair. I'm going to figure this out without you."

"But you don't have to. I'm right here."

"Yes." I nodded over his shoulder. "Right here next to the pictures of your wife and kids."

"It was never like that."

"Only in our minds." I shook my head. He had to see this the way I did. "It was always exactly like that." I watched my hand touch the door handle and felt my heart rip from my chest again.

"Just say the word, and I'll be there."

I opened the door and walked out. I didn't breathe until I was locked in the Escalade Brad had chosen for me.

forty-six

NOTHING SEEMED TO MAKE JENNA less angry. I started to think nothing but a drink would. She was transferred to a rehabilitation facility for her leg and stayed there for a month. I visited twice a week. Once at night and once during the day. I took magazines we used to laugh at, candies she loved, pictures I screen shot from Facebook. Anything to pull her out of her misery. But none of it worked. She was angry and depressed and ashamed and often fought with me over nothing. I wanted the old Jenna back, even if she was drunk.

She seemed to lighten up when the boys were around. Regardless of her state of being, she would always put them first. Her homecoming was on her oldest's twelfth birthday, and she asked if I could get a cake and make it like a party for him. Jenna made a big deal out of each of the boy's birthdays. Of course, the old Jenna was always ready for a party.

I ordered a sandwich tray, sent out invitations to his friends, and had John contact their family. We would party the day Jenna came home. It would just be a different kind of party than we were used to.

My cleaning lady was vacuuming while I unpacked my bags filled with paper products and streamers. I heard the vacuum stop and the front door open.

"Is Meredith here?" It was the unicorn. *For the love of God, why today?* I forced myself to the door, only wanting to hide in the garage until she left, but I was sure she saw the giant Escalade out front.

"Hi," I said, and smiled at my cleaning lady.

She quickly returned to work, not caring who was there.

The unicorn pushed past me, carrying several trendy "mom bags" overflowing with items. I closed the door and followed her into the kitchen. By the time I got there, she was already unpacking her bags and making herself at home.

I just stared at her.

"John told me she's coming home tomorrow and that you're throwing John Jr. a birthday party." I still didn't know what to say. "I'm here to help."

Then I knew what to say. "No, thanks." I shook my head as I spoke. "It's really sweet of you, but I've got this. Really, we don't need any help." The unicorn just kept moving, setting up a bunch of ingredients on the counter and searching the cupboards for something. "What are you doing?"

"I'm making a birthday cake."

"I'm going to buy one." *Who the hell makes a birthday cake? Isn't that what bakeries are for?*

The unicorn pulled Jenna's mixer out of the cabinet under the toaster oven and set it on the table in front of her. She didn't appear to be leaving; wasn't packing up her things. "Look. I know we have a lot to say." I raised my eyebrows, confused of who "we" were. And what the hell it had to do with her leaving. She shouldn't have been in Jenna's kitchen. "We, the women in this town, talk a lot of shit." She finally cleared it up for me. "But when someone needs help, we shut the hell up and help." She stayed still, Jenna's mixer in her hand. She was there to help, and all I had to do was let her. And even though I really didn't need help, I wanted her there with me. As absurd as I usually found Sarah, she was my normal. She was my life that never made sense, and I was trying to get that life back.

"Okay." The word was barely audible, but loud enough for Sarah to smile and begin pouring ingredients into a bowl. "What are you doing?"

"I'm making a cake."

"I just told you I ordered one."

"Nothing says love like a homemade cake. Children should smell a cake baking. They should lick the batter off a spatula. Now what is John Jr. into?"

"I ordered him a baseball cake."

"Perfect. I brought my round bowl." Sarah took a large stainless steel mixing bowl out of her bag. "Cancel that horrible cake you ordered."

I walked out of the room, needing some time to regroup.

When I came back, the unicorn had an apron on and was pouring batter into her bowl. She put the bowl in Jenna's oven and then looked at me. "Now what else can I do?"

"I think we're good."

"Nonsense. I'm here to help. You've got cleaning covered. Let's decorate."

The unicorn and I worked side-by-side, hanging streamers and smoothing table cloths. I was on guard for her to ask me personal questions about Jenna, or myself, but she just worked. She never complained. Not even when the table cloths didn't fit and we had to cut and overlap them. It wasn't Pinterest worthy, but she kept moving. She paused at the family photos on the mantle while she was hanging streamers from it.

"Jenna always was a beautiful girl."

"Did you two graduate high school together?"

"No." The unicorn laughed. "She was a year ahead of me, and we ran in different crowds, but she has always been a beauty. Even after giving birth to all those boys. It's a shame really."

"What is?" I braced myself for my anger, for her criticism of Jenna.

"It's like our kids steal our beauty. They steal our lives, and all we can do is helplessly give them every ounce of it because we love them more than ourselves."

Sarah paused for a second and then returned to her streamers. I couldn't take my eyes off her. We were all floating around in the same boat. Some of us medicating ourselves with pain pills, some with alcohol, and some with or without food, or spending money we didn't have, but all of us were trying to surface from our self-imposed drowning. *It's like the hookers and the thieves . . .* Christine's words came back to me. I had an overwhelming urge to hug Sarah.

"Can I ask you something?"

Sarah stopped blowing up the balloon in her hand. She let go of the end, and it flew across the room. "Anything." Her smile was warm and genuine.

"What do you love about this town?"

She didn't hesitate for a second before saying, "How no matter where my children are, no matter what street corner, or baseball field, or friends' house they're at, this whole town is looking out for them."

I supposed they were in their own way. All that bitching about everyone's behavior. These people were keeping an eye on something. "Thanks for coming over, Sarah." It might have been the first time I used her name when I spoke to her.

"Any of us would do the same for each other."

"I hope so," was all I said.

❦

THE PEOPLE ARRIVED IN DROVES. They were used to partying here. Jenna was wheeled in and deposited in a recliner. It kept her leg elevated while at least fifty people kissed her and told her they loved her.

I loved her.

I kept my distance, unsure of how she felt about me today and not wanting to fight on her son's birthday. John stopped me and thanked me for the party. It seemed the life had been drained from him, too. He'd gone from taking care of Jenna when she was too drunk to care for herself to having a whole household to manage. I promised to help.

I stayed in the kitchen, away from the party, but each time someone new came through the front door, I looked for Vince. As far as I knew the Pratts hadn't been invited, but I knew very little about many of the people there.

Brad arrived an hour late. He said he'd gone to get his car washed. He annoyed me. Whether it was washing his car or breathing, he annoyed me. The only people I exerted any effort for these days were James and Liv.

"How long are we staying?" he asked, and I paused for a moment to see the man I married.

"You can leave whenever you want." I'm not sure if I was talking about *just* the party.

"What is your fucking problem?" Brad leaned in and asked with a low voice.

"You're my fucking problem." He wanted it. He was going to get it. My longing for Vince, my love for Jenna, my desperation that I overflowed with in that house he bought. He could have all of it.

Brad drug me by the elbow out the front door. "Seriously, what the fuck is going on with you? The last few months you've been a complete fucking bitch."

I shook my head and stared at the ground.

"What?" He roughly grabbed me by the chin.

"This isn't where I'm supposed to be."

"Well, you've been here for four years. What's so different now?"

With that one question, Brad got too close to my secret, and the colonel walked up behind him. I pushed Brad's hand from my face, and he turned to see what held my attention.

"Everything okay?" Vince's jaw was clenched. He didn't like what he saw.

"Fine. How are you?" Brad asked and relaxed his entire body.

I took the bakery box from the colonel and walked inside as Vince and Brad chatted about nothing. I put the box on the counter and closed my eyes. I leaned over it, wanting . . . everything . . . to be the way it was before.

"Hey, Jenna needs to go to the bathroom. I figure she'd rather you help her than anyone else." Sarah's voice broke through my sadness and forced me back to my existence.

"I'll go," I said and walked toward Jenna. Richie's dad was helping her into the wheel chair—the sight of which made me sick. Jenna only had to go fifteen feet, but she wasn't allowed to put any weight on her foot for weeks. After this party, a hospital bed was being delivered to her living room so she could convert her house into a rehab center.

"I got it," I said and smiled at Richie's dad. He was only helping. He hadn't bothered me at all since the camping trip. I pushed Jenna to the bathroom and saw Vince walk into the house. He'd escaped Brad. Lucky him.

I reached down to secure the brakes, and Jenna glared at me until I looked up at her.

"I got it," she said and pushed my hands away. She hated me, and I didn't know why.

John walked over. He helped Jenna into the bathroom and emerged, closing the door behind him. I was frozen in place. I had nowhere to go. I didn't want to be home with Brad, I couldn't go somewhere with Vince, and Jenna didn't want me here. Where else was there?

"Give her some time," John said. "She's really angry."

"Why is she mad at me?"

"She's not. She's mad at herself, and you're an extension of her." He rubbed my arm, and it reminded me of how gentle he always was with Jenna. "Just don't give up on her. Please."

"I won't. I just miss her." She was my only friend here. She was my life raft. Without her I would go under and never resurface.

"We all do." We heard the toilet flush, and John left me standing in the hall to help Jenna get back in her chair. She didn't deserve this.

I skulked back into the kitchen, hoping to hide from everyone. If the kids weren't screaming wildly on the trampoline out back, I'd make my whole family leave. As it was, I thought about taking Brad's car and escaping, but he'd make the kids leave with him right away, and they were having fun.

The colonel was leaning on the refrigerator. I stopped and thought about turning and walking back out, but the look in his eyes held me there, close to him, where I wanted to be.

"What was that about out front?" There was not a hint of amusement in his voice. His eyes didn't dance the way they used to around me. The dull ache of longing burrowed in the back of my throat.

"Husband and wife stuff."

Vince nodded, his top lip turned up with disgust. That was the way this whole thing should work. The first time he'd met me, I should have talked about my marriage until he'd been completely turned off.

"I wish you'd reopen your email account," he said. I rested my back against the wall by Jenna's whiteboard that had the entire family's schedule from two months ago still on it. "I have so many things I want you to hear." He moved closer to me. "How are you?" He was the only one who cared.

"I'm drowning."

He stepped until he was only inches from me. The rich mahogany smell that would forever represent warmth and safety flooded my senses. "Impossible. You're a mermaid."

I almost smiled. "How have you been?" I asked, my hands fighting my mind to touch him.

"About the same as you, I imagine."

"I'm sorry, then."

"I send you something every day." His voice was soft, pleading with me, toying with my resolve. I closed my eyes, unwilling to see and hear him. "I send it and hope that's the day you reopen the account, that's the day you return." He retreated, finally allowing me some space, and I opened my eyes. "But they're always returned undeliverable."

"I have to go." I could barely hear the words from my own mouth. My jaw was clenched with hatred for this entire situation. My muscles were taught and my mind raced with need.

"I know." I watched as the breath entered and exited his chest. "Just say the word, Mar."

I wouldn't make the kids leave. I would never let Vince and I affect a decision about them, but I hid the rest of the day where no one would find me. Right next to Brad.

forty-seven

"MOMMY, CAN I WEAR THIS dress to the talent show?" Liv held up a black-and-white dress that had an A-line skirt to her knee and wide crisscross straps in the back.

"Sure."

She wasn't satisfied with that answer. "Do you think they'll send home a note the way they did in kindergarten?"

I racked my brain for what note she was talking about. A vague memory of a crop top over a tank top being mentioned as not adhering to the dress code came back, but I had no memory of what the outcome was. "I don't know," I told Liv. "Do you want to wear a tank top under it?"

"No. The back is what makes it pretty."

"Then wear it how you want, and I'll handle any notes that are sent home."

Liv skipped out of my room, and I didn't think another moment about it. She looked adorable, awesome if you will, the morning of the talent show. She let me pull her blue-streaked hair into a pretty side braid. It laid off her face and away from the dress so you could see the back detail. I took pictures of her and James, and emailed them to Brad in Dubai. I sent a little note to make sure to comment on Liv's dress because she was in love with it.

Everything was going smoothly. Until the school called. The

principal wanted me to bring in a change of clothes for Liv, because her dress violated the dress code. Fucking coward. He'd had his poor secretary call. I wouldn't waste my wrath on her. I would save every ounce of it for the pompous ass who ran that school.

I changed into a short denim skirt and tank top of my own. It was plain, almost sporty, but short and inappropriate and most importantly, it also violated the dress code.

I smiled at the ladies who worked in the office. This wasn't their fault. I waited patiently to speak with him. He assumed I would just bring in the clothes and we'd be done with it, but there I was. Sitting outside his office without a change of clothes for Liv in my hand.

"Would you mind calling Liv to the office when Mr. Peters returns?" I asked his secretary.

"Certainly." Her smile was that of a conspirator. She'd been waiting for me to come in.

"Mrs. Walsh, please come in my office." Mr. Peters' receding hair and freckled scalp were a few inches below my eyes. His shirt was off-white, and the way he rolled his sleeves and left a sharp corner on his cuffs pissed me off. He motioned to the chair opposite his desk and sat on the desk, towering over me. I was not impressed. "I didn't mean for you to waste your time and come in. Although it's always nice to see you. You could have just dropped off new clothes."

"That's the thing. I couldn't do that."

There was a knock on the door. Mr. Peters walked to it with confusion covering his face. He opened it, and Liv walked in. She gave me a huge hug and silently mouthed, *I told you.*

"Hi, baby," I said and hugged her again. Putting her at ease, convincing her that I've got this. "Can you turn around and show Mr. Peters your dress?"

Liv did as I asked, and both Mr. Peters and I examined the minute areas of skin exposed under the wide straps of her dress.

"Is this the issue you called me about?" I asked and turned to Mr. Peters.

"Yes, it violates the dress code."

"What part of the dress code?" I asked sheepishly, trying to hide my growing anger, not wanting to scare Liv.

"Students' torsos must be fully covered."

"I see." I smiled at Liv, willing her to believe she was still going to wear this dress she loved so much to the talent show. "Liv would you mind waiting in the hall for us?"

Liv looked from me to Mr. Peters, not sure who was in charge of her in these halls.

"You can sit on the bench right outside my office, Olivia." Mr. Peters showed her out and instinctively closed the door behind her. He returned and leaned on the desk above me again.

"While I respect your position, Liv is not changing out of that dress."

"Mrs. Walsh." He was practically laughing. "She has to change."

"Listen. The dress is loose and to her knee and has sleeves, and she's in love with it. This afternoon she'll get on stage in front of her entire school and a large portion of this town, and she'll feel confident." He stayed silent, but shaking his head. The angry heat rose up the back of my neck. "She doesn't love the dress because it makes some seven-year-old's dick hard." His head shot up, and his eyes bulged. "She loves it because it's pretty. It's not a distraction. No other seven-year-old cares about the back of that dress. If it is distracting to *you*, then perhaps we should investigate the origin of that further." His head jutted back on his neck, and his mouth fell open gasping for more of the putrid air between us. He was disgusted, and he should have been at what I was suggesting.

"Mrs. Walsh!"

"She's not changing."

Silence . . .

"Look. I left a position with the United States Department of Justice to raise confident, well-adjusted, poised children. And I am bored to tears with it." My voice raised against my will. I was losing my control, and I didn't care. He could stick the dress code up his ass. "Do *not* make this school's dress code and your administration of it, my next project. Because I promise you, Liv's crossed straps will keep you up at night for the rest of your life."

I rose, the anger pulling me from my chair. But I wasn't done. "Now. She is staying here all day and will be on that stage this afternoon, wearing her dress without feeling any shame from her school's administration. Do we understand each other?" I took a deep breath and smiled. Just because I was yelling at him and suggesting he had pedophiliac thoughts did not mean this had to be ugly.

Mr. Peters sat still for a few moments, composing himself. "She can wear the dress today, but don't send her in it again."

I nodded and let him think he won. We could have this same argument again later. He opened the door to his office, and there were six adults staring at us, having heard our "conversation."

"Miss Walsh, you can return to your class."

Liv beamed at me. I was happy I wasn't working so I could go in there and fight for her. She hugged me tight against her and pressed her hot cheek against my face. I thought she was going to cry. It was too much pressure for a little girl.

"I'll see you later. Break a leg."

She leaned back, her arms still around my neck. "Love you, Mommy."

"Love you, too." She skipped back toward class.

"Walk, Ms. Walsh!" Mr. Peters yelled.

Liv halted, began walking, and when she turned to me, I winked at her. I left Mr. Peters standing outside his office and walked out the front door.

I knew when Brad heard about my meeting—and he would—he was going to be pissed. His idea of parenting was not dressing in a short skirt to yell at the principal about the dress code. He would have made her change. The same way he'd made me change.

My anger reignited, and by the time I reached the Escalade parked on the street, I hated it and every other element of my life outside of James and Liv. I kicked the driver's door, and then kicked it again to prove to myself I was, in fact, completely out of control. While Brad was in Dubai, I was trapped there arguing with the twerp principal and worrying about Brad's reaction when he finally came home. The dent in the door did little to calm me. I hated the fucking car, too.

I opened the door and climbed in. My short skirt made it hard to reach the seat. I rested my forehead on the steering wheel and cried. I didn't let my mind focus on what I was crying for. My phone in my purse held what I wanted, what I needed. The photos of the colonel that would quiet the anger. They would soothe the hurt, but I'd promised myself I wouldn't go back in there. Instead, I stared at the phone in my hand. The tears stopped. My heartbeat pounded from my chest to my ear. My resolve was already disappearing, before I did a thing. But then I did do something. I texted Vince.

M: *It's me. Saying the word.*

I smiled at the phone and relief flowed through me. He was a drug and I would OD on him. But I didn't care. My phone dinged with a one-word text.

V: *Nibac*

I turned the key in the ignition and drove to the cabin. Spelling it backward was another promise that he'd work harder to keep our secret, but I didn't need it. I didn't care anymore. I just wanted him.

When I pulled off the road, he was waiting by the open gate. He closed it behind me and locked it. We were tucked away in secrecy. I stopped the Escalade and waited for him to climb in. Emotions raged from his eyes. He would take me from the car and either scream at me, or fuck me. I needed both. I needed him to exist in my world, and I would accept whatever he had to say.

Vince opened the door, and my eyes filled with tears again. I turned from him and drove the length of the lane in silence. I could feel his stare bearing down on me from the seat next to me. The heat from his closeness traveled from the back of my neck and wrapped around my ribs.

I stopped the SUV next to his car and put it in PARK. Before he spoke, I opened my door and exited the vehicle. I met him on his side, and he forced me backward to his police cruiser. He looked from the top of my head to my feet in my flip-flops. He was undaunted by my violations of the dress code.

I wouldn't control myself here, not anymore. I raised my hands to his face, but before I touched him, he reached up and took them both in his. The rough skin on his fingers flooded my body with memories of his touch everywhere. A chill spread through my body, leaving me cold and wanting him closer.

He lifted me to the hood of his car and ripped off my underwear without saying a word. What was there to say? I reached for him, and he grabbed my hands and placed them behind me. He unzipped his pants and released his cock, all while never releasing me with his eyes. I wanted him inside me, but it still wouldn't be enough.

Vince plunged into me, and I leaned back, silencing the anger coursing through me. He pulled out and thrust into me again, leaving the school and my children behind and replacing them with a violent calm only he could provide.

He moved me closer to the edge of the hood and fucked me until I told him I was going to come. It was rising up in my body, forcing me toward it, leaving me defenseless, and then I came, jerking toward him as he continued. He leaned back and watched me, never pausing, never slowing as he kept entering me and filling me with the colonel, Vincent Pratt. And finally he came, too.

His movements slowed. Each time he came in me, I caved around myself. I wanted him hard again. I wanted him inside me forever. I wanted to be able to breathe.

Vince brushed my hair away from my face and leaned over me on the car. "Don't ever do that again," he said, his words rough near my ear.

"Do what?"

"Stop talking to me." Talking, fucking, caring . . . I had stopped everything. I had to.

"I'm sorry."

"I know. Just don't do it again. Whatever happens from now on, we'll figure it out together." *We were a team.* He sat me up in front of him.

"Vince—"

He kissed me. He didn't want to hear what I had to say. And I'd let him avoid it for now. "Together, Maris."

A slow smile spread across my face, and I could see it mirrored in his eyes. He was happy, and my God, he made me whole. "Nothing says 'town whore' like getting fucked on the hood of a car."

Vince shook his head because I just never stopped. "That's a police cruiser, I'll have you know."

"I take it back, then. I'm a lady."

He leaned between my legs, my face in his hands, and kissed me again, forcing respectability into me with his tongue. "I had just pulled someone over for speeding when you texted." I kissed the side of his face and hugged him again. I couldn't stop touching him. "I'm sure they were happy I heard from you."

"You let them off?"

"I didn't even get out of my car. I just drove here."

"And so it begins. The dereliction of duty that comes with the illicit." I was the only one laughing.

"Mar, I love you." His words silenced me. It was almost a year ago I'd ridden on the bus with him to Philadelphia.

"Vince—"

"Hear me out." His eyes pleaded with me, and I owed him. With one text, he'd dropped everything to be there for me. "I've loved you since you asked me if I've ever killed anyone on the bus ride to Philly. I love you." I shook my head. "I don't care if you think it's impossible. I do. And I realize this is far from perfect, but I want you too much to care. The only thing I asked from you last time was that you be honest with me, but I wasn't honest with you, and I wasn't honest with myself."

I pushed him back and slid off the hood of the car. I lowered my skirt and straightened my shirt. This was some sort of negotiation, and I wasn't going to engage with my legs spread.

"I love you," he said it again, smiling this time. The familiar barricade to his love rose up inside of me. I'd run from it so many times before, it was my only instinct now. "You need to hear it. You need to hear it every day. I told you we'd never have an affair; that it's not like that. And it's not, because I love you."

"Lots of people having affairs claim to be in love." I dismissed him, but I couldn't deny him.

"I know what you're doing. Trying to make light of this, and I won't let you. I know you love me, too. I know you don't want to live without me. And we can't move forward the way we were."

"What are you suggesting?" I thought Vince might have left his mind on the hood of the police cruiser.

"Don't worry. I know you'll never divorce, but I need more from you."

"I can't give you more. I was terrified we were going to be discovered the last time."

"Not more time. Not unless we can make it work. More of you." He pulled me close and kissed me. He kissed the side of my face and my chin and right in front of my ear, and then whispered, "Tell me you love me." I wanted to do whatever he said. I wanted to scream into the trees that I loved him, but I'd protected us from love for so long, I didn't know how to let the emotion survive.

"Why?"

"Because I need you to."

He was my lovely Vince, standing in his police uniform the same way he had every Halloween as a child, and all he wanted was for me to admit what we both knew was the truth. But how many lines would I cross? How many rules would I break? "No matter what I say, there's no justification for our actions."

"I know."

He took his holster from the front seat of his cruiser and put it on. And the thought of him being hurt shot through me. What if he went back to work and I never saw him again? I'd promised him I'd leave nothing unsaid, but the most important thing always had remained silent.

"I love you."

forty-eight

AND THEN I DID THE unthinkable. I found a way for us to spend the night together. I couldn't even take credit for it. I owed it all to Brad. Brad, and his constant predictability in putting himself first in all situations.

You could always tell a wedding invitation before you pulled it out of the mailbox. It was the only envelope where someone cared about their handwriting, cared what the stamp was like. No one put any effort into correspondence anymore. I held the heavy cream envelope in my hand, and excitement flowed through me. It had been forever since I'd been to a wedding. Brad and I used to love them.

Mr. David Miller and Miss Christine Donahue requested the pleasure of our company as they exchanged their marital vows and celebrated their union. Christine was getting married. It was at the Sagamore Resort on Lake George. Five hours away. Brad would hate the entire idea.

I begged him to go, but only enough for him to think I actually wanted him there. It was the same weekend as his annual golf trip. He wouldn't relent. He looked forward to it the entire year. I could almost remember what it was like to look forward to something the entire year.

I told him I understood, and I did. But I also told him I was going without him. Brad didn't like the idea at all. Weddings were to be attended as couples. We were a couple. And since he had plans, I should have none. But I RSVP'd yes, for one, and that I would love the fish entrée.

Before I mentioned it to Vince, I confirmed with Christine that it was going to be an enormous wedding. Over two hundred people were invited. It was the perfect shield for me to disappear. From her wedding and from my marriage. Vince and Brad took care of the rest. Brad by refusing to choose me, or what I wanted, over what he'd planned to do. And Vince by scheduling his summer fishing trip early this year. At the start of June, and in the Adirondacks. I didn't know what he told his wife. I didn't know if he often went away by himself; to ask would begin the conversation. What I did know was Vince was staying at a cabin less than an hour and a half north of Lake George. It was nestled in the woods around Lake Placid.

IT WAS LIKE THE BOOK club on steroids. I booked a room at the Sagamore for two nights on Brad's credit card. I checked in and snuck out. I made sure none of the ten people I'd know attending Christine's wedding saw me. I drove farther north, far away from my family, and followed the directions to the cabin Vince was already waiting at.

I turned into the driveway and followed it back through the trees and almost to the edge of the lake. He was lying in a hammock, but when I put the car in PARK, he stood up. He'd been there for three days already. He hadn't shaved in as long. He was beautiful. Like, truly fucking beautiful. I wished my mother could see him. I understood how my father felt about her. I would follow this man to hell, too.

I took out my phone and took a picture of him. It was eight o'clock at night. It would be dark soon. My legs were sore from sitting so long. I'd only stopped for gas and the bathroom; nothing else was worth wasting a minute of time I'd have alone with him.

"What took you so long?" he asked as he walked to me and lifted me into his arms. He kissed me, and I stopped thinking. His hands ran up and down my back, settling in my hair and pulling me closer to him. He was generous with his need.

"My boss is a tyrant. I couldn't get off work until noon." Vince was my lover and my boss. I'd taken the job at the police station after we'd reconnected. I worked four days a week while the kids were at school, which would become four mornings a week while the kids were at swim practice in the summer.

I'd expected it to be awkward, but there was never a minute of it. Vince was professional and helpful and, above all, kind as I acclimated to my receptionist duties. I filed and answered the phones and tidied up the office. The officers were great company throughout the day, and during my down time I read case files. The words, the police reports and investigative notes, were specks of life flowing through me.

At first Brad was disinterested. He came around to being annoyed by it. He tried to call me once, and I let it go to voice-mail because I was talking to a junior officer about his schedule. Brad was used to me being at his beck and call. In the end, he accepted it. I was happy, and that made his life easier.

Vince's lips caressed my neck, and he said, "You should watch out for him. I think he wants to fuck you."

"I think that, too." I kissed him again. "It's the way he looks at me. And the way he takes off my clothes and sticks his dick in me."

"Is that what gives it away?" Vince lifted me into his arms and carried me into the cabin. He made love to me. He took his time. We had no where we had to be. No one wondering where we were.

I lay in his arms in the bed without a care in the world. But the realization of how far we'd come seeped in. The memories of how I'd tried to avoid exactly this. We were now in love and spending the night together. We saw each other every day. *This* had gone from a twice-a-month tryst to an everyday love affair.

I drug myself out of the bed and found my phone. I texted Christine that I had a flat, was fine and back on the road, but I wasn't going to get in until late, so I'd see her tomorrow. And, of course, that I couldn't wait for the wedding.

I texted my brother to check on the kids and tell them I missed them.

I texted Brad.

I climbed back into bed and tightened my arms around Vince. He pulled me up to face him, and I held the phone high above our heads and took our picture. I paused to hide it with the one from before. These photos were far out of my comfort zone, and yet I couldn't let them go. Not even when I let him go.

Vince turned my face back to him. "Thank you."

He didn't have to explain. I knew he was thankful for this night together. I knew he wanted this every night, but he also knew I wouldn't give it to him. I kissed him on the lips and laid my head on his chest. I inhaled him, and I fell asleep solidly in the arms of my lover. I dreamt we were vacationing together, and it didn't matter who saw us.

I WOKE UP TO THE smell of bacon and eggs. I rolled toward the window. My phone was flashing with messages. Fear gripped me that something had happened to Liv or James and I'd slept through it. I hit the home key and found perfunctory messages from Brad and my brother with a quote from Liv: "I love you." The last text was from Jenna. Things were still stiff between us. At times, I caught a glimmer of our old banter, but mostly, I mourned our past. With my job, and the kids, I didn't have as much time to painfully dwell on it. The text read, "I miss you."

I started to cry. I sat up in bed with my phone clutched to my chest, and I cried for my best friend. I texted her back, "I love you," and cried some more. Vince popped his head in the doorway and practically ran into the room when he saw me.

"What's wrong? Why are you crying?"

"Nothing's wrong." I shook my head. "Jenna misses me." I pointed the phone to him so he could see.

"Of course she does." He wiped the tears from my face and kissed me. There were times when I was with him that I felt like a little girl. It was because he was the only person left who took care of me. He held me close to his chest. It was hours after I'd gotten there, and still neither of us had clothes on. I wished we could stay like this forever, but *this* wasn't real life. "What time is the wedding?"

His question flooded my mind with all the evidence of our mock love. He would never attend a wedding with me or eat out at a restaurant. We would never exist in the light. Affairs only survived in the dark. "The ceremony's at three."

"I want you to come back here tonight. Stay the night again." He was shy about it, as if he was asking me out on a date.

"I told you this would happen. First it's one night, then what?"

His eyes turned a deep green like the bottom of the Atlantic off the coast of New Jersey, and he took my hand in his. I was alarmed immediately, and he could sense it. He ran his thumb over my palm, trying to calm me, preparing me for his next statement.

"I'm going to leave my wife." My eyes dragged from my palm to his eyes, and I forced myself to inhale. I held it in until he said, "Exhale," and reminded me to breathe.

"Why right now? Why do we have to talk about this right

now?"

"Because it's the only time we have to talk. We have hours all to ourselves. We're not running home to anyone else."

"Is that why you want to leave her? You're tired of the time constraints?" I could hear the bitterness in my voice and I couldn't diminish it. I couldn't be nice. "You've been hell-bent on ruining this since it started."

"That's ridiculous."

"Is it?" I took my hands from his. "You've said all along that you're fine with what I need for this to work, and then you push for more every step of the way. Why can't we just be what we were last fall? Why can't we just be lovers?"

"Because we're better than that!" His voice roared through the cabin. "And she's better than that. Take us out of this for a minute. Don't you think she deserves someone who wants *her* the way I want *you*?" I closed my eyes. I wouldn't face what Lynn Pratt deserved any more than I would let myself consider Brad. "Talk to me." He'd regained control. He was close to me, and always close to ending this.

"If I took into account what she deserves, I would jump off a bridge and never surface. You are the most selfish thing I've ever done. And as long as both our families are intact, I can tell myself there will be no collateral damage. You have no idea what you'll set in motion. It will fuck up your family for generations to come."

"Or not."

"Your daughter has watched you tell her mother that you love her her entire life. What will 'I love you' mean to her now that you no longer do? What will the sound of your wife crying do to your son? What will he think of you then? There is someone to blame in this situation, and it's you." And then, because by God he'd unleashed the beast inside me, I added, "It'll be difficult for such a good man to survive this fall from grace."

"Fuck you, Maris."

I stared at him without a hint of emotion. I was tired of holding up my end of this argument. Tired of protecting everyone else from his romantic ideas.

And then he walked out of the room.

I pulled the summer dress I'd stashed in my tote over my head and brushed my teeth. I found the skirt, tank, bra, and underwear I'd worn the night before. Few items meant few to keep track of. Each was carefully stored back in my bag. I replaced my toothbrush and makeup bag in my tote. My phone and charger, my car keys, my hairbrush. I searched under the bed for nothing. Sure everything was secure in my bag.

The cabin was a waste. We'd done all this work to spend this time together, and all it gave us was the realization of how little we were in each other's lives. We would have been better served with ninety minutes at his hunting cabin. From the back window, I could see Vince at the water's edge, dressed in only a pair of shorts. He was staring out across the lake. He was waiting for me to come touch him. To wrap my arms around him and bury my face in his chest. To hold him until the words we'd just spoken to each other no longer mattered, but I couldn't. His claim that I could do anything screamed through my head, and I silently admitted I wouldn't.

I walked to my car, and he met me there.

"You promised you wouldn't do this," he said.

"Do what?"

"Run. Stop talking to me." He stood between me and my car door, not letting me escape. "Every time we come close to moving forward, you revert back to covering the evidence that we ever existed." His not touching me bothered me more than if he'd grabbed me. "You promised you'd give me more."

"How can I give you more?" My voice broke, but I wouldn't cry. "You know how I feel about this. You've known since the beginning."

"But we're not at the beginning anymore." It felt like the

ending, and I didn't want that either. I'd created the perfect relationship in my mind that could never be anything but in my mind. The sight of him was making me hate myself, but I wouldn't take that out on him because he deserved better.

"You're the finest man I've ever known." I took a step toward him, and his warmth moved me closer. I nuzzled my lips near his neck and kissed him there. I stood on my toes and kissed his cheek. I pulled his face down and said in his ear, "And I'll love you forever." I stepped back and stared at him until he moved out of the way of my car door. "I'm never going to be what you want."

I climbed in the Escalade and drove away.

forty-nine

I NUMBED MYSELF WITH THREE glasses of bourbon, wisely so, since the vows almost had me jumping in the lake.

"I promise to love, cherish, and be faithful, in sickness and in health, in good times and bad, for richer or poorer, as long as we both shall live." Blah, blah, blah, blah, blah.

A hint of bourbon crawled up the back of my throat, and I swallowed it down with a smile to the couple sitting next to me. The bride and groom were lovely, the Sagamore was lovely, it was all so fucking lovely, and I couldn't seem to pinpoint what was bothering me more than anything else.

The ceremony ended, and the cocktail hour came to a close as I watched the bridal party take pictures on the dock. Christine and David were on the verge of something brilliant. I mingled with the few people I knew from my old office. Pictures were taken, and I made sure they were posted online. There would be no question I was exactly where I said I was. Vince would see them when he stopped at a rest stop for gas on his way home. He would see me in my green one-shouldered dress that made my eyes a deep moss color, and he'd hate me. He'd regret the first grade field trip to the Franklin Institute and consider it the worst day of his life thus far. And even though I knew it was ultimately for the best, I hated myself for it.

I danced a little. People liked it when you danced at their wedding. I would participate. Ethan was a fellow attorney from the DOJ, and when he asked me to slow dance, I accepted. It wouldn't be posted online, but he was entertaining enough. We hadn't spoken in-depth since Brad and I married, and the time off had stunted our mutual interests. When the song ended, and he let me go, I walked straight to the bar. I ordered another bourbon, but before the bartender moved, I switched it to red wine. Bourbon reminded me of Brad. Wine reminded me of me.

I left some singles in the tip jar and took my glass down by the water. The nights were cool on the lake. Too cool for swimming, but perhaps tomorrow before I left for the long drive home. The music from the wedding floated from under the tent and across the giant lawn. Their beginning was a fairytale, much more so than my ending.

The cool night air traveled down my back. I sipped my wine to chase it away. When I turned, Vince was standing on the dock behind me, smiling at me in the moonlight. I closed my eyes and let the reality of him standing there sink in. It filled every corner of me that wanted him more than anything else, every cell that had mourned me leaving him. When I opened them, I smiled back at him, and knew the warmth inside of me was love.

"You're like a moth to the light when it comes to water."

"And you're like a stalker." He came closer, too close for public, and walked past me to the edge of the dock.

"Were you thinking of swimming tonight?"

"I was thinking it's too cold." The light loved him. It clung to his skin and danced in his eyes. "I thought you'd be home by now."

He looked out at the water, too, and shook his head. "No. I'm going to stay with you tonight." I remained silent. He had more to say, and I needed to hear his voice, to feel him near me. "You were right. I'm asking too much, and I promised I wouldn't."

"It's what you want. You'll find it with someone else," I said, and my chest ached at the words, and my shoulders caved in the slightest angle, and he saw. He took one step toward me and stopped. "Not here." My words were barely audible, but they never had to be said in the first place.

I opened my purse and took out my room key. "I'm room three-fourteen." He took it from me, and the touch of his hand practically dropped me to my knees. For a second, I knew I'd never live without him. "I've got to go say goodnight."

The air felt clear between us. It always was, I thought, because he was so honest, but there were ideas in his head he couldn't share.

"I saw you dancing." He pulled me into his arms, and we rocked to the leftover notes of the music coming from the tent. "I wanted to dance with you."

"I wish it had been you." I heard my words, but I didn't know what I was saying. They were just sounds, nothing compared to the feel of his arms around me.

"Do you know him?"

I leaned into him, wanting to feel his body against me. "I used to work with him. He was Number Seven." Vince leaned back, questioning me with his eyes. "From the list of my ex-lovers."

He paused for a second and fell back into the rhythm of the music. He held me tighter to him and I rested my head on his shoulder. "Go say goodbye," he said near my ear and kissed me there.

I let my hand fall from his. I walked backward and turned to navigate the hill. I was practically skipping. *I could fall. I could break my arm. I could fly away to heaven.* I didn't care because Vince was there, and he wasn't asking for anything. We were going to figure this out together.

My goodnights were rushed. For some, I had a headache and couldn't possibly keep up for the after-party. For others, a simple goodbye. For Christine, I saved an enormous hug. I tried to convey congratulations, but I feared it was filled with good luck. And when it was polite, I returned to my room.

The door was ajar. I paused in the hallway, wanting him. Letting my need spread through me, the anticipation of having him in my bed building. I hung my head and leaned with my hand on the wall to steady me as my longing reached the quiet places of my body that screamed for him, stealing my thoughts and my conscience.

He opened the door and pulled me inside, pressing my back against the wall and kissing me hard. It could have been a good-bye. He held my face in his hands as the door shut behind me, and we were alone in my room.

"You are exactly what I want." He kissed me again, and if he'd asked me in that moment, I would have divorced Brad. I could feel it rising in my chest, coming before I was ready to face it. "I'll never ask you for another thing." My face in his hands; my heart in his grasp. "But just say the word, and we'll be together."

I kissed him. Forced the thoughts from my head with his mouth and his body. I wouldn't speak another word until morning.

fifty

JAMES HAD SLEPT IN. HE must be getting sick—he never slept late. He lingered in front of the open refrigerator door, staring inside. It drove Brad crazy when they left the door open.

"Close the door," Brad said and ate another spoonful of cereal.

"Where's the milk?" James surveyed the counter and opened the refrigerator door again.

"What milk?" Brad asked and returned to reading something on his phone.

"The milk for cereal," James said, and I looked at Brad's bowl.

"You used all the milk?" I asked, and Brad put his phone down. He was suddenly the center of attention.

"Yeah."

"What about the kids?"

"What about them? Make him some toast?"

I shook my head and found the bread in the drawer. "I used to make him milk from my breast. I would never finish the milk before the kids have eaten." I tried to understand how he could have done it, and he was watching me as if I was crazy. Maybe I was crazy.

"I'm not going to argue with you over milk." When I walked by, he grabbed my elbow. "I'll argue with you about whatever you want, but not milk. We're better than that." Brad smiled and somehow swayed me. He really did. I softened. I had a glimpse into our old life.

"I made him milk from my breast," I said dramatically, trying to hold back the laughter. "What have you done?" Brad laughed, too. "No, seriously, since your initial DNA donation, what have you done for these children? And do not say, 'I work.'"

"I picked you." Brad kissed my cheek, and my heart stopped for a moment. They were the first words of appreciation he'd said to me since I'd quit my job. The first glimmer of acknowledgement, and although it was an off-handed compliment half-joke to him, it meant the world to me.

◦⌒

LIV'S LEGS FLEW WELL OVER her head as she swung in the backyard. The swings were always my favorite, too. I wanted to fly. Her hair flew in front of her face as her legs pumped backward and then blew behind her as she soared forward.

"I love you, Mommy," she yelled into the kitchen doorway I watched her from.

"Love you, too." I took a deep breath. I could pull this off. I could raise these children to flourish, and I could be with Brad, and I could have Vince. And it didn't matter where I lived, or that I only worked twenty hours a week at the police station. It would be more than enough.

"Watch me! I'm flying."

"I see you. You are flying."

Brad walked into the kitchen.

"You have to come see Liv. She's swinging so high, the whole swing set is rocking."

He came and stood behind me, and we both watched our daughter as she soared through the sky. "She loves it," he said, and sounded almost sad. It caught me off guard. I thought annoyed was Brad's only emotion.

"Hey, Brad?"

"Yes." The annoyance returned.

"What do you love about this town?"

The silence behind me followed his breath down my back. It left me chilled with the familiar longing of isolation in its wake. Even in Brad's presence, I felt alone. Or was it especially in Brad's presence? "Funny you should ask." His tone had an edge of anger. As if he was pissed about something and waiting for the perfect time to fight about it. "I was thinking, maybe you're right. Maybe we should move."

I didn't even turn around. I wasn't going to ruin the moment of watching Liv swing with a discussion with Brad about moving. Brad loved it here. He'd made us move here, made us live in this house, years ago. We weren't going anywhere. *But why would he bring it up now?*

Brad moved closer and swept my hair to one side. He put his hands near my collar bone and ran them down to my shoulders, massaging them with a foreign touch. The slight edge to his tone rested at the end of his fingertips as he pressed his hands into my skin.

"Would that make you happy, Meredith?" He tightened his hands on my shoulders, kneading the muscles beneath his grip.

"You're kidding," I said, challenging him, not wanting to pay attention to this conversation. Liv leaned way back until her head almost touched the ground and her feet almost reached the sky. Brad's hands moved up to my neck and tightened there.

"Just say the word."

My breath caught. My instincts kicked in and I exhaled slowly, not letting Brad feel the difference. His hands still rested near my neck, and everything seemed to move in slow motion except Liv yelling to the sky that she was awesome as she soared through the air.

"I'll let you know," I said with a controlled lightness. I

tapped his hands, stifling the fear with a fake jovial movement.

Brad let go and I stayed, watching Liv, feeling safe in her presence. She would protect me from whatever he knew.

Brad went to the bathroom, and I continued to stare out the window as the rotting sense of death rose up inside me. I swallowed hard to force it back down, but it was there now and wouldn't be ignored.

I emailed the colonel. There was no subject and nothing in it.

Please see the next page for an excerpt from the stunning second installment of the Faraway series, and find out how Meredith, Brad, and Vince's story ends . . .

The Lion's Den
Available for preorder now.

Chapter 1

Chief Vincent Pratt

I USUALLY DIDN'T CHECK FOR an email from her while I was on duty. Meredith was here with me every weekday morning, but today was Sunday and she was home with her family, and I was working. There was no nine-to-five for police officers. Not even the chief.

So I looked. I knew there wouldn't be a new email, but when I missed her I'd read the old ones, anything to hear her voice, to have her tell me something. She wrote me every day, every night before she fell asleep in her husband's bed.

Her bold-faced address at the top of my inbox spread excitement through me like electricity. Until I saw there was no subject. I leaned my arms on my desk, my phone in my hands, and held my breath as I opened it.

There was no content. The world stopped around me. It was the rule I never thought would come up, the one I was sure we'd never need. I went back to my inbox hoping for another email explaining this one had been sent by mistake, but Meredith Walsh never made mistakes. I was her only one.

The day she'd read her rules to me I'd thought she was paranoid, but I didn't care. I'd follow her rules if she needed me to. No calling, no texting, no using her name. She was the most thorough person I've ever met. I'd laughed at her as she read them without any clothes on, but still so seriously. I wasn't allowed to fall in love with her, but I knew I'd already broken that one. And this one—if I ever send you an email with no subject line, and nothing in it, you are to delete your account immediately and *not* contact me—I wanted to break now.

In the year I'd known her, we'd not spoken for a few months. They were the worst of my life. Worse than boot camp, the police academy, and Kuwait. Worse than anything, and now it was going to begin again and I'd have to wait for word from her.

I scrolled down my inbox. Every email was from Meredith. She was the only one with the address. No one else in the world knew it existed, like our relationship.

I searched for ones she told me "I love you." Those were my favorite. It took her forever to even believe we could love each other; that love could be a component of an affair, but I loved her before I had an affair with her. I loved her the first time I saw her.

I found the one she'd sent last Thursday morning before she came to work. I'd read it and instead of work I wanted to drive her somewhere, anywhere we could be alone. But what Meredith really wanted was to not have to be alone. The subject of the email was: I always dream of you.

I had a dream last night we were out to dinner and everyone in town stopped by our table to say hi. You were wearing the Phillies t-shirt which forced me to touch you the first time. Yes, I think it was the shirt that caused THIS. After dinner we met John and Jenna for drinks.

We were real.

The frustration I'd felt when I first read the email came flooding back. It killed her that our relationship only existed in the dark. That we'd never do the things other couples do, but Meredith created the situation. She insisted she'd never divorce her husband. I scrolled up to my reply.

We are real. We're just different. You are a huge part of my life. Whether the rest of the town knows it or not. I love you.

I scrolled through the list of emails I couldn't bear to lose, and considered printing some out or forwarding them to my personal account, but Meredith would kill me. I found account preferences and selected "Delete Account and All Data."

There was nothing left to do, but wait for her. A forbidden text, a Facebook message, both of which I knew would never come. If she sent this email, her husband knew something, or suspected something. She wouldn't risk a shred of evidence of our relationship being found. I'd spend every minute until I heard from her looking for a sign. I'd check the windshield of my car hoping for a handwritten note. I'd watch the door to the police station every time it opened hoping she found an excuse to come in on her day off. I knew I'd drive by her house while out on patrol today, anything to catch a glimpse of her. But I wouldn't make it through the night without hearing from her. Not tonight. Not any night.

☙

I PULLED THE POT OFF the burner and put my cup directly in the flow of coffee. I couldn't wait for the archaic machine to finish brewing the whole pot. I hadn't spoken with Meredith, and I hadn't slept a minute last night. I'd driven by her house twice yesterday, there was no sign of anyone. Even after dark, no lights were on. It was as if she'd disappeared.

She'll be here soon. Swim practice started early. Her son's age group was at 8:30. She'd be here. She was going to walk through the door and I already had an excuse ready for why I needed to talk to her in my office with the door shut.

I switched my full cup of coffee for the pot under the hot stream, and tried to calm down. This was yet another rule we were going to break because I wasn't ever going through a night like last night again. Daniels came in and grabbed a cup off the counter. One of the cups Meredith bought for us.

"Hey, Chief. Did you hear about Meredith?"

My chest tightened, trapping the air inside of me. It collapsed around my heart like a vice.

"No. Hear what?" Daniels moved around like nothing was a big deal. Like Meredith hadn't sent a warning that her husband knew she and I were having an affair.

"She fell at her house. I just saw Jack from the Rescue Squad at Wawa. He said they transported her yesterday. I was hoping she called out sick. That you heard something."

"No calls." I wasn't sure if I was speaking out loud. "Was she okay?"

"Unresponsive."

I put my cup down without a word and walked out of the station. When I turned off Main Street, I switched on my lights and sped to the hospital, breaking every rule. Not caring. It wasn't going to matter after I killed Brad Walsh.

about the author

ELIZA FREED GRADUATED FROM RUTGERS University and returned to her hometown in rural South Jersey. Her mother encouraged her to take some time and find herself. After three months of searching, she began to bounce checks and her neighbors began to talk; her mother told her to find a job.

She settled into Corporate America, learning systems and practices and the bureaucracy that slows them. Eliza quickly discovered her creativity and gift for storytelling as a corporate trainer and spent years perfecting her presentation skills and studying diversity. It was during that time she became an avid observer of the characters we meet and the heartaches we endure. Her years of study have taught her laughter is the key to survival, even when it's completely inappropriate.

To keep up with all of Eliza's new releases and giveaways, sign up for her newsletter at *www.elizafreed.com/love-letters.html*.

acknowledgments

TO EVERYONE I HAVE TORTURED with questions about their marriage, their childhood, their parents' divorce or their own, thank you for being so honest with your expectations and your disappointments. Life is beautiful, but not easy.

Thank you to my editor, Rhonda Helms. You make me want to write a hundred books just to watch you work your magic on them.

To Linda Busacca and the rest of the team at Brunswick House. Publishing this book has been an amazing experience because of you.

To everyone at Perfectly Publishable who makes me look this good.

To Christine Grygiel for reminding me how much I love a character I can root for.

To Deborah Hite for circling the town a hundred times and letting me talk through the facets of infidelity.

To Marcia Carter for still talking to me even after a glimpse inside my head. Together we could run a criminal enterprise.

To Professor Keith O'Shaughnessy, who taught me among other things, the difference between "the tree at the edge of the lot," and "the weeping willow the ladies of my town watched the parade from."

To Tricia Steiner who, even from miles away, still makes

writing horrible first drafts a soul-filling conversation about life.

To my husband, for being so much better than Brad Walsh.

And thank you to my mother who gave me life, my own and hers.